RED ZONE

A COLLEGE SPORTS ROMANCE

FALL LAKE BALLERS
BOOK THREE

ISLA VAUGHN

ARROWSCOPE PRESS, LLC

Red Zone

(p) ISBN-13: 978-1-951919-71-9

(e) ISBN-13: 978-1-951919-70-2

Publisher: Arrowscope Press, LLC; www.arrowscopepress.com

Editing— Amanda K., Line Editor, Caroline P., Proofreader, Angie G., Beta Reader, Red Adept Editing

Cover Design—T.E. Black Designs; www.teblackdesigns.com

Interior Formatting & Design— Arrowscope Press, LLC; www.arrowscope-press.com

CHAPTER ONE

LIAM

Football was my sanctuary, my future—until I collided with my past on the sidelines.

The snap echoed through the air, and I was already running. The catch was clutch. With the ball cradled in the crook of my arm, I looped around and headed back, ready to do it all again. I toed the line as the ball snapped into Kylian's hands, and as our QB1 dropped back into the pocket, I rocketed off. I could do this in my sleep, despite Coach's order to run the route until it became muscle memory. I cut left and extended my arms. Kylian's perfectly thrown spiral dropped into my hands like a gift from the heavens.

The crunch of pads colliding and shouted plays filled the practice field. Sweat dripped, muscles burned, but this was the grind I loved. Add in my closest friends, Ares and Kylian, and we created magic on the field. We'd had a stellar season. *And why wouldn't we?* This was it, my senior year and only a handful of games until the championship, which we were projected to make—possibly even win.

Two more times Kyl and I executed the same drill, a hair too close to where the QB2 was running a similar one with

Desmond, the second-string wide receiver. The meathead had confused the route and almost ran me over once. From the corner of my eye, I saw him barreling toward me from an over-thrown pass. I sidestepped, but he cut right and clipped me anyway. I grunted. Thrown off balance, I scrambled, staying on my feet but slamming into someone on the sidelines. Twisting, I half laughed at the absurdity of the situation. Reaching down to help whoever I'd bumped into, I froze.

My vision tunneled as I stared down at the piercing blue-green eyes blinking up at me. Skye Finley. The girl who'd ghosted me. *What the hell is she doing here?*

"Skye?" *Holy fuck—what a cruel twist of fate.* My heart jumped as I gaped at the leggy brunette sprawled on the turf.

Lips downturned in a grimace, she narrowed eyes that had haunted me since freshman year—the last time we were together before she'd disappeared on me after our whirlwind two-month fling. Long-buried emotions flared to life, gnawing at me and leaving me unsettled.

Images of stolen kisses strobed through my mind, late-night study sessions that turned into staying up until dawn, losing myself in her, the laughter, and even the passionate arguments. We had an intense connection that I'd never experienced before or after, but the most memorable was the pain of her leaving, something I'd vowed never to expose myself to again.

"Hi, Liam."

A mix of resignation and something I couldn't identify laced her greeting. Her hand clasped mine, sending jolts of electricity pinging up my arm and across my chest like lightning.

"Cartwright!" Coach Becket shouted, stomping down the sideline until he stood next to Skye. "Watch what you're doing, son." He turned to her and, with a softer voice, asked, "Are you okay?"

"Yep. I'm good, Uncle Tommy. I mean, um—" She cleared her throat, gaze darting to me then the field. "Coach." Pink tinted Skye's cheeks as she shoved her hair back from her face, tucking it behind her ears while carefully avoiding my stunned gaze.

Coach bent and retrieved the camera that I hadn't noticed and handed it back to his *niece—what the fuck?* I stepped back, fighting the magnetic pull Skye had always had over me. My fingers flexed against the football I'd caught. My other hand curled into a fist as I fought against the urge to grab her hand again and pull her close. She and I, we weren't anything. Not anymore. Another look at her panicked eyes with the pupils blown wide from shock, and I saw our destruction all over again. No way would I go back for more of that—despite how much I wanted to slide my hands into her silky hair and slant my mouth over her plump, kissable lips. No fucking way—I had a career to secure, and messing around with the coach's niece was the kiss of death.

"Listen up, team."

Coach's voice broke into my inner monologue, and I felt the press of bodies as the team gathered around. He must've called everyone over while my greatest mistake had played through my mind, warning me what not to do.

My mantra for the past three years as a football star at Fall Lake University had been simple: no love, no complications. I hadn't come by that motto without reason. But seeing Skye made me question everything.

I couldn't shake the unsettling feeling lurking beneath the surface after the reality of my two closest friends, Kylian and Ares, trading in their wild ways for steady relationships. I'd sworn to avoid that path after my parents' brutal divorce left me jaded. The clincher was freshman year—the only time I'd decided to let a girl in, resulting in devastating heartbreak.

While my two friends were blissfully happy, I knew my place —alone, one-night stands, no attachments. That was my fate, and I would stick to it.

Vow reaffirmed, I shifted back to put more space between myself and Skye. Kylian and Ares flanked me with the move.

Coach gestured to Skye, who'd drifted to his side. "I would like to introduce Skye Finley, who is interning with us for the rest of the season and handling our social media. I don't need to remind you to be on your best behavior and to treat her with the respect she deserves." The threat hung heavy.

Skye slipped her camera strap around her neck, pulling her long, wavy dark-brown hair from beneath it. She offered a small wave as many of the players acknowledged her.

"The next few games will make or break our season. It may seem like our spot in the playoffs is a sure thing, but complacency is where teams fall apart. That will not be us. Not only do I expect each and every one of you to do your best, fighting for a spot in the playoffs, but also remember—NFL scouts will be watching. This is your chance to shine."

His words reaffirmed where my focus had to be as the weight of my future pressed down on me. The speech was short and impactful, then we were dismissed. I put blinders on, half listening as I trailed behind Kylian and Ares to shower and change.

The locker room buzzed with post-practice noise—teammates joking, the clatter of cleats against the floor, and the sharp pop of lockers slamming shut. I leaned against the bench, trying to focus on anything but the nagging memories clawing their way up. The familiar knot in my chest tightened, a shadow of old fights and broken promises.

"Cartwright!" Kylian's voice snapped me back to the present. He lobbed a water bottle across the room, and I caught it without thinking. "Tell Ares he's full of shit. I read the defense fine—he just ran the wrong route."

Ares rolled his eyes, his jaw set. "I wasn't off. You didn't see the safety creeping up."

"Both of you are wrong." I twisted the cap off the water

bottle and took a swig. "But keep arguing, and Coach will bench your asses next game." An empty threat, but a good one. "That should settle it."

Kylian snorted, shaking his head. "Classic Liam, dodging conflict. You're too good at mediating."

Mediating. Yeah, I'd been doing that since I was a kid. Back then, it wasn't about football plays; it was about stopping my parents from tearing each other apart. I could still hear their voices echoing through the walls—my mom's sharp tone, my dad's booming retorts, and the silence that followed when one of them finally stormed out.

Their relationship was a *War of the Roses*–style dumpster fire. And it had screwed me up in ways I hated admitting. It was the reason I kept women at arm's length, why I couldn't let anyone get too close. Letting someone in—like Skye—was a risk I wasn't sure I could take.

After they'd finally split, Mom took off and got herself another family. My older sister and I'd never heard from her, but we weren't parentless. Sometimes—okay, often—I thought we would have been better off if our drunk-off-his-ass dad hadn't volunteered to stick around.

I shoved the thought aside, gripping the water bottle tighter. "Someone has to keep you idiots in check."

"Yeah, yeah." Kylian clapped me on the back. "Don't think I didn't see you zoning out just now. What's eating you?"

"Nothing," I lied, straightening. "Just thinking about the upcoming game."

But it wasn't the game. It was everything else—the past, the future, and the mess in between.

"You're sure?" Ares's voice softened, cutting through the haze. "If something's up, we've got your back."

I forced a grin and clapped him on the shoulder. "I'm good. Focus on fixing your routes instead of worrying about me."

The words felt hollow, but I wasn't about to unpack my

baggage in the middle of the locker room. Not with pro scouts watching, playoffs on the line, and my dreams dangling just out of reach.

I showered and changed, caught up in my head as we left the locker room soon after and made the short drive to Kylian's off-campus condo, where Ares and I also lived. We let ourselves in. I followed Kylian, dropping my bag to the right of the door then moving aside so Ares could enter. It was quiet inside, echoing the emptiness I'd felt after seeing Skye. I glanced around the open floor plan from the decked-out kitchen to the living room with the oversized couches and large-screen TV.

"Where are the girls?" My stomach growled, and I glanced longingly at the kitchen. I'd hoped Kylian's fiancée, Aurora, would be cooking something when we got home.

"Brielle is hanging out with her sister and convinced Aurora to go with. I think they're shopping?" Ares shrugged, his backpack landing with a thump next to where I'd left mine.

"It's too quiet without them here, isn't it?" Kylian asked, voicing what was running through my mind.

I grunted a response. Brielle, Ares's girlfriend, might as well have moved in. She was here more often than not. I wasn't complaining, or not really. It'd been more of an adjustment when Aurora had shacked up with Kylian, invading our space last year. But if I was being honest, I loved them filling the room with their feminine energy and laughter. It didn't hurt that Aurora was a goddess in the kitchen. With her talents, that girl had a gold mine of a career, and we all reaped the benefits.

The other side of me was glad they weren't home. The easy affection the couples had only accentuated my loneliness that I refused to broadcast.

I made a beeline for the fridge. Homework could wait—and so could the pending discussion with the guys about Skye—my stomach couldn't. I swore it was eating itself with how loud it rumbled. Yanking open the door to the fridge, I peered inside.

Score! Aurora had left us some sort of casserole. I pulled it out, tearing off the instructions, and instead of reheating it in the oven like the note probably said, I cut a giant piece and nuked it in the microwave. When I flipped over the sticky note, a laugh burst out of me.

"She called it?" Kylian dropped onto one of the island's barstools.

"Yep." I tossed him the note from Aurora addressed to me for when I disregarded her reheating instructions and instead noted how long for the microwave.

Ares grabbed two more plates, slid one to Kylian, and they both cut two equally large pieces. The microwave dinged, and I took my food out so Ares could put his in. None of us said anything as we tucked into dinner.

The silence wouldn't last, and I was glad because I needed to vent about seeing Skye. After I shoveled the last bite, rinsed my dishes, and put them in the dishwasher, they were done with their dinner too.

I went to the living room, where I fell onto the couch then rested my elbows on my knees, head cradled in my hands. *Skye.* My body ached from fighting the need to pull her into my arms despite the initial shock. *After all this time, why does she still have the power to bring me to my knees?* "What the fuck?" I groaned. "She's Coach's niece?"

"Did you know?" Kylian grabbed an apple from the bowl on the island then sat on the opposite couch.

I jerked upright and glared. "You're kidding, right?" My head rested back against the cushion, and I marveled at the sheer insanity of the situation. "If I'd known her connections—"

"Please." Ares snorted then fell onto the couch and faced me, his arm stretched over the back of it. "It was freshman year, and you were unleashed. No one could have rationalized with you over consequences." He shrugged. "It wouldn't have mattered then because Coach Becket wasn't our coach until sophomore year."

I paused in defending myself. Even I couldn't disagree with what I was like as a freshman. And though he wasn't our coach then, he was now. "But"—I swiped my hand down, chopping through the bullshit—"now that I know, it makes things easier."

"Does it?" Ares's brows climbed his forehead.

"You were pretty gone for her," Kylian chimed in with another truth bomb I didn't want verbalized.

But he wasn't wrong. The fallout from our fling had resulted in sleepless nights of missing her laugh, the feel of her beneath me, the vision of a future I'd never thought I would have—and that was only after being with her for two months. I'd fallen for her, hard and fast. *Love at first sight?* I'd never believed in it—until she happened. "She cut ties. She made her point crystal clear." She didn't want me the way I had wanted her.

"Why was that?" Kylian asked the question I'd never been able to answer.

"You never told us why she broke things off," Ares pushed.

"It didn't make sense." That last conversation played in my head as it had all those years ago.

My mind tripped back to freshman year, when Coach came down on me for a shitty practice.

"Listen up, Cartwright," Coach Macintyre had said. "You're distracted and gonna fuck this up. Is the NFL your goal, or isn't it?"

"Yes, Coach." My stomach churned with worry. I had a scholarship to play football at a D1 university and a firm goal to make it professionally—which meant I had to make the scouts notice me during the games. If he benched me for screwing up in practice like I did that day, I could kiss my dreams goodbye.

"It's a girl, isn't it?"

I winced when images of what Skye and I had done all night long—resulting in my lack of sleep and several fumbles on the field today—flooded my mind. I didn't need to confirm anything to Coach. He saw it on my face.

"Girls are dream killers, Cartwright."

"We're just casual." I rubbed my chest as I said it, trying to downplay how much she consumed my thoughts.

"That girl is in your head. If you're distracted by 'casual,' you won't have a future."

Body sore from a brutal football practice and Coach's words replaying in my head, I'd exited the athletic building to find Skye waiting for me. My gaze crawled over her long legs, lingering on her curves to her gorgeous eyes and plump lips. I wanted to bury my hands in her dark, wavy hair. She was the only girl who had ever held my attention. With long strides, I closed the distance between us, my hand going to her hip and the other sinking in her thick hair to pull her close.

She slapped her hand against my chest and pushed. "Hey, we need to talk."

Halfway to her lips, I froze at the phrase no guy wanted to hear. Her mouth turned up in a shaky smile as she backed up a step, and I leaned against the side of the building. The bricks were warm from the afternoon sun.

The memory was like quicksand, and I extracted myself from it as best I could. "It didn't make sense. She'd asked me an impossible question."

"Which was?" Kylian prompted.

"She wanted to know if we had a future together. It was totally out of the blue. Of course, I told her no." Coach's lecture had been fresh in my head when she'd asked me—and the conversation about girls being dream killers was too similar to what my dad would have said, which was a mindfuck in itself. "My goal was, and always had been, a career in the NFL. Nothing would change that."

"And she didn't elaborate? Was she talking marriage or just an exclusive relationship? Or did she have something against your NFL goals?" Ares scrubbed his hand over the stubble on his jaw. "Some girls don't want a life with a professional athlete because of all the bullshit from other women, late hours, or the travel."

I shook my head. "No. That doesn't make sense. We weren't at a point where the future was relevant because we'd only been together a couple of months. And she even proved that point when she said something crazy like, 'Well, it was fun while it lasted. See you around.'"

"You didn't try to stop her?" Kylian leaned forward.

I scowled, my fists clenching all over again. "It was a good-bye. I saw it in her eyes. Then that fuckhead Calvin walked by and made some smart-ass comment."

"That was the fight? It was right after you talked to Skye?" Ares's gaze locked onto the scar that ran along my left cheek-bone from that day.

"Yep. That was when it happened."

Calvin had run his mouth about Skye dumping me for someone better, and his cousin Mav's name had come up. I'd lost it. Things were already heated. Mav wasn't far and inter-vened. Things went from bad to worse. Mav tried to break us up. Calvin grabbed Mav's hockey stick and wacked me in the face, resulting in my scar. And the kicker was, I saw Mav later with his arm around Skye.

Silence hung heavy between the three of us until Kylian broke it. "Maybe it's for the best. Unless her being around changes something for you."

"She changes nothing," I snapped. I couldn't let her. She'd turned my world upside down. I had too much riding on the year for her to mess with my head again. *Still...* "Why the hell is she here after all this time?"

"She probably never left." Kylian kicked his feet onto the coffee table. "We're at a D1 school with fifty thousand students, and she's a different major than any of us. It's not surprising you never ran into her when she didn't want you to anymore."

"And now she does?" I scowled. "Don't sugarcoat it for me, QB1."

Kylian rolled his eyes. "I get it. This sucks. After she ditched and blocked you, the last thing you expected was for her to invade our turf."

"Yes, that." I was screwed. "How can I concentrate with her there during practices, games, and who the hell knows what else?"

"You do your job." Kylian's game face snapped into place, and he leveled me with the same high intensity that got us to perform our best on the field and win. "You're a legend in the stadium. You have nothing to worry about. Don't let her get in your head. Just focus on the game."

Neither stated the obvious—I'd probably dodged a bullet freshman year. But even though I hadn't known who she was connected to then, she'd taken a wrecking ball to my life. She'd left me, and after, I couldn't stop imagining her everywhere and nowhere. And now, she was the social media liaison for our team. It was time for truth, and if my roommates wouldn't drop it, I would.

"She's here. She's the coach's niece, and she's impossible to ignore." But even as I said it, I knew the deal—it wasn't a game I could walk away from. Skye Finley had already changed the rules. *I'm so screwed.*

CHAPTER TWO

SKYE

My leg bounced beneath the table as I tried to steady my nerves, cradling my caramel mocha latte like it could shield me from the last few hours. I probably shouldn't be having caffeine. I was nervous enough as it was. Another heavenly sip convinced me I could handle the extra jolt. It was too damn good, and I needed something comforting.

The bell jingled over the door to Brewed Awakening, the café on campus that fed my coffee addiction. It was one place I knew Liam never went, so it'd been safe to frequent while I had taken classes and actively avoided him for the past few years, minus the one semester I took off.

I shivered as a cool breeze blew in with the hulking guy who'd just entered. Something settled inside me at the sight of Maverick Davis, my oldest and best friend, with his tall frame and easy smile. He didn't bother to order, as I had his boring black coffee waiting for him. Across from me, the chair scraped against the floor as he pulled it out then lowered himself into it.

"Okay, Skye, I got your SOS." He leaned in, his toned muscles rippling under the black Henley. He searched my face with his piercing blue eyes, framed in long dark lashes that were seriously wasted on a guy—especially one I was immune to, as Mav was like a brother to me. "What's going on?"

"I ran into Liam—literally—at my new job."

Mav angled himself closer by resting a thick forearm on the table, blocking me from a nearby table of guys. "You knew you'd see him when you accepted the internship. I thought you were ready." His brows furrowed. "Otherwise, I wouldn't have pushed you to take it. Bet he was shocked to see you."

"Yeah, he was." I rolled my eyes. "But seriously, I thought I could mostly stay in the background, and he wouldn't recognize me." I twisted a lock of hair around my finger—a horrid nervous habit I couldn't seem to break. "Shit, Mav, it was like seeing a ghost." I didn't say that one touch from Liam was like a live wire to my body. He lit me up inside, an impossible addiction that I'd barely quit the first time. All those old feelings came rushing back. If not for my daughter and Liam's unwillingness to alter the trajectory he'd planned for his life, I don't think I could've done it.

"Not liking the dreamy look on your face." Mav grimaced. "Stop thinking whatever you are. It's weird."

That made me laugh. Ever since his sister died when we were little, our relationship had changed. Though she had been a year older than me and Mav, she was my closest friend. Her death severely shook us. We'd clung to each other and forged a sibling relationship that got us through losing her. So, yeah, I got why he didn't like the direction of my thoughts. It grossed me out to think of him having sexy thoughts about girls too.

"Go back to how Liam ran into you." His jaw clenched. "Do I need to mess him up?"

I snorted. "No. It was an accident. When he turned and saw me…" I closed my eyes and relived the emotions that'd shifted through his eyes like quicksilver, from shock to desire to anger. I shivered. "My hope that he wouldn't remember me imploded —and not in a good way."

"Does that change things? I know you thought you wouldn't be seen—which I told you was ridiculous—but what's the worst that can happen? You left him. Don't you think he'll ignore you after the initial shock wears off?" Mav took a sip of his coffee. "He's not a relationship kind of guy. Unless he could be—if you tell him?"

I refused to touch that last question with a ten-foot pole. I'd heard enough about how Liam hit it and quit it from a few athlete-obsessed girls in several of my classes. Their gossip convinced me I'd done the right thing by walking away, even if it'd shattered my heart.

I'd just found out I was pregnant. My defenses were up, and I probably didn't handle things the best way when I asked Liam what he would do if circumstances changed and he couldn't go into the NFL. I should've known that wasn't an option.

"Nothing will stand in my way," he'd said, and my heart had shattered.

I knew then what I had to do. "Not even for me?" I'd tried to keep it light, but so much was at stake, and I was uncomfortably vulnerable.

"I like you a lot, but no. The NFL is my future, and if you're not on board with that, then we aren't meant to be together."

My stomach rolled on a wave of panic from the unwanted memory that clashed with the ache of seeing Liam again. It drove home the uncontrollably wild way he made me feel. It didn't matter anymore. I'd made my choice. Lily was mine—*but what if he found out? Would he challenge me on parental rights like my dad did with my mom? Would he even care?*

"You're making decisions for him, Skye. Don't they deserve to know each other?"

"I'm protecting her, Mav."

"Are you? Or are you protecting yourself? Secrets have a way of coming out, Skye. And if he finds out from someone else…" He let the thought hang, his gaze steady on mine.

"It doesn't matter. It's done. Maybe I shouldn't have taken on the internship. It's so much, and I don't want to steal more time from my daughter." I slowly rolled the almost-empty cup between my palms.

Mav cupped my hands and leveled that look at me that he got when he intended to lay down some deep truth. I stilled, waiting for his advice, needing the solidarity he offered.

"You've got this. Just set boundaries and remember that you're juggling a lot. You're a great mom. On top of school, you're doing your TA job and trying to manage a public relations internship. It may be too much. I mean, I hear you. It will all look great on a resume, but you've gotta cut yourself some slack. If you're solid that keeping him out of Lily's life is the right thing to do, then Liam isn't a factor in your world, right?"

The question hung between us. My only answer was a scowl.

Mav shrugged, resolved to drop it if I wanted to be stubborn. "Fine. You're sticking to your decision. Then don't give him any headspace."

I nodded along to his words. He was right. I could do it. I released the cup I'd been cradling, turned my hands into his, and squeezed. "Thanks. I needed this." I pushed out a breath, the tension leaving my shoulders for the first time since yesterday's deer-in-the-headlights moment with Liam.

"You good with seeing him daily?"

I bit my lip, pondering his question rather than responding with my typical knee-jerk reaction. "I don't know. I mean, it's been years. I'm over it, or I thought I was. But after seeing him again? It's just... hard. I didn't expect to feel anything." I shrugged, not wanting to worry about why I ended things with him in the first place or if I did the right thing. I did. But a part of me felt like I should have at least told him I was pregnant with his child. When I'd confided in Mav, he'd made his thoughts crystal clear that I should tell Liam, but he'd stood by me and supported my decision. I'd decided to have and raise her on my own. I couldn't lose Lily. My biggest fear was that Liam would get a big NFL contract and sue me for custody.

"Maybe this is your chance to clear the air with Liam. To tell him."

"No. Stop. You've pushed that already. Let it go." I didn't think that would be a good idea. "The whole encounter is probably karma finally catching up with me. Besides, I've heard about how much of a player Liam is. Has that changed?"

Mav frowned. "No, but that doesn't—"

"Why are you defending him? Didn't you guys have that fight after I ended things? You didn't exactly help by throwing a punch back then, you know."

He sighed, running a hand over his face. "Yeah, well, some guys deserve to be hit, and I'd do it again if he hurt you." His expression turned weary. "That was long ago, and my cousin was involved."

"Your cousin is a problem." But that was a discussion for another day. I had enough on my plate, and adding to Mav's wasn't helpful. "Look, I'm not risking it. Liam never wanted a family or to get involved in anything serious outside his goal of becoming a professional athlete. I'm taking our collision and eating turf as a sign that I should keep my distance. I've got enough on my shoulders without adding Liam to the mix."

Mav said nothing, which brought a boatload of guilt. I didn't like that one bit. As my oldest and closest friend, I knew him far too well. I needed commiseration, and while he gave me some of that, he also pushed me to be up-front with Liam. That wasn't going to happen. And since Mav knew my secret and I wasn't willing to discuss it, we needed a change in subject—stat.

"Now that we're done talking about me, tell me what's new with you. Any more news on the agent or hockey front?" He already had an agent, Trevor Faraday, who was one of the best in the NHL.

Mav shrugged, released my hands, and leaned back in his

chair. "Trev's in talks with two teams. He's calling tonight, and we'll probably hash out details then."

I studied his relaxed demeanor. The NHL was his endgame, but unlike Liam, he wasn't wound tight about it. "You take it all in stride." I gestured to his coffee like he held the secret to his zen. "How do you just show up and not worry?"

He shrugged. "Because I've already done the work. Now, I just need to let it pay off."

I rolled my eyes. "Must be nice. Some of us don't have it that simple."

"You could do the same, Skye. Stop running."

I narrowed my eyes, not liking the implication "I'm not running. I'm doing the internship. I saw Liam. I'm moving past it." Mostly. "Let me know how it goes with the agent and potential placement, okay?" I glanced at the time. "I've got to head out. Thanks for letting me vent."

After another sip from his disgusting black coffee, Mav unfolded his large frame from the chair and drew me in for a hug. I stayed an extra few seconds before pulling back, the clock ticking in my head for when I had to pick up my daughter.

As I stepped out into the cool breeze, Mav's words echoed in my mind. *You could do the same, Skye. Stop running.* If only it were that easy.

Fifteen minutes later, I stood in front of the doors to Little Sprouts Daycare for the designated pickup time. A few more seconds, and Miss Jill opened the door. Lily raced under her arm, pigtails bouncing, carrying a backpack nearly as big as she was. I bent, opening my arms, and she launched herself into my embrace. Laughing, I stood with her and spun around to her delighted peals of laughter. My heart felt two times lighter as I showered kisses all over her face, inhaling the smell of crayons and fruit snacks. For a moment, all my worries faded.

"I missed you, Lily-bean."

Two tiny hands clutched my cheeks. "Missed you, Mommy."

Having my daughter in my arms was all I needed to reaffirm that I'd done the right thing and that Liam needed to stay in the dark, where he belonged—firmly in the past. As I peppered kisses across her cheeks, Lily wrinkled her nose the same way Liam used to when he tried not to laugh at the onslaught. God, even her grin sometimes felt like a mirror of his. *How long before someone else notices?*

Her tiny arms wrapped around my neck, anchoring me in the moment. For now, she was mine and mine alone. But the storm I'd been running from was closer than ever, and Liam didn't look like the kind of man who would let me outrun him again.

CHAPTER THREE

LIAM

I tore across the turf, following the new route Coach Mack wanted the wide receivers to practice. I dug in, weaving through defenders, shaking free of a tackle before cutting hard to the right. Kylian's perfect spiral fell into my hands like a gift. I tucked the ball in and sprinted to the end zone.

When I jogged back, tossing the ball to Coach Mack, I caught a glimpse of Skye's long hair dancing in the wind as she bent along the sideline, snapping pictures. She was everywhere, and no matter how much I tried to ignore her, she had a way of getting under my skin. I didn't know what pissed me off more—that she'd left without a word or that seeing her still made my chest ache in ways I hated admitting.

After staying up until two a.m. the previous night trying to make sense of my chemistry homework and stressing about the test I'd probably bombed, I gave up. My mind kept drifting between plays I needed to memorize and the final looming ahead. That was when I caved and scrolled through the team's Instagram account. Since she'd taken over, the engagement had skyrocketed. The pictures were... well, they were outstanding. She had talent and a way of humanizing us, getting people even more invested. Her approach reminded me of the NFL documentaries that followed a few professional athletes.

We practiced three new plays until they were smooth. When training drew to a close, Coach Mack motioned me over. "Cartwright, a word?"

I kept my gaze trained on him, not Skye, who was packing her stuff nearby. "What's up, Coach?" I halted before him, tugging off my helmet and tucking it under my arm.

"Got a call from Professor White."

My heart plummeted, and sweat broke out across my forehead. That couldn't be good. "Oh yeah?"

"Don't give me that nonchalant bullshit. You failed your last test. You know what that means?"

I didn't answer. I knew damn well it was rhetorical. He would have my ass if I even tried to play it off like it wasn't a big deal.

"You're on thin ice, Cartwright. Fail another test, and you'll lose your eligibility—and scouts won't bother sticking around to see you ride the bench."

Coach Mack's words faded as panic set in. School didn't come as easily to me as it did to Kylian and Ares. Not to mention I'd fucked off my first two years, not caring about my grades. It didn't help my GPA or my current position with the last two semesters of upper-level classes. My communication classes tended to offset some of the lower grades in other courses, but it was too little too late. I was fucked if I didn't get a passing grade in my stupid science course I had to take. It was one of my weaker subjects, and I'd put it off as long as I could.

I didn't want to ask, but I needed to know. I cut in when the wide receivers coach drew in a breath, pausing from his lecture. "I'll do anything you ask, but am I still starting in the game this weekend?"

Coach Mack's beady eyes narrowed further, judging my

sincerity and commitment. He gave a curt nod. "So long as you set up tutoring for Monday night."

My lungs expanded as air whooshed in on the news, and I took my first full breath since he'd started talking. "Yeah, of course. I'll go to the athletic center after practice."

"No. Not this time. You'll be coming in late to address your less-than-stellar grade and will need extra help, which means, after Coach Becket got involved, the academic advisor set up sessions with Professor White's TA. Check in with them to find out where you're supposed to be Monday night."

I would agree to anything so long as it meant I could keep playing. Especially since the head coach had gotten personally involved in setting up my tutor. "I'm on it."

"Cartwright." Coach Mack's glare intensified. "You get one chance. Don't fuck it up. If I hear you missed a single session with the new tutor or your grades haven't improved, Jackson will take your starting position, and you'll ride the bench."

"I hear you, Coach. You won't be disappointed." I promised, all too aware of what was at stake.

***

The atmosphere in the stadium for Saturday's game against Iowa was electric as it raced over my skin and fueled me to push harder, run faster, and be better than every one of our opponents who stood in the way of the job I needed to do. I loved it—lived for it. It was my destiny, and I wouldn't let anything stand in the way of establishing myself and attaining my goals.

It was a crucial game, and I could feel the scouts' eyes on me from the stands as they watched, clipboards in hand. I glanced to the sideline where Skye snapped pictures. Our eyes met for a moment, and a surge of determination flooded my already-pumped-up blood.

Every time I lined up for the next play, my eyes flicked to the sidelines. She was there, camera in hand, oblivious to how much space she still occupied in my head. I shook it off. *Football first.* Everything else could wait.

We lined up at the forty-yard line in Iowa's territory, the tension palpable. The formation was tight—two wide receivers, including myself; Ares, our star tight end, pulled in close; and a running back.

The home crowd roared, but we were in the zone. Kylian called what I knew would be the game play. We were locked in. The ball was snapped. Kylian caught it, scanning the field as I split off to the right, drawing the defenders away from Ares.

Everything unfolded in a flash. Kylian dropped back, eyes sweeping for options. The defense closed in fast, but our QB1 was calm under pressure. His gaze locked onto Ares, sprinting five yards out. With a flick of his wrist, the ball was out of his hands, spiraling toward Ares, who snatched it out of the air.

Double-teaming in anticipation of a pass to me, the defenders dropped away, changing directions to intercept Ares. I lowered my shoulder, ramming into the chest of the closest one to clear the way. Ares twisted and tossed the ball in an underhanded backward pass to Jackson right before a giant lineman took Ares down.

I raced alongside Jackson, working to clear a path for the touchdown. We made it to the twenty-yard line. Out of nowhere, a safety zeroed in, taking Jackson down hard. Before hitting the ground, he lobbed the ball back over his shoulder just a few feet behind him. The timing was perfect as I snatched it out of the air and charged ahead.

Tucking the ball, I turned on the speed. Cleats digging in, I barreled past an Iowa defender, fighting for every inch. The defense was caught off guard and scrambled, but it was too late. I wove through the defense like lightning. Fifteen yards, ten, five. The defensive backs chased in vain as I sprinted to the end zone. The crowd erupted as I crossed the line untouched for a touchdown.

Up by six points, I tossed the ball to the ref and returned to my team. Despite the beautifully executed play that was a piece of football magic, we weren't done, leaving the opposing team stunned and the Fall Lake crowd roaring with approval. We'd just pulled off something spectacular.

We lined up, going for the two-point conversion with seconds left in the game. Determination buzzed through our line. The ball was snapped, and I dodged a lineman in a perfect hole Ares created. Once in the end zone, I faked out a defensive end then turned, catching Kylian's eye, making myself an option. He launched the ball. I jumped, stretching my arm up. In a one-handed catch, I came down inbounds a second before the ref blew the whistle, signaling the end of the game.

As the team and our fans cheered, I scanned the sideline until I found Skye in the chaos. I wove through my teammates and the crowd until I stood in front of her on the packed sideline. She stood, slinging her gear bag over her shoulder, and I racked my brain for something to say.

"Great posts on socials." My voice came out softer than I intended.

She looked up, a small smile playing on her lips. "Thanks. You guys have given me some great shots to work with."

Silence settled heavily, charging the air between us with years of unspoken words hanging in the balance. A shadow fell across her, breaking the spell and causing me to tear my gaze from hers.

"Ready to go, Skye?" Maverick's tone was casual, but his eyes held a challenge as he looked at me.

"Didn't know you two were still so close." I kept my voice and facial expression neutral.

Skye glanced between us, her brow furrowing. "Mav's always been there for me."

I clenched my jaw as they walked away. That scar on my cheek burned, a reminder of the fight that had changed everything. He'd gotten in the way back then, and it looked like he still was. But I wasn't backing down. "Guess some things never change."

Mav glanced over his shoulder, paused, and smiled faintly but without humor. "Yeah. Some things don't." Before Mav turned to leave with Skye, his voice carried low enough for only me to hear. "You're not as smart as you think, Cartwright. And if you don't figure it out soon, someone else will."

She'd moved on—Mav made that clear. *But the way she avoided my questions, the flicker of panic in her eyes?* It didn't add up. Skye was hiding something, and I wouldn't let it go.

CHAPTER FOUR

SKYE

Books littered the coffee table, but I didn't have time for them. I needed to edit the pictures from this weekend's game against Iowa. It was unusually quiet without Lily and Aunt Eileen, but I was so grateful to her for taking my daughter shopping and giving me an hour to get the pictures done and uploaded before I had to be at the field for a couple of candid shots of the athletes.

A few clicks through the pictures, and I couldn't help but pause on two, Jackson and Leroy—a wide receiver and a defensive end who, from my experience, had exclusively ridden the bench but had acquired significant game time recently. Developing and earning crucial minutes in big games wasn't unusual for players. Still, it surprised me—especially with Jackson and Leroy. Or at least Jackson. He was in one of my classes, and I'd noticed how much he'd bulked up over the past month. It was the class we had before practice. He would drink the contents in his shaker bottle then dart off as soon as class ended to get onto the field.

The only reason it interested me was my research in Professor White's lab with a few others about the negative and detrimental effects of performance-enhancing products. I wanted to ask what he was using. It couldn't be illegal, because the athletes were randomly drug tested, and the guidelines for the NCAA were strict.

I clicked on a few pictures and uploaded them to the football team's Instagram account, adding personal notes to hopefully engage fans. Jackson had more time than Leroy, but it was still impressive, especially going from zero field time to a full half of explosive blocking that had cleared the way for at least one of Liam's touchdowns. I closed down a few images then was faced with an action shot of Liam.

He'd been everywhere—on the field, in the crowd's roar, and worse, in my thoughts. Watching him stretch for that one-handed catch shot a pang of something through me that I refused to name. I hated how my heart still reacted to him and that no resolve could silence the memories of late-night talks and his whispered promises to make it big. He'd kept the details of those promises to himself, but I'd learned the hard way they didn't include me.

Everything about him screamed athleticism and God-given talent. *I know he'll achieve his dreams, but did he have to crush my soul in the process?* My hand shook as I tried and failed to minimize the image of what we'd had together—the fairy tale, magic, escapism, the star-crossed lovers' vibe, then heartbreak. My self-confidence had shattered in one final conversation when I realized that, in his eyes, I was not good enough to include in his life goals.

Devastated, alone, and rejected, I'd had to regroup and realize that I was independent and I could do it all on my own—raise my child and build a life for myself as a single mother and still seek education to better my life and my daughter's, without running to Liam for help. I'd realized quickly how resilient I was and that I would never get back together with him no matter how much I missed him.

My encounter with Liam after the game had left me shaken. As Maverick had led me away, I'd refused to look back. It didn't matter if Liam was staring after us or if the flicker of something in his eyes had been longing or anger. I'd made my choice a few years ago, and nothing—not Liam's charm or his questions—would make me undo it.

I resolved not to let his larger-than-life personality affect me through memories or a photograph. I clicked through the last few pictures, sighing with relief. The house was calm for once, and I had an hour to breathe. A knock at the door shattered the moment.

Glancing at the time revealed I had another hour before I had to leave. Shuffling through my mental checklist of things to do before then, I opened the door without looking through the side window to see who it was—big mistake. My hand froze on the doorknob, dread pooling in my stomach. *What the hell is he doing here?* I wasn't ready—not for him. *No-no-no-no.* My body went on lockdown as my fingers bit into the door.

Towering over me in a letterman jacket and jeans that hugged his powerful thighs was Liam, as if I'd conjured him from my warped imagination.

Lily. Oh God. A gust of cold early-December air blew in, sending a volley of goose bumps dancing over my skin beneath my long-sleeved T-shirt. I slammed the door in his face, eternally grateful that Aunt Eileen had taken Lily shopping as a mini panic attack took possession of me.

As he pounded on the door and shouted for me to let him in, I visually ticked through everything that was in the living room —her stuffed bunny, the mini kitchen, and if that wasn't enough, there were pictures of *my* daughter—because there was no "our" in this situation—everywhere.

The pounding accentuated how I couldn't ignore him forever. Reluctantly, I opened the door and tilted my chin higher to glare into his green eyes. "What are you doing here? My uncle isn't here."

"You've got to be kidding me." Liam pulled out his phone and stared at the screen before meeting my defensive stance again. "You're my tutor?"

"Ah, what?" My eyes widened farther as I tried to block the entryway with my body.

"The athletic office gave me this address and told me to show up for chemistry tutoring, which I now assume you do. You should've gotten an email." His jaw clenched.

Oh no. I thought through my calendar—I had a mandated athlete tutoring session today, and I'd forgotten. I squared my shoulders and crossed my arms. "Fine. Let's get this over with."

A muscle ticked along his sculpted jaw, and he crowded me. I stepped back, and he entered.

"Sure, come on in, Liam," I snapped.

"I had no idea you lived here, Skye, or that this was Coach's house."

I crossed my arms over my chest and took a badly needed defensive stance. I didn't like him in here. His presence felt too big for the room, suffocating me. I hated how easy it was to remember what it felt like to have him close, and I hated myself even more for still caring.Careful not to touch him, I moved to the couch and opened my laptop. Quickly minimizing the picture of him, I opened my email. "Dammit." He wasn't wrong. I had an email from the athletic advisor's office and one from Professor White about tutoring Liam twice a week. Worried about upsetting Professor White and jeopardizing my TA position within his lower-level chemistry classes, I gave in. I could only hope Aunt Eileen wouldn't return until Liam left. Taking a deep breath, I motioned for him to have a seat. "Yep. Looks like you're stuck with me. Show me what you're having problems with."

More Liam time—not even at a distance but up close and

personal—was the last thing I needed. I moved farther on the couch in an attempt not to let any part of our bodies touch. He was like a live wire and could set me off with one of his smoldering looks. I couldn't risk it. Resisting him in the past had been almost impossible, but now... the stakes were higher.

He slid his backpack from his shoulder, opened his laptop, and pulled up his last dismal assignments and test results, not looking me in the eye the entire time.

Could his bad grades affect him more than I'd ever thought possible? I brushed the speculation aside. It was doubtful.

I knew what his endgame was—the NFL. And he probably couldn't get the jersey chasers to take his chemistry tests because Professor White was inordinately strict and didn't give athletes an ounce of leeway.

My phone pinged with an incoming text. Mav's name flashed across the screen, and I snatched it from the coffee table, where we were working. A glance out of the corner of my eye to see if Liam had noticed told me all I needed to know by the muscle jumping in his clenched jaw—he had. But he kept his head down, working on the chemistry discussion question I had given him.

I shot off a quick message: *I'm tutoring Liam for chem—fuck my life.*

Mav: *(laughing emoji, devil emoji) You can't hide from this forever. He's going to figure it out.*

Me: *(tongue sticking out emoji)*

We'd had that discussion more times than I could count. The thing was, Mav worried about Liam stepping up for Lily too. I wasn't alone in my concerns. He knew all about how my parents had been in a custody battle until their lives had tragically ended and how my dad had been in the NFL with an endless supply of money to make things impossible for my mom. That made Liam's dreams an issue for me. When I finished the conversation with Mav, I set my phone back on the table, screen-side down.

"What's this?" Liam picked up a notebook with a crayon drawing Lily had done that morning peeking out. "Did your niece draw it?" He glanced at the pictures on the wall across from us.

My stomach dropped as his fingers brushed Lily's drawing. I snatched the notebook away in a flash, my pulse hammering as I set it face down on the end table. *Too close. Way too close.* "Something like that."

I launched into work, not giving him an inch to ask any more personal questions or to peer too closely at the pictures all around us. I went over his last test, expanding on the things he'd gotten wrong, coaxing him to come to the correct answers for a half hour until I thought he had a basic handle on it, but we clearly had a lot of work to do.

More than once, his leg grazed mine. When his hand touched the back of mine, I almost jumped out of my skin. Emotions and feelings running rampant, I tried desperately to keep us focused and my mind where it needed to be—on tutoring, and maintaining distance.

When his gaze kept returning to the pictures on the mantel above the fireplace, I lost it. All the pent-up resentment for how things had ended and what I'd heard of him moving on exploding in verbal warfare. "Pay attention. You can't coast on your looks or godlike football status to pass this class. You have to be present and put in the time instead of partying and working your way through jersey chasers."

His head slowly turned from the framed pictures of my family to face me, meeting my gaze with chilling precision. "I work goddamned hard, Skye. You, of all people, should know that. Football takes forty fucking hours every week between practice, watching film, the weight room, meetings, and games.

Add in another twenty hours of homework, classes, and sleep if there's time. What the hell do you think I do every day?"

Before I could tell him all the explicit things I'd had to listen to from his adoring female fans, the garage door opened, and Aunt Eileen walked in with my daughter in tow. Fear shot through me, and my chest tightened as Lily's chatter filled the room. Every detail screamed Liam—her green eyes, her dark hair, even the defiant tilt of her chin. I wrung my hands, praying he wouldn't connect the dots.

Please, God, not now.

"Mama, I gots butterflies! And hearts. Pink!" She skidded to a halt in front of us and stomped her cute little foot. Pink hearts lit up on her shoes, and she clapped, excitedly squealing.

I must've responded because Lily grinned then raced to the kitchen when Aunt Eileen called her for a snack, apologizing for interrupting our study session. Liam's gaze lingered on Lily, his brow furrowing like he was trying to place a memory just out of reach.

My heart pounded. *Say something. Distract him.* I gathered his book and computer, shoved it into his backpack, and slammed it into his rock-hard stomach. Suppressing a shiver at what I knew was underneath his navy henley, I jumped to my feet, threw his letterman jacket at him, and ushered him out. Slack-jawed, Liam glanced between me and over my shoulder, where I knew he could see Lily sitting at the kitchen table, swinging her legs like she always did.

"We'll meet at the library on Thursday. Same time. Don't be late." I practically shoved him out then slammed the door and twisted the lock for good measure. My hand trembled against my mouth as I leaned my forehead against the solid wood.

No matter how much my heart wanted to believe in fairy tales again, I couldn't let Liam close enough to destroy the life I'd built for Lily and me. Not again. I'd shielded Lily from everything he could take away. I couldn't let him break it all down. Not again.

CHAPTER FIVE

LIAM

The door slammed behind me, the sound echoing along the empty street as I made my way to my truck. The cold bit at my skin, but I barely felt it. My head spun, and no amount of freezing air could clear it.

Lily.

Her name was on repeat in my mind, her little voice echoing alongside it. *"Mama, I gots butterflies!"* She'd been so proud of those pink shoes, stomping her feet to make the hearts light up. And those eyes—bright, piercing green. *My green.* Or maybe not.

I shoved my hands into my pockets, my breath puffing out in uneven bursts as I tried to make sense of it all. Skye had a kid. That much was obvious. *But everything else?* None of it made sense. Three years—that was how long it had been since she'd walked away without a word. *If Lily were mine, wouldn't she have told me? But what if she didn't? What if she couldn't?*

I climbed into the truck, gripping the steering wheel like it was the only thing keeping me grounded. My thoughts were a mess, spiraling in a hundred different directions at once. I thought about Lily again, the way she'd burst into the room without a care in the world, chattering to Skye like they were the only two people who mattered. *And Skye...*

The way she froze when Lily appeared, the panic in her eyes when she looked at me—it was like she was bracing for something. Like she would be caught.

But if Lily were mine, why would Skye hide it?

I let out a sharp breath, my grip tightening on the wheel. One reason kept coming back, no matter how much I hated it. *Maverick.*

The thought of him made my stomach churn. Mav had always been close to Skye—too close. Even back when we were together, I'd caught glimpses of the way he hovered around her, always there, always protective. I'd chalked it up to their friendship, but after Skye left, it hadn't been hard to imagine him stepping in.

And now?

The way Skye had looked at me, the way she'd shut down the second Lily entered the room—it wasn't just fear. It was guilt.

My chest tightened as the thought took root, unwanted but impossible to ignore. *What if Lily isn't mine? What if she's Mav's?*

It made sense—too much sense. I let out a bitter laugh, the sound sharp and hollow in the quiet truck. Of course, she would have chosen him. Mav was solid, dependable, the kind of guy who wouldn't let her down. He wasn't selfish. He wasn't reckless. He wasn't me.

I slammed my head back against the seat, staring up at the ceiling as I fought to pull myself together. I didn't have any proof—no real reason to believe Lily wasn't mine. But I didn't have any proof she *was* either.

And those eyes...

I groaned, scrubbing a hand down my face. I was seeing what I wanted to see. That was all. It was a coincidence. But the more I thought about it, the harder it was to shake the memory of how Skye used to look at Maverick. How easy it would have been for her to turn to him when things fell apart. Jealousy burned, sharp and bitter. I didn't want to feel it, didn't want to care. But the thought of Skye with Mav, of Lily calling him "Dad"—it was too much.

I shoved the keys into the ignition and pulled onto the road, the truck growling beneath me as I drove aimlessly through town. The streets weren't busy, and the cold seeped in through the windows, settling deep in my chest. I didn't know what to think, what to feel.

Part of me wanted to believe Lily was mine, that I still had a place in Skye's life, no matter how small. But another part of me—the part that thought I wasn't good enough, that I left nothing but damage in my wake the way my dad did—couldn't help but wonder if it was for the best that I'd already been replaced. Maverick had always been there. And now, there was Lily.

It would be so easy to walk away, to let them have their perfect little family without me screwing it up. But I couldn't. Because as much as I hated it, as much as it terrified me to admit it, I wanted to know the truth—even if it destroyed me.

⸻

Practice the next day was alive with activity, but my attention was shot. Every time I looked to the sidelines, there she was—Skye, camera in hand. After yesterday's revelation about her daughter, my mind couldn't stay in the game. The ball sailed past me, and I stumbled, missing an easy catch.

"Cartwright!" Coach Mack bellowed. "Get your head in the game."

I'd nodded, my face burning with embarrassment.

After practice, Coach Mack pulled me aside again. "Cartwright." His voice was low and serious. "I've noticed you've been distracted lately. Is everything okay?"

"Yeah, I'm good." *What can I say? My chem class is kicking my ass, and I'm terrified I won't be able to play because of my grades, so I could lose my chance with the scouts? Or the other thing that has plagued me since I learned it—Skye is a mom?*

"Look, son, I know you've got a lot on your plate, but you need to stay focused. The scouts are watching, and mistakes like in practice today could break your future. Don't force my hand and make me put Jackson in over you. I'd hate to see you throw away everything you've worked so hard for."

The weight of expectation sat heavily on my shoulders, so much so that after practice, I called Fiona to see if she'd had dinner yet. I needed my sister to remind me of the pact we'd made as kids—to make something of ourselves despite our shitty role models growing up. Fiona had accomplished her goals when she became a detective. It helped remind me that if she'd made it, I could too.

The afternoon sun dipped low as I drove toward Fiona's. The light turned green, but instead of heading straight to my sister's, I tightened my hands on the wheel, turning toward Coach Becket's house. I told myself I wasn't looking for her. *But who am I kidding?* The need to see Skye, even from a distance, overruled reason.

As the two-story house came into view, I slowed. A black Jeep stood in the driveway. When I was two houses away, the front door opened, and Skye walked out with no one other than Maverick Davis. He swung the laughing little girl in his arms while Skye went to the passenger door of the Jeep.

A pang of something—jealousy, loss, regret—burned through me as I watched him hold the little girl. Their laughter carried on the wind, taunting me with what I could never have, what I'd never deserved.

I didn't stick around. I pulled past and exited out the other end of the neighborhood, hoping she didn't see me and think I was stalking her.

The drive to my sister's went by in a blur, and I found myself on autopilot as I parked on the street and climbed the steps to her townhome, then rapped my knuckles on the blue door. Her place wasn't super upscale, but in her words, it was more "blue-collar cozy." It fit and was a step up from our origins and our dad's hoarder-style dump on the city's south side.

Fio answered the door, her dark-brown hair pulled back in a low ponytail as she waved me in. "Hey, bro. Hurry up. You're letting in all the cold air."

I grinned, inhaling the comforting aroma of Italian sauce. "What'd you make?" I hoped for lasagna. Fio's was the best. Not that I would ever admit that to Aurora, but something about my sister's reminded me of living there with her and all the time we'd spent together while Dad fucked off doing who knew what in his corner of the city.

I'd taken off from my dad's place to live with Fiona as soon as possible the summer before college. I even stayed with her during holidays or long weekends when I could. It was the same in college. This was home.

My newly found good mood took an instant nosedive when I spotted Dad passed out with a fleet of beer cans near the recliner. Without deviating, I made a beeline for the kitchen, where spaghetti, meatballs, and garlic bread were waiting. Hot on my heels, Fio knew what I would say when we were far enough away, and I turned to confront her.

"What the hell, Fio? Why is he here?" I gestured toward the living room, where Dad snored amid a pile of empties.

Fio grimaced. "He lost the house."

"Why is that your problem?" The words were out before I could take them back.

"Because he's family, whether we like it or not." Her voice was a soft reprimand.

"And when he hocks the TV for beer money? Is he still family then?"

The memory burned like an old scar. Dad had broken into

my room, stolen the money I'd saved for the combine—and decimated my shot at the NFL. His drinking had hijacked my future before I'd even had a chance. With no other choice, I'd accepted the scholarship to Fall Lake University and enrolled, altering my future and adding a few more years to achieving my goal.

The cop mask she wore when we fought about Dad fell into place, and her jaw hardened. "I've got it handled. This is a temporary development, not something you need to worry about."

"Bullshit. You have a job. What's he going to do with all that unsupervised time in here?"

"He won't ever be at the house when I'm not. I've got connections." Her arms crossed over her chest—her tell that she was digging her heels in and gearing up for a fight she would not lose.

I knew better than to engage when Fio was like that. I settled for a warning. "Don't let him fuck up what you made for yourself. He's poison, and you know it."

"I appreciate your concern, but as I said, I've got it handled. You focus on what you need to do—school and securing your future. I got what I wanted. It's my turn to deal with him."

I grunted a nonresponse. It wasn't that I didn't appreciate what she'd said, I just hated laying anything on her doorstep, and our dad could derail the best-laid plans.

Fio grabbed a plate and shoved it into my hands. "This conversation is over. Let's eat."

I couldn't fight her on that and piled my plate high. Grabbing a glass of water, I followed her to the small table. It was later in the evening, after my failed attempt at finding clarity, by the time I sat across from Fiona at her kitchen table. We tucked into our food, neither of us talking until we were almost halfway through our meal and the edge of my hunger was sated.

"How are Ares and Brielle?"

Fio had been there when Kylian and I went with Ares to rescue Brielle after her dad's illicit past had come calling. "They're good. She practically lives at the condo." I swallowed another bite. "It's not that bad having Kylian's fiancée and Ares's girlfriend around."

Fio laughed, setting down her fork and shoving away her plate. "Maybe you're finally coming around to considering a relationship."

I glanced through the open-concept living room to where Dad was passed out in the family room and pointed my fork in his direction. "How can I take that risk?"

"You can't know until you try." Her voice softened. "You're not Dad, and really, will you let his shortcomings define you?"

I didn't bother answering because it was hard as fuck not to do that. I battled the past constantly, but every failing grade and what'd happened with Skye freshman year were reminders of how I wasn't good enough. I badly needed a change of subject. I'd had enough heavy to last a lifetime. "I have to get tutoring for that stupid chemistry class."

"Why did you have to take chemistry? That's not an easy class."

"My advisor screwed up and thought I'd filled my science elective. That was the only thing I could take by the time he figured it out. As it was, I started chem the day after add/drop closed."

"Shit. That sucks. How's the tutoring? Is it helping?"

"Skye is my tutor."

Water sprayed across the table as Fio choked on her sip. While she coughed and wiped her mouth, I sopped up the rest that'd landed on the table, thankfully just shy of my food. I would've been annoyed if her spit take had ruined the rest of my dinner.

"The girl you were so hung up on? The same one who you practically stalked the campus trying to find for a solid month?" At my nod, her eyes lit up. "Maybe you can try dating her again."

I snorted at that impossibility. "She has a kid."

"How old is the kid?"

I shrugged. "How should I know? Two? Three?" I didn't need to ask to know Fio was doing the same mental math that I had.

"Could it be yours?"

"She had dark-brown hair, but so does Skye." But one thing still hit me hard. "And bright-green eyes."

"Shit, Liam. Do you think—"

"She's probably a hockey player's kid, and I think that was who Skye dumped me for." The kid's eyes were similar to mine, but Mav had greenish-blue eyes, so Lily was more likely his.

Fio tilted her head, scrutinizing my expression too closely. "If he's not in the picture, you could still date her."

Life was complicated enough. "No. She's a flight risk to boot —possibly similar to Mom." Who'd left us to start another family.

Even with all that, why can't I get Skye out of my head?

I slid into a back corner booth across from Kylian and next to Ares at Last Call, an off-campus bar that was always crowded after games. Despite it being a weekday, the place was packed. It usually was, as it was the go-to college hangout, the it place. And it had been for me, too, until I had a come-to-Jesus moment in a conversation with my roommates and our head coach. With it being my last year, the countdown to the combine, and scouts watching our every move, it was time to quit my reckless behavior, stop drinking, and get serious.

Aurora practically lived at the condo, and her meals were a constant reminder of how domestic life could be. I'd never thought much about it before, but with Skye back in my life—even at an arm's length—it was harder to ignore that I wanted someone there for me too, even if I couldn't have it.

The steady stream of girls and all the partying that I'd enjoyed over the past few years had come to a grinding halt. I didn't miss what it represented, its purpose: to ease my loneliness and distract me from how happy my closest friends were with their girls and that their paths weren't meant for me. I'd come to accept it rather than bury my head in the sand and pretend everything was fine.

"Thanks for meeting me."

"No problem." Kylian pushed a glass of ice water in front of me. "After your—"

"Change of heart"—Ares shoved my shoulder—"we were surprised you wanted to come here."

I shrugged. "I wasn't ready to go home. Dad was passed out in his usual drunk state at Fio's. It fucked with my head for a minute. And I don't know, I just wanted a breather somewhere that didn't remind me of all the responsibilities and expectations pressing in."

"Dude, you'll be fine," Kylian said. "You were all over ESPN after the game this weekend. You've got nothing to worry about."

Slouching back against the booth, I ran my hands through my hair. "Maybe." But that could change with one career-ending injury. Nothing was guaranteed.

"What else is bothering you?" Ares folded his arms and braced his weight on the table. "You seem more stressed than usual. Is this really about your dad or the draft? Or did something else happen?"

"You know the tutor I'm required to see for chem?"

"Yeah." Kylian's gaze locked on me as he waited expectantly for my response.

"Fuck it." I clenched my jaw before letting the story pour out of me. "It's Skye. The address was for Coach's house. She lives with him and his wife."

"Okay." Ares drew out the word. "Not ideal, but he must've set it up because it was at his house."

"He was involved in it, according to my advisor and Coach Mack."

"And?" Ares continued. "That means Coach will see you're committed to improving your grade."

"Yeah, I guess."

"Is it messing with your head? Maybe you should get another tutor," Kylian said.

"That's part of it. It's not just about seeing her again," I admitted, the words heavy on my tongue. "She's everything I want but can't have. Seeing her with Mav only worsens the pressure—scouts, coaches, Skye—every part of my life feels like it's tearing me apart." I confessed, running a hand through my hair for the millionth time.

Kylian and Ares exchanged concerned glances while I bared my soul and grappled with conflicting emotions that were too big to manage.

"Have you thought about talking things through with her? Maybe making another go of dating?" Kylian asked.

"She walked, man. I tried to talk to her, to get her to understand why I said what I did, but she blocked me. If she could walk away that easy, then there's no denying that she doesn't want me." I took a deep breath then dropped the truth bomb that had plagued me since I'd left Coach's house. "Besides, she has a kid."

"Does that bother you?" Kylian leaned back, giving up all pretenses of drinking the water before him.

Does it? "Yes and no. I like kids." But that wasn't the problem. It was how things ended between us.

Both Ares and Kylian had hard and fast rules about family. They had moms who would do anything for them, who always had their backs, and who they loved beyond all reason. I didn't have that, and I listened to them when it came to the things like family and relationships. I was too emotionally screwed up to trust myself, and I tried to make sure I wasn't letting my past infect my present and future—which was a constant battle I failed at more often than I liked to admit.

Ares's fist clenched on the table. "She's a single mom. You can't mess with her unless you're serious."

"I know." The words tasted like a lie. I didn't want to ruin her life—or mine. But no matter how hard I tried, staying away from Skye felt like fighting gravity. Impossible. My confession hung in the air, heavy from finally being spoken.

Ares leaned back, folding his arms.

"She's everywhere lately," I said, my voice sharper than I intended. "Practice, tutoring, the sidelines... It's like she's haunting me." In my head, on the field, in Coach's damn living room. And no matter how hard I tried, I couldn't shake the way seeing her again knocked me completely off balance.

I gripped the glass of water like it was the only thing keeping me grounded. The noise of the bar buzzed in the background, barely registering. I wasn't there to unwind—hell, I didn't even know why I was there. All I knew was that sitting at home, alone with my thoughts, wasn't an option.

"She's probably not trying to run into you," Kylian said evenly, but his gaze sharpened. "She moved on, right? Maverick and all that?"

The mention of Maverick made my stomach churn. "Yeah. Sure looks that way."

Before either of them could respond, the door to the bar swung open, letting in a gust of cold air. All three of us turned instinctively, and my chest tightened when I saw Skye enter. She stepped inside, glancing around like she was looking for someone. Her dark hair caught the dim light, and even in the chaos of the crowd, she stood out like a beacon.

"Damn," Ares muttered. "She's here."

"Looks like she's meeting someone," Kylian added, his tone careful.

My jaw clenched as I tracked her movements. She hadn't noticed me yet, her eyes scanning the room, and I couldn't look away. She stood just inside the door, her expression carefully neutral, though I could see the tension in her shoulders. She was looking for someone, and I already knew who. *Maverick.*

Sure enough, Maverick leaned casually against the bar, and when he saw her, his grin widened. Something inside me twisted as he pushed off the countertop and closed the space between them. He pulled her into a quick hug, his arm slung over her shoulder like it belonged there.

I clenched my jaw, biting back the jealousy that surged through me like wildfire. *What the hell is he to her?* Brotherly, my ass. He was always there—on campus, after our last game, now here. Always close, always in her orbit.

Maverick said something, and Skye laughed lightly, but when he motioned toward my booth, her whole body went still. Her shoulders stiffened, her gaze following his gesture until it landed on me. I knew the exact moment she spotted me. Her lips pressed into a tight line, and for a second, I thought she might turn around and walk out. But she didn't. Instead, she squared her shoulders, lifted her chin, and started toward me, her movements measured and deliberate. Her defiance lit something in me that was equal parts infuriated and captivated. She'd always had that effect on me.

Ares exchanged a look with Kylian then turned to me. "We'll give you some space."

"What?" I snapped, dragging my attention away from Skye to glare at them for deserting me.

Kylian smirked knowingly. "You're wound tight, and we're not sticking around to watch you implode. Talk to her, Liam."

"I don't need—"

"Yeah, you do," Ares interrupted, sliding out of the booth. "And you're welcome for us clearing the way."

Before I could argue, Kylian and Ares were gone, leaving me alone to stew in my mess.

"Liam." Skye slid into the booth across from me, her tone neutral, like she was trying to pretend it wasn't awkward as hell.

"Skye." I leaned back, forcing myself to appear calm, casual, though my pulse pounded in my ears. "Didn't expect to see you here."

"I could say the same." Her gaze flicked to the glass of water in front of me. "I thought this place wasn't your scene anymore."

"It isn't." I shrugged, swirling the ice in my glass. "I needed a distraction."

She raised a brow, a flicker of skepticism in her eyes. "Funny. I wouldn't think the great Liam Cartwright needs distractions. According to your rant, football keeps you busy enough."

I flinched, the jab hitting harder than it should have, but I forced a tight smile. "It does. But sometimes, it's not enough."

The weight of those words hung between us, thick and charged. Skye's fingers fidgeted with the strap of her bag, and for once, she didn't have a quick comeback.

"I was thinking about freshman year," I said suddenly, my voice quieter. "The night before our first big game. You remember?"

Her gaze snapped to mine, her expression instantly guarded. "Of course, I remember."

"You stayed up with me," I said, the memory clawing at my throat. "I was a wreck—nervous as hell—but you kept me grounded. Made me believe I could handle it."

Her lips curved into a faint smile, but it didn't reach her eyes. "You didn't need me to believe in you, Liam. You always knew who you were."

"That's not true." I leaned forward, my elbows resting on the table as I lowered my voice. "I didn't know shit back then. Hell, half the time, I still don't. But you… you made me feel like I didn't have to pretend. Like I could be myself."

Her breath hitched, and for a moment, her composure cracked. Her eyes darted away, and her fingers twisted tighter around her purse strap. "That was a long time ago."

"Not long enough for me to forget," I said, my voice softer, more vulnerable than I wanted it to be. "You disappeared after our last disagreement, Skye. No explanation, no warning. I thought… I thought we had something real."

Her head jerked up, and for the briefest second, guilt flickered across her face. But she quickly masked it, shaking her head. "You never indicated that. I specifically remember you saying we were just casual."

I flinched. She wasn't wrong there.

"And… it wasn't that simple."

"Then explain it to me," I pressed, my frustration bubbling to the surface. "Because I've been trying to figure it out for three years, and I still don't have a damn clue."

Her throat worked as she swallowed hard, and I could see the hesitation in her eyes. She was about to say something, but before she could, a shadow fell across the table.

Maverick.

He set a drink in front of Skye, his expression casual, but his eyes held an edge as he looked at me. "You okay?" he asked her, his voice light, but there was no mistaking the protective undertone.

"Fine," she said quickly, taking the drink. "Thanks."

My gaze stayed locked on her as she turned toward him, her posture stiff, her movements abrupt. She was hiding something —I could feel it.

Maverick lingered a second longer, his gaze meeting mine with a faint smile that didn't reach his eyes. "Good seeing you, Cartwright."

"Sure," I said, my tone clipped as I leaned back in the booth.

He turned to walk away, Skye by his side, then he paused just long enough to lean in close, his voice low enough for only me to hear. "Figure it out, Cartwright. Before it's too late."

His possessive words hit like a direct blow to the chest. *She doesn't want me.* I sat there, frozen, watching them disappear into the crowd.

CHAPTER SIX

SKYE

Glass shattered at my feet, a sharp crash that jolted me back to reality. I closed my eyes and willed my hands to steady. It was just a beaker, not the end of the world. But my nerves were another story. I needed my study to be successful, but it was Liam's stupid grin that kept replaying in my head, throwing me off balance.

I muttered under my breath, brushing the shards into a dustpan. My chest tightened at the uninvited memories of his touch —strong, warm, infuriatingly gentle—lingering from our last tutoring session. *Why did he have to be so... him?*

"You okay?" Joe turned to face me, concern flickering in his deep-espresso eyes.

"Yeah, just clumsy today." I summoned a smile I didn't feel.

The weight of his gaze stayed on me as I finished cleaning up, but I avoided looking directly at him. Joe didn't need to know how much my current distraction was tied to a certain wide receiver.

I noticed Joe's disheveled hair and swollen lips then remembered seeing Megan slipping out of the lab as I came in. I laughed. "I'm fine, but it looks like you're more than fine. What were you and Megan doing before I came in? Did she finally agree to go out with you?"

"I took your advice." Joe's sheepish grin tugged at my mood despite my frazzled nerves. "Megan said yes."

"Good. Don't screw it up." I waved him off with a laugh, sweeping up the glass and trying not to let my shaking hands give me away. "When did this happen?"

"Last night."

My brows climbed my forehead. "You dog. Bet you were here 'working'"—I air quoted—"last night. Maybe she didn't even go home." I glanced around the lab. "Just tell me, should I avoid working anywhere because of… contamination?"

"Shit, Skye." His cheeks flamed red, and he ducked his head. "You're all good. But yeah, we were… working all night, and she said yes when I asked her out."

"So it's official?" I'd known Joe since last year, when I'd started being a TA for Professor White's introductory chemistry class. Joe was at the top of his class and was Professor White's go-to assistant. We'd become friends when he covered for me during a few emergencies with Lily. I'd noticed how he pined for Megan, another grad student who had access to the lab for her research on the harmful effects of pain meds and performance-enhancement drugs in high school and college student athletes. Because he'd been such a great friend and had helped me out when I'd needed it the most, I'd decided to coach him on how to ask her out. Guess he'd finally manned up and taken my advice.

"Yeah, we're going out Friday night."

I dumped the glass in the trash. "Was that before or after you two got busy?"

"Jesus, Skye."

I laughed at his discomfort before deciding to go easy on him. "I'm glad things are going well for you."

"Yeah, thanks." Joe glanced at me as he scribbled something in his notebook. "How's tutoring?"

"It's fine," I said too quickly.

His head snapped up, eyebrows raising in curiosity. "Fine, huh?" He leaned back, crossing his arms.

"I was asked to add an athlete to my schedule. Liam Cartwright."

"Really?" Joe's smile fell away. "I saw the two of you at the stadium last night. You've been spending time with Cartwright."

My stomach tightened, but I forced a casual shrug. "I'm tutoring him, Joe. It's part of my job."

He frowned, his expression shifting from curiosity to something more serious. "I know guys like Liam. They take what they want and leave the rest in pieces. Be careful, Skye."

"Ah, nothing's going on with Liam. I'm just tutoring him."

"Still, I know how he is with women and relationships. I'm just saying this because you set me up with Megan, who won't ditch when fame hits."

"As I said, nothing's going on between us." I couldn't keep the chill from my voice if I tried.

He ducked his head, seemingly chastised.

"How's your research on foxglove going?" I eyed his notes. It was one of two separate studies he'd been burning the midnight oil on this past summer and semester.

"Really good." A genuine smile curved his face.

"Do you need a hand with that?" He waved to my abandoned work.

"No. I'm good. I'm too preoccupied to focus. I need to get out of here anyway."

Aunt Eileen was picking Lily up from daycare, feeding her dinner, and getting her to bed, which gave me the flexibility to spend the evening with the team. I'd planned to film some of the players walking through campus for a short day-in-the-life post after candid practice shots to hype the next game. It wasn't my favorite part of the job, but it was important for building engagement. In addition, I needed to work on the players' stats for the once-a-week posts I'd started doing to get everyone who liked that sort of thing hyped for the upcoming games. Mostly guys, but some girls followed that data religiously as well.

"Sure." His response was distracted as he refocused on his experiment, already absorbed in his work.

As I bent to tuck the dustpan back under the counter on my way out, the lab door creaked open.

Megan stepped back in, her gaze bouncing between Joe and me. She carried an air of curiosity that didn't feel entirely innocent. "Hey, Skye," she said, her tone casual. "I saw you at the game last weekend. You've been spending a lot of time with the team lately."

I nodded, brushing my hands on my jeans. "I'm their social media manager. Most of what I do is behind the camera, but I'm also taking on some athletic tutoring."

Megan's eyes sharpened slightly. "Must be interesting, being around them all the time. I bet they're under a ton of pressure."

"Yeah, it's a lot, but the coaches keep them focused," I said, my tone measured.

"Do you ever hear about, you know, the pressure they're under?" She tilted her head, feigning casual interest. "I mean, with scouts watching them, the combine coming up, and all those insane stats you post, it's got to be intense trying to measure up."

"Probably," I said cautiously.

Megan leaned against the counter, her lips twitching into a sly smile. "You ever wonder if any of them might... I don't know, look for an edge? Hypothetically speaking."

Her tone was too breezy, too specific to feel innocent. I stiffened, not liking the direction her questions were going. "Not here. They know better than to risk their futures over something like that."

Megan shrugged, her smile not reaching her eyes. "I'm sure you're right. I was just curious. You hear stories, that's all."

"You heard wrong," I said firmly. "Our team knows better than to jeopardize their careers over something like that."

"Of course." Megan laughed falsely. She turned to Joe, her voice shifting into something huskier. "We still need to go over those samples later. Don't forget."

Joe nodded, his focus fixed on his notebook.

"Catch you later, Skye." Megan threw me a wide smile before disappearing toward the back of the lab.

I stood frozen for a moment, the exchange replaying in my mind. Something about her questions rubbed me the wrong way, but I brushed it off as curiosity gone too far. With a final glance at Joe, I grabbed my bag and headed out the door, ready to shake off the strange encounter.

Backpack slung over one shoulder, I hurried through the quad toward my car, eager to get to the stadium. It was easier driving to the athletic center and practice field than walking. Ten minutes later, I was on the field, my backpack parked on the bench as I snapped pictures of the players in action. I had to be careful not to reveal any of their plays but to take individual shots or group ones where they were just talking or lifting in the gym.

Later, as I stood on the sidelines, camera in hand, my focus was supposed to be on all the players, but my lens kept drifting to Liam. He wasn't just running drills—he was commanding the field. Every movement was sharp, deliberate, as if he could will the world to see him.

I shook my head, lowering the camera. *What is wrong with me?* I couldn't keep letting him pull me in. Still, something about him was different now. He wasn't the cocky freshman I remembered. There was a quiet intensity to his game and the way he encouraged the rookies, clapping them on the back or offering tips between plays. It tugged at something in me that I didn't want to name.

Shoving the camera strap higher on my shoulder, I forced myself to focus on pictures and stats for anything post worthy. Liam didn't fit into the careful plans I'd laid for my life. I couldn't afford to lose sight of that, no matter how much he made me feel like I already had.

When the numbers blurred, I glanced at the team still running drills on the field with a more critical eye. Megan's question about the players circled in my head. It took only a few seconds to key into what bothered me about the players' attitudes. A few of them were exhibiting unusual behavior, where their movements seemed almost too quick, their strength beyond what I'd thought I remembered from earlier in the season when I'd studied the team before taking on the internship.

I watched the scrimmage on the field where number eighty, Louis Leroy, one of the defensive ends, tackled another player with such force that the sound echoed across the field. My suspicion grew, and I shifted on the bench, pulling up the team's stats on my phone to study the reoccurring theme I'd spotted earlier—players who didn't see a lot of field time and weren't getting noticed before now were, and their stats showed a remarkable difference from last year. The numbers for some players didn't make sense. Leroy's numbers had skyrocketed, but the way he moved—almost too fast, too strong—made my stomach churn. Something about it didn't add up, and the numbers on my screen weren't helping.

What could that mean?

My gaze flickered to the field, where Liam caught a pass and bolted down the sideline like he had something to prove. He was magnetic, impossible to ignore. Even now, in the middle of piecing together a puzzle that could change everything, my mind circled back to him. To the way his laugh had sounded last night when he'd called me out for avoiding him. To how his green eyes seemed to see through every wall I'd built.

I forced my eyes back to my phone. My body tingled with the sense that I was being watched, and I dropped my phone to my lap, whipping my head toward the field.

"Hey, social media queen," Liam called out, jogging over as practice ended.

My pulse kicked up, and I quickly masked it with a smirk. "What? Need tips on how to smile for the camera?"

He grinned, the dimple in his cheek flashing. "Just making sure you're getting my good side."

"Every side's your good side, remember?"

The words slipped out before I could stop them, and his eyes locked on mine, the teasing glint fading into something deeper. My breath caught.

"I remember," he said softly before turning back to the field.

But I didn't miss the thunderous expression on his too-gorgeous face that conflicted with his light tone. He affected me too much, and my mood turned mercurial.

"What? What did you really want to talk to me about?" I snapped.

"Why didn't you tell me you had a kid?"

My defensive walls erected abruptly. "It's not relevant to being your tutor, which by the way, is just a job. It doesn't mean we're friends. I don't owe you anything, nor are you entitled to information about my personal life."

"Really? After everything we've shared?" His kissable lips curved into that sexy, irresistible grin that invaded my dreams on lonely nights. "You're taking that stance with me?"

Why the hell am I thinking about kissing him? Even when he was being an absolute jerk, my body betrayed me, tugging me toward him with a magnetic pull I couldn't explain—or resist. "Get serious. Let's talk about what's going on here, which has nothing to do with the past. If you expect to improve the shitastic grade you have in chemistry by the final exam, you'll need to get serious with a study plan. That means at least three nights a week, not two, and also on Sundays—preferably hangover and jersey-chaser free—or you'll lose everything you've set your sights on so rigidly."

"You think I'm still that guy? The one who only cared about parties and the next girl? News flash, Skye—I grew the hell up while you were busy running away."

"You didn't grow up, Liam. You just shifted focus. You still bulldoze through everything in your path, and God help anyone who gets in your way."

"Come on, Skye. Look around." He spread his arms wide, muscles rippling with the movement. "You used to know who I was—"

"That was a long time ago. And you moved on real quick after we split up."

His eyes narrowed dangerously. "From what I remember, so did you."

I jumped to my feet so he couldn't tower over me as much. "Stop throwing our past in my face. It was two months. That's a blip in time and hardly amounts to anything." *Except for the conception of our daughter.* The thought blindsided me, and I cringed.

"Maybe"—his spring-grass eyes heated with flecks of fiery gold around the pupils as he crowded me—"what you're really doing here, day in and day out, is trying for another go. Everywhere I look, there you are, snapping my picture, and lo and behold, you're the tutor I'm required to see several times a week. Surprising, because you up and quit on me when you weren't sure if I would be the paycheck you were digging for. Is that why you're back in my life? Mav not promising a long-term relationship?"

"Fuck you." I clenched my fists at my sides. "You're an asshole."

"I'm right, aren't I?" That tick along his jaw worked overtime. "If it weren't, you would be working for the hockey team where your boyfriend is. After all, he's headed to the NHL, and rumor says he's already got an agent."

Ares skidded to a halt behind Liam, grabbed his elbow, and pulled him away. "Chill out, man."

Liam's intense stare lingered as he let Ares pull him back, only breaking when he whirled around and gave me his back. Anger roared through me, and I sucked in a deep breath, fighting the urge to chuck my phone at his retreating form. I counted to ten, willing my blood pressure to lower as I caught sight of my uncle's approach from the field to the sideline where I stood.

"Skye."

His deep voice jolted ice into my veins, and I relaxed my tense muscles. He didn't know Liam was Lily's dad, and the last thing I wanted was to cause problems between Liam and his coach or his chances of Uncle Tommy speaking well about him to scouts.

"Are you okay? One of the assistant coaches heard you and Liam arguing."

"Yeah, totally fine." I faked a smile. "It was just about school. Liam's frustrated by chemistry, and he needed to vent. Nothing major." I slung my bag over my shoulder and shoved my phone in my pocket. "I'm going to get some video around campus to add to a few posts, maybe follow some of the players walking out of the building just for a day-in-the-life clip."

He let the silence hang between us, his gaze dancing over my face as if he could decipher the truth from my features. No way. I had that shit locked down with my game face on. I'd perfected it early in my pregnancy while living with my aunt and uncle. While she knew the truth about Lily's father being a football player, my uncle didn't—and he couldn't without it potentially causing an issue for Liam.

"I want to try to catch up with a few players and get their consent to film them leaving. See you at home?"

"Be careful," Uncle Tommy said.

"Always!" With a wave, I whirled around and hurried through the building. The argument with Liam had already taken enough time for most of the team to shower or head for the weight room. I needed some film of them lifting, too, but not today. Liam's presence was more than I could handle, and since he was still here...

It didn't take long before three huge football players headed toward the exit. Good thing I recognized one of them. That only made it clear I had to familiarize myself with the entire team, not just the starters and the usual subs.

"Mitchel."

I jogged over to the guys as they paused halfway out of the building. They turned as a unit. Mitchel grinned then wiggled his eyebrows, and the tension in my shoulders eased.

"What's up, Coach's Niece?"

I snorted. "Knock it off, Romeo." Mitchel was a teddy bear—a huge one—but a total player. "Kissing my ass won't do you any good. You should work on your angles instead of chasing the quarterback. Try it in the Indiana game 'cause that quarterback has speed."

Mitch barked out a laugh then ruffled my hair. "What're you, the new positions coach in training?"

"Just call me coach, and we'll be good." I winked as the other two players crowded our group. "But all kidding aside, can I follow you guys out and record you leaving the building for a short video through campus just past the fountain?"

"You can follow me anywhere, darlin'," Rodrigues drawled as

he sidled up to Mitch, his eyes roaming from my head to my toes and back again.

Liam rounded the corner and joined the guys, a muscle jumping overtime along his jaw as he slapped the rookie in the ample gut and pushed him back. "Ease up unless you want Coach to bench your ass for the rest of the season." He waited until the new guy looked suitably chastised. "You need to think of her as your little sister." He shoved Rodrigues out the door ahead of him. "Whatever you need, Skye, let's get it done."

Counting to ten, I prayed for calm around Liam, resigning myself to spending a little more time with him since he'd hijacked my original group. What mattered was the content I could get, and having Liam in the shot guaranteed more likes and responses.

I set my phone to record and positioned myself behind them as they filed out the door, joking and talking with one another. Streetlamps cast a soft glow along the winding path we took rather than the exit that led straight to the parking lot.

I ended the video and shouted thanks as three of them broke off at the fork before the fountain. Liam hung back, watching me. I ignored him. Before I looped back to head to my car, I moved closer, wanting a picture of the fountain all lit up without another soul around it.

I loved the architecture and design. It was the first time I'd been back there in so long. I hadn't risked going near it until now, as it was too close to the athletic building, and I had the potential to run into Liam. However, the fixture was very similar to Buckingham Fountain on a much smaller scale. At night, lights highlighted the details and alternate colors. I snapped a few pictures from a distance then moved closer, noticing something odd about the section around the base. The water had been drained a while ago due to the weather, but something large occupied the basin.

Is that...?

I closed the distance for a better look. The lights flickered, casting colorful patterns across the carvings. At first, I thought it was a shadow—a trick of the light. But as I stepped closer, the outline sharpened into something unmistakable—a body lying face down, head turned to the side, its unseeing eyes staring in my direction. My stomach twisted, bile rising. I stumbled back, a scream lodged in my throat until it tore out of me at eardrum-shattering decibels.

Strong arms wrapped around me. "Shit," Liam muttered. "Skye, look away."

For a few seconds, my gaze remained locked on the unmoving body until I was physically turned, my head cupped, and my cheek pressed against a warm body. The scent of cinnamon and warm spices penetrated the haze of horror. The world blurred as Liam held me tightly. His warmth was a shield against the icy fingers of panic creeping up my spine. I wanted to disappear into him, to let his strength carry me far from the nightmare unfolding before us.

Footsteps pounded the pavement, sounding like a herd of elephants as the guys I'd been filming returned. Liam's arms loosened, and I clung tighter. He paused for a second then lifted me and moved farther away. "You're all right, Skye. I've got you."

His voice was low and soothing, but it only worsened the storm inside me. With a volley of shivers along my spine, I buried my face in his jacket, needing his strength like I'd sworn I never would.

"Holy shit," Mitch swore. "Is that Jackson?"

Liam tensed, his head whipping up from where he'd rested his chin on me. My arms drifted up from his waist to wrap about his neck. I clung to him, the warmth of his embrace at odds with the cold dread settling in my bones. I didn't want to face Jackson's lifeless body or the fragile balance of our world that had cracked wide open. I wanted not to give a fuck about what I'd seen or what would happen. All I wanted was for Liam to hold me, to make me forget everything—and that was more dangerous than what we would soon find out about how Jackson had ended up in the drained fountain.

The police were called, and Liam and I moved away from the action with enough distance that I could pretend none of what I'd seen was real. His arms tightened around me, his warmth a shield against the icy fear clawing up my spine. My breath hitched, and I buried my face in his chest, inhaling the familiar scent of warm spices and something distinctly him.

I tilted my head back to meet his eyes, those green depths searching mine with an intensity that stole the rest of my breath. His hand cupped my cheek, his thumb brushing away a tear I didn't even realize had fallen.

The world around us faded—the team's shouts, the horror of what I'd seen—until it was just him and me. His gaze flicked to my lips, and my heart thundered in response.

"Skye..." His voice was barely a whisper, but it hit me like a plea, threatening to undo everything I'd built to keep him out.

I didn't move away. Maybe I couldn't. The pull between us was undeniable, a gravitational force stronger than reason. My lips parted as he leaned in, his breath mingling with mine, and for a fleeting, reckless moment, I wanted to close the distance. But then the world came rushing back—the shouts of the players, the reality of the body in the fountain—and I jerked away, my face burning.

"We can't." I stepped back, wrapping my arms around myself. "This doesn't change anything."

Liam's hand dropped to his side, his jaw tightening. "Maybe it should." He didn't wait for me to respond as he turned to stride toward the group gathered around the fountain.

I stood frozen, feet rooted to the ground, my heart pounding and my chest aching with everything I couldn't let myself feel. The numbers, the players' strange behavior, Jackson's lifeless body—they all pointed to something bigger. And I wasn't sure I was ready to face it.

A sharp pressure coiled in my chest, winding tighter. "Liam!"

He turned, brows furrowing at the panic that had to be clear in my expression before returning to my side, his hand sliding back into mine. I clung to him, not wanting to be alone.

CHAPTER SEVEN

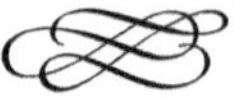

LIAM

The police arrived quickly, and since a dead body was involved, Fiona, as a detective, showed up too. Skye hadn't let go of my hand, and I didn't plan to leave her side. I hated seeing her as rattled as she was, and I was thankful that the person questioning her was my sister. I knew Fio would have a gentle touch, and I was grateful it wasn't some dickish rookie brushing Skye off or not handling her kindly or telling me to take a hike so he could grill her at her most vulnerable.

A sad smile curved Fio's lips. "Thanks, Skye. That's all I need. You're free to go home, but maybe have someone drive you?"

"I couldn't agree more," Coach Becket said from behind us.

Skye still didn't release her death grip on my hand, and I braced myself for what Coach would say, as he'd obviously seen. "Coach."

"Cartwright." Coach slapped me on the back, his expression grim. "I have to notify the president and the dean." He notched his head in the direction of where Jackson had been found. "Do me a favor and take Skye home."

"Of course." I wouldn't leave her alone, not after the trauma she'd just suffered with finding Jackson.

Coach wrapped Skye in an awkward hug, and she maintained her grip on my hand, returning to my side as soon as he released her.

"Take care of my niece, son." Coach held my gaze before seeing whatever he needed from me and turning to talk with some of the other coaches and police.

We walked to my truck in silence, her trembling too noticeable for me to ignore, and I pulled her against me, slinging my arm around her shoulder. She went willingly, and that told me everything I needed to know about her mental state.

"I'm sorry you had to see Jackson like that." I cringed at the visual of my teammate's unresponsive body, shocked to the core that he was gone.

"It was… awful. And he's done so well this season. It's… I don't know. Do you think he could've been taking something that caused his death? The detective said there weren't any signs of a struggle. I mean, he warmed the bench last year, then bam, he's making plays and getting mentioned on ESPN for his explosive talent. It's like it came out of nowhere."

"I'm not sure. We'll hear more after the autopsy."

Skye shuddered.

I got it. No one wanted to think about—experience— someone our age dying or having an autopsy. "The detective, Fiona, she's my sister."

"Oh." Her eyes widened. "I had no idea. Well, I should have seen the resemblance. I was just…"

"I understand. It's hard to take everything in when your mind is reeling from such an awful discovery. Life is… it can be brutal and ugly."

Her brows furrowed, and I kicked myself for going so deep. I should've kept things on the surface as much as possible. But it was Skye, and she was my kryptonite. Always had been.

"Why do you say that? You sound like you're speaking from experience."

I pressed my lips together, not wanting to let her in more than I'd already done.

"I see the walls coming up, Liam." Her hand rested on my arm. "Please don't shut me out. Not tonight."

"My parents' relationship was toxic. They drank too much, fought all the time, then toward the end, when Mom got into drugs, she went to rehab and never came back. My sister and I survived together, but her leaving… It messed with all of us, including Dad. He's still a drunk. But my mom? She turned her life around once she left. She has a new family now, and she's never looked back."

We paused in front of my ancient truck, and I was more than glad for the distraction. I opened the passenger door for her and waited until she was seated before shutting it and rounding to my side. Once in, I started the car and turned the radio down to a low background noise. Streetlights cut through the darkness.

Coach's house wasn't far, but I wanted to do what I could to get her out of her head on the way. "So, have you seen the new Marvel movie?"

"What?" she turned to me, eyes slightly dazed. "Oh, Marvel. Yeah, no"—she snorted—"I don't get to watch anything that isn't *Barbie*, Disney princess movies, or a handful of truly mind-numbing cartoons on TV."

"Don't knock Disney movies." I put the turn signal on for her street. "I was forced to watch every one of them when my sister and I were young. I pretended to hate it half the time, but truthfully, they're entertaining. And don't get me started on Ariel. I think I had a crush on her from nine to ten years old."

She shifted and watched me instead of the street. "I would pay money to see you sit through an afternoon of princess movies."

"Challenge accepted."

The truck rolled to a stop in front of her house, but I didn't shut off the engine right away. Skye stared out the window, her hands resting in her lap, her knuckles white where she gripped the strap of her bag.

"Want to tell me what's going on in that head of yours?" I kept my tone light, though the vibe in the air was anything but.

She let out a soft, humorless laugh. "You don't want to know."

"Try me."

Her eyes flicked to mine, dark and stormy, before darting away again. "It's just… Jackson. Everything about tonight. Then you showing up and being… this." She waved a hand toward me, frustration bleeding into her voice. "It's confusing."

I leaned back, gripping the steering wheel. "Confusing how?"

She turned fully toward me then, her gaze sharp. "This. You. Acting like you care. After everything—"

"I do care," I cut in, my voice firmer than I intended. "I never stopped."

Her breath hitched, and she blinked rapidly as if trying to ward off tears. "You pushed me away, Liam. You made your choice."

I clenched my jaw, forcing myself to stay calm. "I didn't push you away because I wanted to. I did it because I thought that's what I needed."

"Well, you got what you wanted," she snapped, her voice breaking.

The pain in her voice slammed into me, and I exhaled sharply. "I was scared, Skye. Scared of screwing up my life, something I was pretty good at doing."

She shook her head, her laugh bitter. "Well, congratulations. It looks like you're doing quite well for yourself."

"Does it?" I shot back, leaning closer. "Because all I've done since then is regret it."

Her lips parted, but no words came out. The air between us was charged, every unsaid word, every unhealed wound crackling like static.

I reached out, my hand brushing against hers where it rested on her knee. "You're the only thing I've ever been sure of, Skye," I said quietly. "And I was an idiot for not fighting for you when I should have."

Her breath came in uneven bursts, and her eyes searched mine like she was trying to find the truth in my words. Slowly, almost hesitantly, her hand turned under mine, her fingers curling slightly.

"Liam…" Her voice was soft, barely a whisper, but it was enough to pull me in.

I leaned closer, my forehead almost brushing hers. "Tell me to stop," I murmured, giving her the chance to pull away.

She didn't.

Our lips met, and the years melted away, leaving only the two of us and the connection that had never disappeared. The kiss was soft at first, tentative, but it deepened quickly, a slow burn igniting into something neither of us could ignore.

When she pulled back, her breathing was ragged, her eyes wide and glassy. "I… I need to go."

Her words cut deep, but I nodded, my hand falling away. "Okay," I said softly, though it felt like a lie. The ghost of her kiss lingered on my lips, and I let out a shaky breath. Tonight had changed everything, and somehow, nothing at all.

She fumbled for the door handle, her shoulders tensing as the door to the house opened. Her aunt stood there with Lily in her arms, light spilling around them from the living room.

Skye's focus shifted to her waiting family. "Thanks for the ride."

The click of her seat belt unfastening was enough to spring me into action. I wasn't leaving her alone. Not yet. Not after our unexpected connection. I wanted to stay close to her, even knowing it might end in heartbreak. I got out of the car and hurried to her side as she opened her door. Her mouth formed an o as she let me grasp her hand to help her get out of the truck. It was probably over the top, but I craved the feel of her hand in mine—any touch from her—and I needed to assure myself that she was okay. Relief flooded me.

Her hand trembled before she got it under control, and she pasted a fake smile on her face as we reached the door. "What are you still doing up, Lils?"

"She just woke," Coach's wife said. "I was about to read her a story and get her back to sleep."

Something melted inside me as Skye's adorable daughter pulled her thumb from her mouth with an audible pop. Her dark curls framed her sleepy green eyes as she watched us in her Little Mermaid pajamas. "I wants story. Aunt Leen said so."

"Okay, baby girl." Skye moved close and reached for her daughter, who launched herself at her mom.

"Hi, I'm Eileen," Coach's wife said.

I nodded, extending my hand. "It's nice to—"

"Oh"—she whirled at the sound of a phone ringing—"excuse me. It's probably Tom."

I shifted from extending my hand to Coach's wife to pressing it against the small of Skye's back. "Come on, let's get this little princess her story."

"What?" Skye's head whipped around to me. "No, you don't have to stay." Some color returned to her face, pink staining her high cheekbones. "I appreciate the ride home, but you can go."

"Story." Lily's innocent eyes locked on mine in a surprisingly demanding glare.

"I'll read you one, butterfly." I bopped her nose, and she giggled, her arms extending to me. I caught her and swung her into my arms. She was light and small, but something about holding Skye's daughter felt right. A gentle nudge to Skye's back, and she closed the door behind us, shutting out the chilly air.

"I don't feel right about this." Skye worried her bottom lip with her teeth. "You should probably go."

"No, Mama. Story." Her little arms tightened around my neck.

"You heard the princess." That earned me another giggle from the little angel who seemed entirely on my side and a ticket into getting closer to her mom. "Lead the way to her books."

Skye's gaze was wary, but she shook her head and decided to give in. Her face said it was probably due to the strain and exhaustion more than anything else. I followed her up the stairs and down the hallway to a room decorated for a princess. The walls were a pastel pink. And while the full-sized bed had a simple cover, the toddler bed had a bedspread washed in pink, purple, blue, and yellow with silver stars. A white canopy stretched above the bed, and the translucent fabric was pulled back toward the little headboard. A large picture on the wall closest to her bed featured all the Disney princesses. A small bookcase stood directly beneath it.

Lily squirmed, and I set her down. As soon as her tiny feet touched the cream-colored carpeting, she raced to the book-case, pulled out a *Beauty and the Beast* book, and thrust it high toward me.

"Did you brush your teeth, Lils?" Skye wrung her hands as her gaze darted from me to her daughter.

"Yep, I dids." Lily nodded with a seriousness that was too cute.

"Okay, well"—Skye glanced at me nervously again—"get under the covers so Liam can read you a story."

"Two." Her eyes narrowed, tiny shoulders tensing as she prepared to battle with her mom.

"I have time for two, but get under the covers like your mom said, butterfly."

Skye helped Lily settle under the comforter of her toddler bed then curled up on the her full-sized one. I wanted to tuck Skye in just like she'd done with her daughter, but I wouldn't push my luck. It was just short of a miracle that she'd let me this close.

I settled on the floor beside Lily's bed, a little too far from where Skye lay for my liking, and cracked the book. Three pages in, a feather-soft touch traced the scar on my cheek. I held still as Lily explored the mark, waiting to see what she would say.

"You have an owie?" Intense concentration shone in her tired eyes.

"It happened a long time ago. It doesn't hurt anymore." Kids were brutally honest and unapologetically curious. Plus, I didn't mind. "Just left a mark."

"'Kay." She snuggled back under the covers, the topic forgotten as quickly as it had popped into her head.

I finished the book then moved on to the next one she'd picked as her eyes drifted shut. When she was fast asleep, I kept reading for another few seconds to be sure then let my gaze wander to where Skye lay nearby. Her face was softer as she slept, having passed out midway through the first story. She hadn't heard her daughter question my scar or seen her touch my face. I wondered what she would have thought if she'd witnessed the exchange.

After returning the books to their shelf, I lifted a blanket at the bottom of Skye's bed and carefully covered her. Then, I shut off the light, leaving the door cracked open as I moved into the hallway. At the bottom of the stairs, I ran into her aunt.

"The girls are asleep," I said, feeling like I was intruding.

Eileen studied me, her gaze flicking between my face and the stairs, lingering just long enough to make me uncomfortable. She had dark-blond hair and wise brown eyes that looked at me a little too closely. I felt like I was under a microscope as her gaze traced my features.

"Is everything okay?"

"You just look very familiar," she said.

My pulse quickened. "You've probably seen me at the games."

I flashed her a grin, and her eyes widened. As I stepped outside, the weight of her scrutiny followed me. I didn't know what else to say. It was weird talking with Coach's wife when he wasn't around. On that note, I shouldn't be there, but leaving Skye alone after what she'd discovered wasn't an option either.

Rattled, I said goodbye and headed out. *What the hell was that about? Does she know about my relationship with Skye from a few years ago?* If so, I was screwed because if Coach found out, I would be in serious trouble.

CHAPTER EIGHT

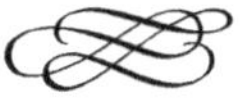

SKYE

I was officially obsessed. With a click, I closed the laptop and the striking picture of Liam in mid-catch. "This is crazy," I muttered, shaking my head. My hand flattened over my stomach, willing the flutters to stop. They wouldn't, and I couldn't deny how he made me feel or the solace I'd felt having him take care of me—*and Lily*—last night.

"Mama. Mama!" Lily flew into the kitchen, brandishing her Little Mermaid doll in one hand and Belle in the other.

"Whoa, munchkin." I smoothed down her wild curls. "That's some crazy hair you've got going there. Are you trying to match Ariel today?" I bent and peppered kisses all over her face as she giggled.

The front door opened, and I could hear my aunt talking to my uncle, who must've come home for lunch. I loved that he tried to do that as often as possible just to see her. Us, too, but their love was still in the honeymoon stage. It was sickeningly sweet and something I wanted with all of my being, something I'd determined I would never have with Liam way back when. It'd colored my decision, and after last night, doubt crept in that I'd made the right choice.

Shoving those unhelpful thoughts aside, I pasted on a smile and picked up Lily. "What do you want for lunch today, Lils?"

"PB an' J." She cuddled close.

"Okay, you sit here." I placed her in her booster seat at the table. "And I'll get your lunch."

She grinned and immediately started playing with her dolls as my aunt came in. Uncle Tommy paused in the doorway, grimacing as his phone rang. He ducked out to the living room to answer. I half listened as Aunt Eileen cooed over Lily then opened the fridge and handed me the strawberry jelly before getting the chopped salad she'd made for us an hour ago.

"How are you doing?" she asked as she dished the salad into three bowls then grabbed an apple and carrots for Lily.

"Okay. I sent Detective Cartwright the pictures and video I took last night." I spread peanut butter on one slice of bread and jelly on another before cutting off the crust. "What about Uncle Tommy? Did he learn anything new about what'd happened?" I didn't want Lily to know about it, which was why I'd asked away from the table.

"No, nothing yet. I do have some questions for you, though." Eileen's eyes narrowed, and her sharp intellect turned their dark brown to a burnished amber. "That young man looked familiar."

I shrugged, but by the knowing look in her gaze, it was clear my secret wouldn't hold. "It's the dimple, isn't it?"

"Yep. All that. Especially since Lily has the same features and mannerisms."

There was no point in denying it. She'd known Lily's father was a football player, but I'd kept Liam's name from her and definitely my uncle. "That was Liam, Lily's father."

Her mouth formed an o as she leaned a hip against the counter, two bowls in hand. "Does he know?"

Heat flooded my cheeks, and I busied myself by peeling the skin from Lily's apple. "He still doesn't know. Last night was...

unique. We don't typically get along." Or we hadn't since I'd come back into contact with him.

"He seemed enamored with Lily—and you."

I bit my lower lip before releasing it. "He wasn't ready to be a dad. I never told him. Please don't say anything."

She studied me for a few seconds. "I'll keep your secret, but I don't like lying to your uncle. This needs to come out, sooner rather than later."

I crossed my arms over my chest. "I appreciate you keeping this to yourself. As for Liam knowing, I'm still not sure that's the best idea. You know how things were between my parents."

After Dad decided to file for custody rights, it was ugly until the day they both died in a horrible accident exiting the lawyer's office. A truck hit a car and jackknifed onto the sidewalk where they were standing.

"Skye, honey." Aunt Eileen set down the bowls and squeezed my arm. "You can't project what happened between them onto someone else. Liam is a different person."

"You don't even know him," I snapped, uncomfortable with the dark emotions swirling in my mind from memories and past mistakes.

"Well, don't write him off yet." She kept her voice low so only I could hear. "That young man has feelings for you."

"Please." I rolled my eyes. "All we do is fight. He doesn't think of me as anything but annoying." I shot a covert glance to where my uncle had gone, somewhat reassured he couldn't hear anything as his voice carried from the one-sided conversation drifting in from the living room. "And I can't even think about anything more because Liam's on the team. Can you imagine Uncle Tommy's reaction? Liam's chances for the NFL would be seriously compromised, and that's all that matters to him."

Aunt Eileen's lips pressed together tightly for a moment. "Just... let me worry about Tommy when you decide to tell

Liam the truth. He seems like he would make a wonderful father."

I closed my eyes as she left me to my thoughts. The guilt was an enormous boulder in my stomach. Pushing out a breath, I wiped all the uncertainty from my face and took Lil's food to the table.

Uncle Tommy entered the kitchen, his phone back in his pocket. He paused at the table and studied me for a hot moment. "Are you all right? After yesterday? Liam said you got home okay."

"Oh, yeah. It was a horrible shock, and I'm still trying to work through it, but Liam was great. He made sure I got back, like you asked him to, and even read two stories to Lily."

The blanket covering me when I woke this morning gave me pause. *Had he done that?* It was messing with my head so badly. I preferred to think of Aunt Eileen coming in to check on us and covering me instead of the version of Liam I'd been privy to last night—which was so at odds with the combative experiences we'd had since our reconnection.

"Liam." Lily perked up at his name, slapping her little hands on the table. "I wants Liam over."

Uncle Tommy grinned. "You like one of my football players, Lily? Your mama will have to bring you to a game." He tweaked her nose, making her laugh. "We'll make a football fan out of you yet."

"Game!" Lily bounced in her seat. "I wants Liam, Mommy."

Really? I shot my aunt a panicked glance, but she was no help. How he'd been with me last night—reading to Lily—softened the edges of the walls I'd built around my heart. He wasn't supposed to care, wasn't supposed to make me feel safe. Yet, he had, and I hated him for it because it made me question the decisions I'd made to protect Lily and myself. "We'll see about going to a game sometime, Lils. It's pretty cold right now to sit for hours in the bleachers. Maybe next season."

Lily's lip trembled. "I wants Liam to play. Pwease, Mama."

I reached over and tickled her stomach, ignoring Uncle Tommy's pleased expression. He had no idea and wouldn't be so indulgent if he knew who Liam was to Lily and me.

"I have a fun idea, Lils. Next time I take pictures of the guys inside, I'll bring you. Okay?"

My daughter, appeased by my promise, tucked into her sandwich, and the subject was dropped. We got through lunch. I cleaned Lily up then sent her off to play in the living room. As Lily's giggles faded into the background, I wiped down the counter, my mind buzzing with everything left to do that day. I had no time to dwell on Liam or Aunt Eileen's knowing look. Work, as usual, was my escape. I needed to get ready to meet with Professor White.

I wasn't scheduled to take any social media footage until tomorrow since it was another home game. I would have to travel to some away ones as well because they'd made it into the pro bowls, but that would come later.

Aunt Eileen appeared in the doorway. "Everything okay? Are you headed out?"

"Yeah." My smile was distracted. "You got her? I have to get to my meeting with Professor White."

"Sure, hon. You go."

Forty-five minutes later, I left Professor White's office with an updated schedule for covering two of his classes and only one TA study session to worry about at night. He'd wanted to know how tutoring was going and relay what my pay would be from the university, which I was more than happy about, especially since I'd increased Liam's sessions so he would pass the class.

Closing the door to Professor White's office, I turned quickly and slammed into a blur of curly blond hair as she bounced off me. I grabbed her elbow to steady her. "I'm so sorry."

She shoved her hair from her face, revealing laughing hazel eyes. "No, it was probably me. I wasn't paying attention. Oh, Skye." Megan smiled. "What're you doing here? Joe said you didn't have any classes today."

"I had a meeting, but I thought I would stop into the lab for a minute." I shoved my hands in my pockets and grinned. "I heard you two are dating. Congrats."

She blushed and rocked back on her heels. "Yeah. I still can't believe it. For one, he's a grad student and a genius. I never thought he would be interested in me."

"Please." I rolled my eyes. "He's been secretly crushing on you for the past few weeks. It's about time he made his move."

"I heard you encouraged him." She laughed then squeezed my arm. "Thank you for that."

We chatted for a few more minutes until she had to leave for class. I wandered down the hallway then pushed open the door to the lab. I told myself I was there to pick up my notebook, but the truth was, I needed the distraction. Anything to keep my thoughts from drifting back to Liam and how he'd looked holding Lily. I glanced around at the spotless workstations then to the cluttered area where Joe worked. Several chemicals surrounded him along with what looked like two different trials.

I paused at his workstation, pretending to study his trials while my mind drifted. Seeing how good of a father Liam could be should have made things easier—it should have justified my choice to keep him in the dark. But instead, it only made everything harder. Still, I couldn't help but think about how he was at the top of his game, laser-focused on his NFL future, and his stats had only improved this season, proving where his priorities remained. My camera lens had captured it countless times, but seeing it in person was different.

"Skye?" Joe's voice pulled me back.

"Sorry," I mumbled, distracted. "Just thinking."

Thinking about how Liam's focus extended off the field—his patience during tutoring sessions, the way he actually listened when I explained something—it wasn't the Liam I'd known freshman year, the one who'd bulldozed through life without looking back.

I tilted my head, finally seeing the experiments in front of him. "How do you keep track of everything? I mean, you're working on what?" I peered closer. "Two different trials?"

He tapped his temple. "Eidetic memory. It makes things easier." He caught my gaze flicking to the stack of notebooks on his desk and added, "I'm helping Megan with one of her trials, too —it's a lot, but it keeps things interesting."

As Joe explained his experiments with foxglove, specifically digoxin extracted from the leaves to help treat and cure atrial fibrillation, my gaze caught a notation in his lab book—*or was it Megan's?* The word "undetectable" was underlined twice, and the ink smudged as if someone had paused on it for too long. My chest tightened. It had stuck with me since I'd overheard it on the sidelines, spoken in hushed tones by someone I couldn't remember. *Is it connected to Louis's meteoric rise on the field?*

I wanted to ask Joe what the word pertained to, but the timing didn't feel right. *What if I'm jumping to conclusions?* Still, the question lingered like a shadow at the edge of my thoughts.

Joe's thesis centered on a foxglove-based drug for heart conditions—completely different from Megan's performance-enhancement trial. *But why would I see a term like undetectable in either of their notes? Unless... could there be a crossover I didn't know about?*

As I left the lab, the weight of Joe's cryptic notes and the lingering image of Liam with Lily pressed down on me. I had too many unanswered questions, and I was tired of running from them.

CHAPTER NINE

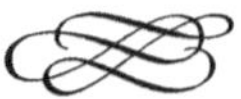

LIAM

Head bent against the sudden gust of cold air as I exited the business building where Kylian, Ares, and I had our last lecture on Friday, we jumped right back into the conversation we'd been having before class.

"I still can't believe Jackson is dead." It was surreal, and not in a good way, despite my all-too-real view of life. "Did you see anything like that coming?"

"Nope. He ran drills yesterday with Matthews when we were working on the new plays," Kylian said. "He seemed fine."

"He wasn't supposed to work with Matthews." I frowned, remembering a conversation I'd overheard between the wide receiver coach and the quarterback coach. "Coach Mack wanted him to practice routes with us to improve the timing. It would've made sense."

Ares shifted closer so he didn't knock into a group of girls we passed on the path through campus. "He should've been practicing with us if he was starting, and I think he was supposed to start today instead of Trevor."

I made a mental note to tell Fio, as any details mattered. I'd seen how she worked on cases long enough to know that. I pulled my phone from my pocket and thumbed off a quick text to fill her in, whether the info mattered or not.

"I heard you took Skye home." Ares bumped into my shoulder, almost making me drop my phone.

I glared at him as I shoved it back into my pocket. "Coach saw me with her and asked me to."

"How's she doing?" Kylian asked as we turned onto the sidewalk that led to the parking lot. "I heard she was the one who found Jackson."

"She was pretty shook up. I stayed with her and read some books to her daughter until she and Lily fell asleep." Despite the circumstances, I couldn't help smiling at how much I'd enjoyed spending time with them.

"See?" Kylian slapped me on the back. "You do have a domestic side."

Ares joined in on Kylian's laughter. "Don't fight it this time. Skye's good people."

I rolled my eyes. "As if you know her."

"I know enough." Ares shot me a serious look. "Besides, this side of you was always there. You volunteer the most out of everyone for Coach's outreach programs."

"Kids love you," Kylian said. "And keep in mind that I never saw myself with Aurora, either, but sometimes, things just feel right. Going all in with her was the best decision of my life."

I couldn't fault him there. Aurora was amazing, and he was happier with her.

"Helping out with my nephew, no matter how busy football and school gets, will always be my priority," Ares said. "I know you would feel the same if you let Skye and her daughter in."

Ares's sister and her husband had died in a car accident a few years back, and he'd stepped up, taking on more of a big brother parental role when his mom took Preston in. It hadn't been easy, but he never complained.

"I wouldn't trade the time I spend with Preston for anything.

What we do for kids makes a difference in their lives. And I'm sure Skye appreciated you helping and showing kindness to her daughter."

"Maybe. I don't know. Skye was rattled, and I'm sure that was the only reason she was okay with me being around her kid." With a wave to Ares and Kylian, I slid into my car. The weight of the upcoming game pressed on me. But it wasn't just Indiana or the scouts on my mind—it was Jackson, Skye, and how everything had seemed to collide at once.

We'd split to drive to the athletics building, and I was glad to drop the conversation. The game against Indiana tomorrow would be front and center in all our minds, as it should be. Scouts would be present. I needed more ESPN time and hopefully more exposure to get the attention of top agents and a team that wanted me. Regardless of how often Skye and her daughter invaded my mind, that had to be my primary focus. I had a plan and needed to see it through until I achieved my goals.

After practice, weights, and film, I stopped by Fiona's to nab any leftover spaghetti from the other night and see if she'd made headway on the case—and if she would tell me anything at all. When I let myself into her townhome, my dad was awake on the recliner. I'd hoped to avoid him. It looked like I wasn't that lucky.

"Liam, my boy." His words slurred already, and red rimmed his unfocused eyes as I tried to slip past him. "How's the season going?"

I stopped on my way to talk to Fio, who was hunched over some documents at the kitchen table. Football was the only thing I had in common with my dad. He'd spent countless hours throwing me the ball in the backyard and had even gotten me a JUGS machine so I could practice two hundred catches a day. He'd wanted to help me achieve my dreams, and I couldn't ignore the topic when he brought it up.

"We won against Iowa, and I got a mention on ESPN."

"I heard. Great job, son. Now you just need to bring it home."

I nodded, ignoring the tightness in my chest at the pressure to do just that. "Tomorrow's game is another home one against Indiana."

"They've got no game. Their success is in basketball." His voice rose with excitement. "You've got the win in the bag."

"That would've been true a few years ago, but their new coach has turned things around. They've been rising in the ranking since last year. That's why we're facing them this far into the season."

"Well, don't let them win. Simple as that." He toasted me with his Budweiser. "I'll be watching from here."

"Thanks." It was the best conversation we'd had in a long while, and I tried to move on before it went to hell, as it usually did. "I came to check in with Fio about something. Have a good night." I doubted he would be conscious much longer with the stack of empties lined up on the end table next to his elbow.

"I heard about the girl that found the dead football player. That's what Fio is workin' on?"

"Yeah. Skye, our team's social media manager, found him. It was rough for her last night." I knew my mistake before I finished talking. *Why don't I ever learn?*

Dad's face went from pleasant to furious, red infusing his already-ruddy cheeks and nose. "Skye? Didn't you date some girl with that name when you first started playing at Fall Lake?" He pointed a finger at me, and beer sloshed over the rim of the can and onto his stained jeans from the sudden movement. "Don't let a pretty face sway you."

My knuckles tightened around the counter as he ranted, the words blurred, familiar, and suffocating.

"Women can't be trusted. She'll ruin your life, sway you from the end game. You'd better stay strong and say no to relationships, or eventually, she'll kill your dreams then leave you in a ditch for some doctor with a bigger salary and a Jaguar and a mansion in Miami."

Fuck me. It was like watching a replay of every fight he'd had with Mom. But I wasn't him, and Skye wasn't her. "Not everyone is Mom, Dad."

As I moved away, Dad's slurred words lingered in the back of my mind like an old injury that never healed. When I reached Fio's kitchen, I felt the tension knotting in my shoulders, the relief of seeing her not enough to quell the dread of whatever might come next. I went to the fridge, pulled out a container, and dumped the contents onto a plate before putting it in the microwave.

"Please, help yourself," my sister said snarkily.

"Thanks." I winked then moved closer when I saw the pictures she had spread out. Her computer was open to a shot of the fountain and a few of the defensive players I knew Skye had been filming last night. "Those are from Skye?"

"Yep." She looked up from the images to level me with that detective look I knew too well.

"That stare," I muttered, picking at the label on my water bottle. "You'd think I'd be immune to it by now, but nope. Still feels like getting grilled under a spotlight."

She smirked but ignored my comment. "I can see why you had a thing for Skye. Interesting that she had such a tight grip on your hand. She's the one, isn't she?" Fiona's tone softened. "The girl who disappeared freshman year."

I didn't answer, but the silence must've said enough because she smirked.

"Thought so." Her voice was low so Dad wouldn't hear.

I appreciated it, but I wasn't in the mood to get into a discussion about my history with Skye, not after the lecture from Dad. "It didn't mean anything."

"If you say so. But, little brother, I hope you're wrong."

I grinned at her as the microwave dinged, and I retrieved my dinner. "There's nothing little about me."

She snorted then shoved the papers aside so I could sit at the table with her.

"How's the case going? You got my text?"

"Yes, thanks. So far, we don't have any major leads. Did you know Jackson had a heart condition?" Fiona asked, her tone sharper.

I froze mid-bite. "What kind of condition?"

"Still waiting on specifics, but it's the kind of thing that should've made him cautious, especially with the sudden improvement he's had. It doesn't add up."

"No. But the coaches should know. He would've had to disclose that in his medical info in the athletics portal."

"I have an appointment with them early tomorrow morning, before the game."

Her slight hesitation snagged my attention. "You found something else, didn't you?"

She pursed her lips. "There might've been something in his blood," she said, her words deliberate, heavy with unspoken concern.

I leaned forward, plate forgotten. "What does that mean? Something like... drugs?" That wasn't good. *What if Jackson's death impacted the team's unity or our game plan?*

She hesitated, her lips pressing into a thin line. "We're not jumping to conclusions yet. But if you hear anything about supplements or substances going around the team, I need to know."

Is that why Jackson went from benchwarmer to star player so quickly? "I haven't, but I'll keep my ears open." That would be a catastrophe for the team and our odds with NFL scouts.

Early the next day, before the game, I was in the library, sitting next to Skye at a secluded table on the third floor as we completed another tutoring session. The awareness between us escalated to degrees I could barely manage. I didn't know how much longer I could go, how much more I could take before I broke down and kissed her.

Would that be so bad?

Skye shoved her laptop into her bag, her movements deliberate but too quick to be casual. Tension radiated from her, though she wouldn't meet my eyes.

"Thanks for the help." I broke the silence as she slung her bag over her shoulder.

Her gaze flicked to me, and for a second, I thought she might say something, but she just nodded. "Yeah. See you later." She started toward the door, her shoulders tight, as if she were carrying something too heavy to set down.

"Skye, wait," I called, my voice cutting across the empty floor of the library.

She paused mid-step, her back to me, and for a moment, I thought she might keep walking. But then she turned, her expression unreadable, her eyes holding some emotion I couldn't name.

"What?" she asked, her voice quiet but strained.

I stepped closer, narrowing the space between us. "You don't have to do everything alone, you know. Whatever you're dealing with, you don't have to carry it all by yourself."

Her lips pressed together, her hand tightening on the strap of her bag. "I'm fine, Liam. I've been fine for years."

"I don't believe that." My voice softened, and I reached out, brushing a strand of hair from her face. "Not for a second."

Her breath hitched, her eyes flickering between mine, and the weight of unspoken words hung in the air between us. "Why do you care?" she whispered, her voice breaking on the last word.

"Because it's you," I said simply, stepping even closer. "It's always been you."

For a moment, time seemed to stop. The tension crackled between us, electric and undeniable, as her gaze dropped to my lips before darting away.

"Liam…" she started, but whatever she was going to say was lost as I leaned in, giving her plenty of time to stop me, a distinct possibility after how our kiss ended last time.

She didn't.

Our lips met, softly at first, tentative, but the kiss quickly deepened as everything unsaid between us exploded to the surface. She clung to me, her fingers gripping the front of my shirt like she was afraid to let go. I poured everything I couldn't say into that kiss—the longing, the regret, the hope that maybe, just maybe, it was a new beginning.

Then, as if only just realizing what we were doing, Skye shoved me back, her breathing heavy, her eyes shining with something I couldn't name. "I still can't do this," she whispered, taking a step back.

My chest tightened, but I nodded, giving her the space she needed—for now. "Okay," I said softly, though every fiber of my being wanted to stop her.

She hesitated for just a second longer before turning and walking away, her steps quick and purposeful.

CHAPTER TEN

SKYE

I tried to put the time with Liam in the library behind me and looked at the second half of game day as if it were a separate day entirely. It almost felt like it with the cloudless sky and brightly shining sun promising a semblance of warmth. I just finished taking a few candid shots of the audience and the field before the guys came out.

"Hey." A girl with honey-blond hair grinned at me expectantly from the stadium's packed seats. "You're Skye Finley, right?"

I nodded. "Yeah." I tilted my head, recognizing who she was as I placed the brunette next to her as Aurora, Kylian's fiancée. Weird that I chose the exact section where Liam's roommates' girlfriends were sitting for the playoff game. Well, maybe not. We were at the fifty-yard line and in the first row. The seats were terrific, and I could get fabulous pictures without being on the sidelines. I didn't regret the choice—since I'd already captured shots from the sidelines—now that I knew the people next to me.

Players and spectators alike wore black armbands in honor

of Jackson, the football player who had died. It was a heartbreaking and unifying sight.

"I'm Brielle Sinclair, and this is Aurora," Brielle said. "I recognized you from the athletic website."

"Oh." I scrunched my nose. "I hate that picture. I don't know why they had to put it up. My name works well enough."

"What are you talking about?" Aurora laughed. "It's a great picture. Very artistic."

It was artistic but not my favorite. I preferred to stay in the background or behind a camera.

Brielle squeezed my forearm and released it, sympathy clouding her ice-blue eyes. "How are you doing? Liam told us what happened with Jackson and how you found him. Liam's been like a caged animal ever since, super worried about you."

I started, my mouth falling open before I snapped it shut. "Why?"

Aurora grinned as she leaned forward to better join in the conversation. "Girl, you know he's into you, right?"

Heat flooded my face despite the December chill. We miraculously hadn't had any snow yet, though I could use some right about now to help with the wave of embarrassment and maybe hide behind a wall of white. "Liam isn't into me. He's a total player."

Brielle shrugged. "Maybe he was. But I can tell you he's been different lately. Think on that."

A roar went through the crowd as fans leaped to their feet. The stadium shook from the crowd stomping as our team ran out onto the field and saved me from responding. My heart thudded, not from the high energy of the fans but from what Brielle had implied—stupid heart. I just… I was afraid to set myself up for heartbreak a second time. It was probably too late to shield myself against Liam. My heart hadn't gotten the memo from my mind as it fluttered like I was some damn Disney princess who'd just been kissed by the man of her dreams. A happily ever after wasn't in store for me. I needed to remember that. I'd had a front-row seat to Liam's reality check when we'd been together.

I shoved Brielle and Aurora's comments to the back of my mind, focusing instead on my task for the day. It was the start of the playoffs, and Fall Lake University's Falcons were predicted to win against Indiana. But the media had been relentless, questioning if the team could pull it off after the devastating loss of their rising-star wide receiver. The pressure on Liam was more intense than ever, something I knew weighed on him despite his outward confidence.

Over the past two weeks—and especially two nights ago, when he opened up about his rough childhood—I'd glimpsed layers of Liam that had only deepened my curiosity. Now, with him on the field, it was impossible to look anywhere else.

We won the coin toss and deferred, giving Indiana the ball first. It was the right call. Our defense had been ironclad, with new players stepping up alongside the veterans, making it hell for anyone to gain yards.

As the game wore on, I snapped photos and chatted with Aurora and Brielle, but my attention kept drifting back to Liam. Kylian was throwing rockets, completing short and long passes with precision. The crowd roared, but it all felt muted in my ears with my focus locked on Liam.

Liam dominated the field, every move precise and calculated, as if he were born for this. Watching him, I couldn't ignore his magnetic pull. Everyone was watching him—including me. I raised my camera, trying to capture that determination in his eyes—the same determination that made my stomach knot. I alternated between my camera and phone, trying to catch a few live videos to post on social media. The rest would be edited and uploaded later. The game moved fast, and I adjusted the settings on my camera to focus on Liam midsprint. The light hit just right, illuminating his determined expression as he dodged a tackle. *Perfect.* The caption formed in my head: "Unstoppable. Falcons Lead 21–14."

"Liam's on fire today." Aurora nudged me as he made a spectacular catch, weaving through defenders like they weren't even there.

The crowd chanted his name, and his stats flashed on the stadium's giant video screen. I nodded, watching Ares bulldoze through two defensive players, clearing a path for Liam to sprint through the red zone. Touchdown. The stadium erupted, but I couldn't shake the mixture of awe and worry tightening in my chest. Liam made it all look effortless, but I noticed the subtle tells—the way he shifted his weight at the line of scrimmage, his eyes flicking toward the scouts in the stands, even as he lined up for the next play.

"He looks stressed," Aurora added, her voice quieter.

I swallowed hard, feeling the weight of it too. I couldn't imagine him not catching the eye of every scout in the stadium. Liam wasn't just good—he, Kylian, and Ares were unstoppable forces, creating magic on the field that rivaled top NFL players. I'd heard analysts on SportsCenter talk about him the same way. The only question was when his big break would come—not if.

As the crowd roared, I scrolled through photos of Lily on my phone before slipping it back in my pocket. How she'd giggled when Liam had read to her flashed in my mind unbidden. *Would it be fair to let her get attached to someone who might not stay?*

The camera lens followed Liam as he lined up for the next play. My hands shook slightly—not from the cold but from the memory of Liam with my daughter. Lily had adored him instantly, and the way he'd read her a bedtime story... It wasn't fair. He wasn't supposed to be that good, that kind. I forced myself to focus on the field. The ball snapped. Liam took off, and I took a picture, capturing him mid-stride, all power and precision.

Leroy's tackle was bone crushing, the kind that left the

crowd gasping. I winced, lowering my camera. Something about his speed seemed… unnatural. My mind flickered back to Jackson's sudden power and skill. *Was it just hard work, or was something else behind it?*

My phone buzzed with notifications as I posted a slow-motion clip of Liam's last touchdown. Within seconds, the comments had poured in—fans swooning over his athleticism, his smile as he ran off the field. I set down the phone, but not before sneaking another glance at him through my lens. He looked so alive out there. So untouchable.

The crowd erupted as the final whistle blew, but my chest felt heavy. I couldn't shake the image of Liam's smile—or the ghost of Jackson's presence on the field. Victory felt hollow when so much remained unanswered.

After the game, as the crowd began to disperse, I lingered in the stands, snapping a few final shots of the field. Liam was at the center of it all, surrounded by teammates, coaches, and what looked like a few scouts. My emotions were a chaotic swirl—pride in his performance, anxiety about the drug rumors circulating after Jackson's death, and the growing pull I felt toward Liam.

Our eyes met across the distance, and for a second, the noise around me faded. A jolt of connection shot through me, sharper than I'd expected. My chest tightened as I realized just how complicated things could get. My feelings for Liam were no longer just about me—they could impact his career. Since he'd read to Lily and tucked her in that night, something inside me had softened toward him.

He'd been right to tell me the truth all those years ago—football came first for him. It always had. I broke our gaze with a heavy heart, unsure of the future or if we even had one.

Aurora and Brielle waved goodbye as they passed, heading to wait for the guys outside the locker room. I packed up my camera gear, trying to distract myself from the nagging thoughts churning in my mind. Nearby, a group of cheerleaders gathered, watching the players with greedy eyes. I couldn't help but overhear their whispered conversation.

"Liam was insane out there today," one cheerleader said, her voice full of admiration. "He's seriously NFL material."

"Yeah, and he's still single," another added, giggling. "Think he'll finally settle down? Or is he keeping his streak alive?"

Disgusted with their gossip, I pulled out my phone and scrolled through photos of Lily. I couldn't let myself get wrapped up in Liam again. Even if I wanted to—and I could admit that much—I had to think about my daughter. She needed stability. I'd been terrified to tell Liam the truth for a reason. Especially after what had happened to my mom when my hotshot dad had decided he finally wanted me in his life.

I lingered a moment longer, watching Liam disappear into the locker room. The field felt empty without him. I didn't know what scared me more—the idea of letting him in or the thought of what might happen if I didn't.

CHAPTER ELEVEN

LIAM

The sidelines were chaos in the wake of our win against Indiana. We'd played the game for Jackson. I hoped our teammate would have been proud of us. But even with that energy, I couldn't get my mind off something else. I hadn't even felt the cold as wind tore through the empty field. There'd been a moment when I'd caught Skye's gaze in the stands. Something was happening between us, and I didn't want to fight it anymore. I wanted her.

She'd let her barriers down some since the night I drove her home. This was the time to capitalize on that response and worm my way back into her world, which I wanted to do despite the inevitable shutdown that came with a girl like Skye. I needed and wanted her more than she did me—even with that reality check, I couldn't deny the pull I'd always felt for her. She was worth the risk to my carefully constructed rules of self-preservation.

And right now, she had no escape—not when she tutored me several times a week and showed up at practices and games because of her internship. All that gave me more chances to build on the connection that was so clearly present between us.

"Cartwright!" Coach Becket bellowed from down the sideline, standing next to Mark Thompson, one of Kansas City's well-known NFL scouts and someone I very much wanted to impress. He was a former player for the Chiefs as well, one I respected a lot.

I broke away from Ares and Kylian, jogging along the sideline until I caught up with Coach as he and the Chiefs scout headed into the tunnel to the locker rooms.

"I want you to meet Mark Thompson," Coach said. "We can use my office."

I extended my hand and shook the scout's offered one in a firm handshake. "It's great to meet you, Mr. Thompson."

"Mark is fine." He grinned.

We chatted about mundane things until we arrived in Coach's office. Coach took the chair behind his desk and waved for Thompson and me to use the two in front of it.

Thompson leaned back in his chair, crossing an ankle over the opposite knee, his gaze locked on me and assessing. "Thanks for taking the time to meet with me, Cartwright. I've been following you this season. Your stats are impressive, and you have many traits we look for in a wide receiver—your ability to create separation with your route running, your speed off the line, your overall high football IQ, and how you fight for those contested catches. Those are all things we notice, but let's talk more about your game and where we see opportunities for you to grow."

"Absolutely. I welcome your insight on what I can improve." I had to demonstrate I was coachable then show him results on the field after our initial conversation.

He was proving to be a no-nonsense guy, true of everything I'd heard from Kylian and Ares, whom he, among other scouts, had been recruiting hardcore. That it was taking longer for me to gain attention and conversations was nothing short of panic inducing. I had to nail our meeting. Not only that, but his approval and setting his sights on me would only open more doors. ESPN would stand up and take notice, as would other teams.

"We love what you can do after the catch, but we'd like to see you break free of blocks and improve some of the details in your route tree. In the NFL, defenders are faster and more physical. Watch film on Jerome Myers at USC. His footwork and timing on every route help build separation. If you can improve and show consistency there, it'll only prove you've got more of what it takes to make it in the professional league."

There was proof of my competition. "Got it. I appreciate the tip and will work to improve. Thank you."

"Your deep routes are stellar, but sharpen the short ones to become truly unstoppable."

"You would know." I grinned, pouring on the charm. "I've followed your career and strive to emulate your success, among others."

"Good to know." Mark chuckled then turned to Coach. "His charisma is off the charts, just like you said."

"At least you won't have to worry about putting me in front of reporters. I'll do whatever the PR team needs." I would work any angle to make myself stand out in their eyes. If that tipped the scale for me, then so be it.

"What's your weekly routine regarding film, study, practice, and recovery?"

I eased back in my seat and rattled off the hours I spent every day with prep work. Kylian, Ares, and I were the team's hardest working players, which was a big reason why we were the best—or they were. I had some concerns when Thompson brought up my competition. I needed to up my game.

Coach chimed in with my dedication to improving my schoolwork—I did my best not to flinch—and how much I balanced, never complaining when more was put on my plate. Also, the other receivers looked up to me for how I stayed late to help the rookies improve. I was a true team player. I could fucking kiss the man for the gold he spewed. Thompson looked impressed.

Fuck yes!

Thompson nodded along with everything Coach said, making a few notes on his clipboard before turning back to me. "How do you handle adversity?" His gaze briefly dipped to the scar on my cheek. "The NFL creates a lot of pressure. We're always looking for guys who stay levelheaded and keep pushing, even when things don't go their way."

I wouldn't touch the fight freshman year that resulted in my scar. It was long ago, and I doubted he knew anything. What he wanted to know was the kind of teammate I was when the chips were down, even after Coach had spouted off all the team-player stuff about me—I got it, but it needed to also be in my own words. I had this, no problem.

"I can give you a few examples of things I've done for team-mates and friends off the field that never once affected my game." I darted a glance at Coach, who nodded encouragement. From his serious expression, he knew what I was about to share. "Kylian Wilder and Ares Bellingham are my roommates and good friends." They needed no explanation about their positions or status on the team as they were well-known and frequently mentioned on SportsCenter. I explained how Ares's girlfriend had been abducted and what role I'd played in helping my friends and my sister, who was a detective, get her back safely. How my performance on the field never suffered. I could juggle emotional duress without it impacting my game. When I finished, he looked noticeably impressed, and I breathed a sigh of relief. One test passed. *What else will he throw my way?* I was ready. I rubbed my hands together, leaning forward for the next challenge. Something Thompson noticed by the way his eyes lit up.

"That was a helluva explanation and one not many can

compete with. Keep up the work you've been putting in, but remember, there's always room for growth. I want to see you hungry to improve, and from what I've witnessed today, I think you are."

"Thank you, sir."

"Continue to refine your craft, Liam. Stay healthy, and don't lose focus. I know you've got the tools. Keep grinding. You've got a real shot at making it to the next level."

Coach and I stood with Thompson and shook his hand. Coach asked me to stay a few more minutes as he walked Thompson out. When they were out of sight, I shook my arms and rolled my neck, releasing the tension that'd built up. It wasn't long before Coach returned.

He left the door to his office open and clapped me on the back. His thick mustache worked overtime as he furiously chewed his signature nicotine gum. "Scouts want to get a sense of players' personalities, work ethics, and often how they handle feedback. You went above and beyond today. I have no doubt about your physical skills, character, and focused mental preparation. You've got what it takes to succeed professionally, and you showed him what he wanted to see with that conversation. The rest will have to be on the field. I'll be watching you during playoffs and at the combine. Show me what you've got."

"I will." I nodded with every point he made. I would make it happen.

"Do what Thompson said. Study what USC's star wide receiver is successfully doing that you're not. And while you're at it, check out Ohio State and Bama's star receivers too. He may not have mentioned their names, but they're being heavily recruited. Up your game, son. I know you can achieve your dreams."

I blinked furiously. Goddamn. I was so close. His praise and belief in me encouraged me to work harder than ever. "I promise I won't let you down, Coach."

CHAPTER TWELVE

LIAM

I got to the science building early on Monday for a late-afternoon tutoring session. Skye had suggested working in the lab so I could go over the next experiment I had to ace. I didn't know how she remembered the staggering amount of chemicals and elements along with their properties. I could manage a new playbook and have it memorized backward and forward in no time, but with science, it was in one ear and out the other. *Would I ever need it with my sports management and communications degree?* No, which only made it worse. But after the conversation with Thompson, I would work my ass off to excel in every area of my life. I had a goddamned point to prove.

Coach's tension had been palpable all day. Rumors about an emergency meeting after last Saturday's game were already circulating, and I couldn't help but wonder if it had to do with Jackson. His death had left a hole in the team, and if the whispers about drugs or foul play were true, it could mean trouble for us all.

I paused outside the lab door, catching sight of Skye through the glass. She was lost in thought, her fingers absently twirling a strand of her dark-brown hair. I should've been thinking about the emergency meeting or my route tree, but all I could focus on was her. She might be a complication I couldn't afford—but she was also one I couldn't walk away from either.

I took in the curve of her full lips and how her long eyelashes cast a slight shadow on her cheeks. Every time I saw her, it was like gravity shifted. She was strength, determination, and chaos wrapped in a package I couldn't ignore—and didn't want to.

The lab was quiet save for the rustle of papers and the soft clink of equipment from the few people who were also using the space. I hesitated before approaching her, enjoying the moment I could take her in unnoticed. The girl was worth fighting for. That thought kept recurring despite her uncle being my head coach.

"Hey." I slid into the seat next to her.

She started before a slight grin curved her mouth. "Hey, yourself." She glanced at her phone, and her brows rose. "You're early."

I shrugged. "Looks like it worked out since you've already got everything set up for the experiment."

I wanted to take it back the second I said it because that distant wall she wore when she tutored me snapped into place. It was probably for the best, or it was while we got some work done. I shoved my thoughts aside and focused on what she had to teach me. Halfway through our session, the lab cleared out until it was just the two of us.

Our hands touched a few times as she handed me chemicals or slides, and the slight brush of her skin against mine sent pings traveling up my arm and into my chest. Tension crackled between us until it was all I could think of. I moved closer until our legs touched, and awareness buzzed through my entire body—she didn't pull away, and I heard the intake of her breath. Pink stained her cheeks, telling me I wasn't the only one who felt the current between us.

I set down the microscope slide to face her. I had to touch her. I couldn't resist her another second. My hands slid into her long, thick hair as I cradled the sides of her face and the back of her head as I closed the distance. My lips grazed hers slowly. When her body softened and she leaned into me, heat exploded through me, and I deepened the kiss.

Her taste was intoxicating, an addiction I couldn't shake. The sharp ping of my phone cut through the haze, relentless and demanding. Skye's hands pressed firmly against my chest, pushing just enough to break the spell. Reluctantly, I let her go, and we gasped for air, our breathing ragged and uneven. No one had ever unraveled me like that—only Skye. She was everything I'd ever wanted, everything I'd been too blind or stubborn to admit I needed until now.

The kiss felt like stepping off a ledge into the unknown. Skye tasted like every dream I couldn't afford to have. If Coach found out, it wouldn't just be a slap on the wrist—it could destroy everything I'd worked for. But as I looked into her wide, confused eyes, I could only think how much I wanted to do it again.

"We shouldn't have done that," she whispered. But even as she said it, I could see the same hunger mirrored in her expression.

"We should've. And I hope we do again," I promised.

But in the back of my mind, alarm bells blared. As much as I wanted to lose myself in Skye, a small voice warned me to pull back. I was playing with fire. I had to repeatedly remind myself that her uncle was Coach Becket, the man who held my future in his hands. *And after what Thompson said about staying focused?* The timing couldn't be worse. But none of it mattered when she looked at me like that.

She shook her head, put some space between us, and got to work cleaning up the supplies on the desk, probably to escape the conversation we needed to have. Her phone rang, and she ducked her head, breaking eye contact as she moved away, bringing it to her ear as she answered. Her back was to me as she successfully avoided my gaze.

The dual responsibilities weighed heavily, and I finally picked up my phone to see who'd messaged just as a grad student I'd met in one of the TA sessions, Joe Riken, and a girl who was friends with Brittany, one of the cheerleaders, entered. They were deep in conversation, only sparing a glance our way.

I hadn't meant to eavesdrop, but Joe's voice carried across the lab. "Megan, you've been messing with the performance-enhancement study samples. Don't think I haven't noticed."

Megan's response was sharp. "Stop being paranoid, Joe. Everything's accounted for."

My gut tightened as I watched Megan storm back out, her face red. Joe slammed his notebook shut, muttering something under his breath. I didn't like how his voice rose, or how Megan stomped out without looking back. Something about it felt off. I glanced at Skye, her head down as she spoke into her phone from the far corner of the lab where she'd moved, oblivious to the tension between Joe and the blonde. If anything shady was going down, I would make damn sure it didn't touch Skye.

I finally glanced at my phone and winced at the group chat message as Skye ended her call and returned.

I told her quietly, not wanting Joe to overhear. "Coach called an emergency meeting."

Skye whipped her gaze to mine, worry leaching the color from her face. "Do you think they got results for what happened to Jackson?"

"That would be my guess. Come on." I grabbed the rest of the slides and chemicals from her, washed them, and returned them to the cabinet. "I'll walk you to your car."

Joe's accusation lingered in my mind as we left the lab. *Samples being messed with?* It could've been nothing—just two students in a spat—but with everything going on lately, it was hard not to connect the dots to Jackson. I made a mental note to mention it to Fio since Skye said she'd been asking about the chemistry department, specifically Professor White. If something shady was happening in the lab, it was better to get ahead of it.

Reality popped the bubble we'd managed to create in the lab, and I gathered my thoughts. But as my hand grazed Skye's elbow, she glanced at me with heavy-lidded eyes, and everything in me froze, instincts roaring to take her in my arms. She shifted closer, our pace slowing as tension built between us, and her intoxicating lightly floral scent grabbed me by the throat. My fingers brushed hers, a barely there touch that sent a spark zipping through me. She didn't pull away. Instead, her breath hitched, and I couldn't resist the magnetic pull drawing me closer. My hand slid to the small of her back, tentative but deliberate.

Her step faltered, a shiver rippling through her as if my touch ignited something beneath her skin. Slowly, she turned her head, her gaze locking with mine. The look in her eyes unraveled me—every unspoken word, every charged moment between us in the lab condensed into a smoldering intensity that left no room for doubt.

"Do we need to head out yet?" My voice was low, uneven, betraying my restraint. My eyes flicked toward a nearby door, half wondering, half hoping. "Or..."

She followed the direction of my gaze and shook her head, the movement slow, deliberate, and laced with everything she wasn't saying. I wanted her—I couldn't deny it. The tension between us snapped, and I closed the small gap separating us. Her breath caught as I moved into her space, but she didn't hesitate. Her arms slid up, wrapping around my neck, pulling me closer.

I backed her toward the door, the cool wood pressing against her spine as my hand found her waist. For a heartbeat, time felt suspended in the charged air between us, her lips just a breath away from mine. Then I slanted my mouth over hers, claiming what we both knew had been inevitable. She melted into me, her fingers tangling in my hair as I deepened the kiss, heat roaring to life between us.

The door clicked open under our combined weight, and we stumbled into the dimly lit room. My hands gripped her hips, steadying her as I kicked the door shut behind us then reached behind me to lock it. The world outside ceased to exist. There was only her—soft, warm, and intoxicating.

I moved us away from the door and any windows, skirting around desks in the empty classroom, then my mouth found hers again in a frantic kiss that she matched. As our tongues tangled, my hands roamed, skimming over her soft curves. Everything about her drew me in—the soft noises she made, how she fit perfectly against me, and the uncontrollable passion that detonated from a simple touch. I wanted her—always. That had never changed. I wanted all of her.

I broke the kiss, our breaths crashing in the small space between us. "Are you sure about this?" *Please be sure.*

"Yes. I just… don't want to think too much about what I'm doing right now." She slipped out of her coat and grasped the edge of her shirt, easing it up and tormenting me with every inch of bared skin. I helped with her clothes, desperate to see all of her, watching for any signs that she might change her mind. She gave none as she stood beautifully naked before me. She took my breath away.

I pulled a condom out of my wallet, stripped off my clothes, and put it on. There wouldn't be time later, not with the mounting desire crackling through the air. I was utterly addicted to her, desperate to be inside her. I wanted her more than my next breath.

I was so turned on that going slowly wasn't an option. With no clothes separating us, I cupped her ass and lifted her. Her legs automatically wrapped around me, and as I pinned her against the wall, I took her lips in a desperate kiss, ruthlessly invading her mouth until she moaned.

Needing to watch, I broke the kiss. A tremor went through her body as I slid my fingers down her silky skin to brush a teasing caress over her clit. Met by her warm, wet heat, I slipped my finger in, my thumb circling her sensitive nub as I pumped inside her, then I curled my finger until she panted.

"Liam," she moaned.

By the way her legs tightened around me, urging me closer, I knew she was close. Withdrawing my fingers to the sweet sounds of her protests, I aligned the tip of my cock with her entrance and slanted my mouth over hers.

Her hands tangled in my hair, tugging the strands as she kissed me with the same need. She nipped at my lip then ran her tongue over it, and I lost it. Positioned at her slick entrance, I thrust in. Her head fell back on a low moan, and I wrapped my hand around the nape of her neck. The other gripped her ass as I drove deep. Her hips tilted, and she met my furious pace.

I grazed my teeth over the soft skin from her neck to her shoulder, eliciting a whimper as I increased the pressure. She arched against me, and a wave of lust drove me to go harder, faster until her body convulsed around me, and she cried out. Two more pumps, and I followed her, spilling deep inside her. I leaned into her, bracing one arm on the wall as we caught our breath. Goddamn, she was addictive. I'd never been with anyone who made me feel the way she did.

Then she laughed, and the sound was so carefree and sensual that my mouth watered. A fine sheen of sweat coated her, and her firm breasts glistened, tempting me to take her nipples into my mouth and worship every inch of her again. She was so beautiful.

We both groaned as I pulled out, and she slid her legs down to stand. I made sure she had her footing before releasing her to dispose of the condom. Afterward, I ran my hands through my hair, somewhat shaken by how insatiable she made me feel.

Our clothes were a mess, tangled around our feet, evidence of the chaos we'd just created. Skye eased away as she bent to gather her clothes then clutched her discarded shirt to her chest like a shield. Her hair spilled over her shoulders in dark, wild waves, and I could still see the faint blush trailing down her neck. But then she spoke, and the warmth in the room evaporated.

"This doesn't mean anything," she said, her voice soft but sharp enough to cut through me. "It can't." Panic laced her words as she hastily dressed.

In the middle of pulling on my jeans, I paused, the muscles in my shoulders tightening as her words sank in. I didn't like it one bit. "What are you talking about?"

She stepped away from me, toward the door, but glanced over her shoulder, her eyes flickering with something I couldn't pin down—regret, guilt, fear, maybe all of them.

"We've always been like a moth to a flame, Liam. I just... we touched so many times in the lab, and it got to me. I should never, um—this... this was a mistake. Let's just forget it happened."

"Forget it?" I repeated, the words scraping my throat like sandpaper. I finished fastening my jeans then leaned forward. "Skye, I'm not forgetting anything. Not this. Not us."

"There is no 'us,'" she said quickly as she turned to face me, fully clothed. "We had something back then, sure, but now? Now there's too much... everything. Too much baggage. Too many complications. I can't—"

"You *won't*," I interrupted, gently pulling her closer.

She flinched, just barely, and it made my chest ache.

I lowered my voice. "I'm not saying it'll be easy, but it's real, Skye. What we had was real, and it still could be."

She shook her head, her hands trembling as she pulled away.

"No. I don't want to complicate my life any more than it already is. I need to separate... this"—she gestured between us—"the physical, from everything else going on. And I can't do that if I let myself think this could be more."

"You're lying to yourself." I forced the words out, though they felt heavy in my chest.

She released a shaky breath, stepping back. "Maybe I am. But that's my choice to make. Please, Liam. I need this to be a one-time thing. I know I said yes, but please. I need us to go back to how we were when I was just your tutor, never mentioning what just happened again."

Her words felt like a slap. I clenched my jaw, holding back everything I wanted to say, everything I wanted to shout. Instead, I took a deep breath and nodded, the movement stiff and unnatural.

"If that's what you want," I said, my voice flat, detached. But inside, it felt like something had been ripped out of me, and all that was left was the hollow ache of disappointment.

She nodded, relief flashing across her face. "Thank you." And just like that, she turned, leaving me alone in the room that still smelled like her.

I leaned against the wall as the silence pressed in. *Forget it?* Not a chance.

CHAPTER THIRTEEN

SKYE

I practically bolted out of the classroom, my heartbeat thundering in my ears. The echo of the door clicking shut behind me should have been a relief, but it only amplified the emotions swirling inside me. My face burned, my skin still tingling from the memory of his hands, his mouth, his everything.

What did I just do?

The cool air of the science building did nothing to douse the fire that still smoldered beneath my skin. I'd been careful—so damn careful—for the past three years. And now, one tutoring session and a quiet, empty classroom later, and I'd unraveled every inch of progress I'd made. I was ignoring the handful of steamy kisses we'd shared—this was my fault because I let it happen. Liam was clearly my weakness.

It had been three years since I'd been with anyone—Liam was the last. The connection we shared had gone beyond physical, though even that had been explosive. At times, the emotional bond between us felt almost overwhelming, impossible to ignore.

I hurried down the hallway, my sneakers squeaking faintly

against the linoleum as I deliberately chose the opposite direction from the one I knew Liam would take. It wasn't cowardice. It was practicality. Even I didn't believe that lie, but I was going with it. Because if I saw him again, if he caught my arm and gave me that look—the one that always seemed to see past every defense I tried to throw up—I didn't trust myself not to go back for more.

My grip on my backpack strap tightened as I pushed through the double doors and into the crisp night air. The sting of the cold against my overheated skin was almost a relief, but not enough to stop the memories flashing through my mind: the way his lips had brushed against mine, how his hands had anchored me to him like he was afraid I might disappear.

I shouldn't have let it happen. I *knew* better. But I'd never been able to resist him.

I reached my car and slid into the driver's seat, locking the doors behind me like that would somehow keep out the memories. My hands trembled as I gripped the steering wheel, my breathing uneven as my mind betrayed me again. Liam's low voice, the way he'd whispered my name like it was a lifeline. The press of his body against mine, the unspoken promise in his kiss.

I squeezed my eyes shut, willing the images away. I couldn't do it. Not again. Look what had happened the last time. The thought twisted in my chest like a blade, sharp and unforgiving. Falling for Liam once had left me shattered. Picking up the pieces had been hell, but I'd done it—for me, for Lily. And I'd sworn never to let him back in, no matter how much he made me feel like I already belonged to him.

But now? Now, I wasn't sure I would survive another whirlwind romance with him. I couldn't let myself go there. Not when the stakes were so much higher. I pressed my forehead against the steering wheel, drawing in a shaky breath. I had to be stronger than that. For Lily. For myself.

With a deep breath, I straightened, started the car, and forced myself to focus on the road ahead. I wasn't that girl anymore—the one who'd believed Liam Cartwright was her happily ever after. No matter how much my traitorous heart wanted to believe otherwise.

CHAPTER FOURTEEN

LIAM

The crisp air whipped against my face as I stormed across campus, barely noticing the swirl of activity around me. Students laughed, chatted, and hurried across the quad to classes. None of it registered. My chest burned from Skye's recent rejection, and my fists clenched so tight my knuckles ached. The reason had to be Mav. I'd seen him helping Skye and Lily when I'd done that drive-by, and he was around her more than I liked.

Then I saw him—Maverick Davis, my competition. He leaned against a bench like he didn't have a care in the world, his trademark smirk stamped across his face. He radiated that effortless confidence that used to piss me off even when I didn't have a reason to hate him. Now, it was like gasoline on the fire raging inside me.

My steps faltered, but only for a second. Every nerve in my body screamed at me to walk away, but I couldn't. Not this time. Not after everything. "Maverick!" I barked, my voice cutting through the hum of conversations around us.

Heads turned, students casting curious glances. *Let them look.*

He turned slowly, his expression shifting as he saw me. His eyes narrowed, and he straightened slightly, though the cocky edge never left his stance. "Cartwright," he drawled. "What's your problem?"

I stopped a few feet from him, my pulse hammering. "You think you can just waltz in and take my place?" Everything about her ate at me, even not knowing if Mav was Lily's father, if he was the one with the permanent connection to Skye.

The smirk dropped from his face, and his jaw clenched. "Careful, Cartwright," he said quietly. "You don't want to start something you can't finish."

I stepped closer, my voice dropping to a growl. "Answer the damn question. You've been in her life this whole time, right?"

His expression hardened, and when he spoke, his tone was ice. "You could've been there by her side. You did that to yourself when you made her feel like an afterthought."

The words hit me like a punch to the gut. My breath caught, but I swallowed the pain, burying it under the anger that surged back up, stronger than ever. "You don't know anything about what we had."

"Oh, I know enough. Skye and I are friends." His lips curled into a bitter smile, making me want to swing at him. "I know you walked away from something most guys would kill for. She deserves better than being someone's backup plan. You made her think she wasn't good enough to be part of your future. And now you're mad because someone else was there for her when you weren't?"

My hands flexed, fists forming, my vision narrowing on him. "Don't act like you're the hero in this story." Everything in me was so twisted up, I couldn't control what flew out of my mouth. "You're just another guy trying to take what isn't yours."

"What isn't mine?" His voice dropped, low and dangerous, and he stepped into my space, his words slow and deliberate. "Skye doesn't belong to anyone, least of all you. You're mad because you lost her. But let me tell you something, Cartwright. She doesn't owe you a damn thing."

My chest heaved, my throat tight as I struggled to form a response. The world around us seemed to fade, the chatter of students just a dull hum. A few lingered, their whispers cutting through the tension like static.

"You think you've got it all figured out." My composure slipped. "You're not in love with her." My gaze flicked to the girl he'd been talking to seconds before I'd confronted him.

His eyes flashed, but he didn't rise to the bait. "Believe what you want. But the truth is, Skye made her choice, and it wasn't you. You're pissed because you can't rewrite the past. That's on you, not me."

The words echoed in my head, each landing like a blow I couldn't block. My fists loosened, falling to my sides, and I stepped back, the fight draining out of me.

Maverick watched me for a moment longer then straightened, his expression calm but firm. "Figure out what you want, Liam. If it's Skye, maybe start by being the man she deserves."

Then he turned and walked away, leaving me in the middle of the quad like an idiot. The crowd's whispers barely registered. All I could hear was his voice, his words replaying on repeat.

I'd needed someone to strike out against, and my envy of Mav's closeness to Skye had been the perfect outlet. I hadn't expected him to say something that resonated. I needed to stop thinking of Mav as a roadblock and focus on what mattered—Skye.

The walk to the athletic center felt longer than usual, my mind a tangle of emotions I couldn't unravel. Mav's words echoed in my head, cutting deeper with every replay.

"Figure out what you want, Liam. If it's Skye, maybe start by being the man she deserves."

My jaw clenched, my fists tightening at my sides. I didn't need Mav's advice—or his judgment. But damn it, he wasn't wrong. I'd spent so long trying to bury my feelings for Skye, pretending I didn't care, and now I was paying the price. I shoved the door open and headed inside, the hum of voices and the squeak of shoes on the gym floor greeting me. A few guys lingered near the bulletin board, their heads turning as I approached.

"Cartwright," one of them called out. "Coach is looking for everyone. Emergency team meeting in the conference room."

I nodded, my stomach sinking. An emergency meeting wasn't typical, but it was becoming the new norm. And after everything that had happened—Jackson's death, the whispers about substances—it couldn't be good.

By the time I reached the conference room, most of the team was already seated. The atmosphere was thick with tension, conversations muted and cautious. Coach stood at the front, his arms crossed, his usual calm demeanor replaced by something harder, more severe.

"Settle down." Coach's voice cut through the low murmur of voices.

The room fell silent as we turned our attention to him.

"First things first." His gaze swept over us. "I know you've all been feeling the weight of what happened with Jackson. It's been a tough couple of days, and I won't pretend like we're past it. But we have to talk about something that's come to light during the investigation."

A ripple of unease passed through the room. I straightened in my seat, my pulse picking up.

Coach took a deep breath, his expression grim. "The medical examiner found anomalies in Jackson's blood. I can't go into specifics, but substances were present that shouldn't have been there."

The air seemed to leave the room, every set of eyes fixed on him.

"Now," Coach continued, his voice steady but firm. "We don't know where these substances came from, how Jackson got them, or why he was using one in particular. But I'm warning all of you—this is a wake-up call. The NCAA has strict policies for a reason. Any violation—*any*—will ruin your career before it even starts. Don't think you can outsmart the system, because you can't. Random testing is happening more frequently, and I promise you, the consequences will be severe."

A heavy silence hung in the room, the weight of his words sinking in. I glanced around, trying to read my teammates' faces. Some looked worried, others just confused. But a few—guys like Leroy and Marc—shifted uncomfortably in their seats, their eyes darting away from Coach's gaze.

"Do I make myself clear?" Coach's voice boomed.

"Yes, sir," we mumbled in unison.

"Good." He nodded, his eyes narrowing. "If anyone here has something to confess, now's the time. My door is always open. But if I find out anyone's involved in something that puts this team or this program at risk..." He let the threat hang, his expression saying everything his words didn't.

He dismissed us shortly after, but the unease lingered as we filed out of the room.

I stayed back, leaning against the wall as the others shuffled past. My mind raced, piecing together fragments of conversations, actions I'd seen on the field, and the stats Skye had mentioned. My gut twisted as I remembered the conversation with Mav earlier.

Mav was right about one thing—I needed to figure out what I wanted. And I wanted Skye. *But this mess with Jackson and the team?* It wasn't just about football anymore. Something bigger was happening, and for the first time in years, I wasn't sure I could fix it.

Pushing off the wall, I headed toward the gym. I only knew one thing for sure. Whatever it took, I wasn't going to let it destroy the future I was fighting for—or the people who mattered most.

CHAPTER FIFTEEN

SKYE

I paced the living room's length while Lily played with her dolls on the coffee table. My social media posts for the team were getting tons of attention. People seemed to love the individual highlights of team members, but I needed another new angle. I'd already done several posts showing a shocked and grieving team winning for their lost teammate. But I wanted to do something else. Only a handful of weeks remained until our team was on track to play in the championship game, and I needed to find more ways to gain new superfans.

The posts I'd created for the Falcons had already increased fan engagement by thirty percent. If I could push that number higher, it would strengthen my portfolio and give me an edge in landing a job with a professional team's media department. My internship was a huge opportunity, and no matter how much I tried to lie to myself—it gave me a chance to spend time with Liam.

I couldn't deny his pull. It went far beyond physical. And despite my vow not to give in to the undeniable attraction and chemistry we had, maybe we could go slow. Be friends—if not for our sakes, then for Lily's.

He'd begun showing me a softer side. He'd opened up about what had molded him into the strong individual who had drawn me in before Lily came into the picture and forced our hands—his unknowingly.

A week had passed since the Indiana game, and they had a rare bye week this weekend. Tutoring Liam was going well, and I felt he was in good shape for the upcoming final before winter break, which was right around the corner. With all the time we'd spent together, I felt closer to him on a different level than I ever had. He was constantly on my mind.

Screw it. I snatched my phone from the table, where Lily hadn't yet noticed the device, as she was playing with a Barbie she'd become enamored with. I clicked on Liam's contact and pressed the phone to my ear, looking to the ceiling for help, which was ridiculous.

What if he says no? Worse—what if he says yes, and it becomes a disaster? But as I watched Lily playing with her dolls, her giggles filling the room, I realized it wasn't just about me anymore. She adored him, and the thought of seeing her happy, even for a few hours, made the risk worth it.

He answered on the third ring, the sound of weights clanging in the background telling me exactly where he was.

"Hey, Liam." I cringed at how high-pitched my voice sounded and quickly cleared my throat. "It's Skye. Are you busy?" *What the hell?* Of course, he was. I squeezed my eyes shut.

When I opened them, my too-intuitive-for-her-age daughter was studying me intently. A deep laugh rumbled through the speaker, causing a delicious shiver to travel through me.

"I'm wrapping up a workout. What can I do for you, Skye?"

So many things. No—I shook my head to clear memories from our past that I wouldn't mind repeating. But that wasn't what this was about. "I had an idea for a feature about a day in the life of a college athlete. Are you interested?"

He hesitated. "Whatever you need, I'm in."

I straightened. The stress that'd caused my shoulders to hover close to my ears eased a little until I glanced at my daughter. "There's just one issue." I cringed at my word choice. Lily was never an issue. "I'll have to bring Lils with me."

Lily squealed and clapped her hands. "I see Liam too!" She jumped to her feet and raced around the table to the stairs.

"Bring the little princess. It'll be fun."

"You say that now." I stared at the spot Lily had vacated as she'd raced to her room. "I bet she's packing her backpack with books and toys you'll be required to entertain her with."

"That doesn't bother me even a little. I love kids."

My stupid heart flipped, false hope filling it with longing that shouldn't be there. *He didn't want me then, and now isn't different, which means he probably won't stick around for Lily.* I wasn't even touching the off-the-charts sex in the science building. I had to remind myself why I'd made my decision, or else I might break down and tell him everything. "I have some pictures of you at the gym already. I thought we could meet at the park near campus." I rattled off the address where I took Lily sometimes. They had a playground, a trail through the woods, and a few obstacle courses that might be fun to take shots of Liam on.

I wanted to include a schedule that Uncle Tommy had shared with me about what his football players endured every week as well as candid shots of Liam and other athletes as they went through their routine, highlighting individual moments and what made them unique that could be a little more relatable to the general public.

Liam volunteered for most of the athletic department's outreach programs. I'd talked with the contact in the department who handled that and found out a date close to Christmas so I could attend and get some pictures. That article would come out before the championship game, but if it went the way

I thought it might, the exposure to the team would be through the roof.

"Sure. I can wrap things up here and meet you two in a few minutes. Or do you want me to pick you up?"

"Oh, no. I'll meet you there. I've got her car seat and stuff in my car."

He sounded mostly normal aside from that slight hesitation in the beginning, not mad that I'd told him to forget anything had happened between us. Some of the tension in my shoulders eased. We agreed to a half hour as Lily came barreling back, flinging her bag at my feet that had her favorite stuffed bunny poking out of the top.

I disconnected the call and shoved my phone in the pocket of my jeans. "What did you pack?"

Lily rattled off everything she had to bring, pulling each item out and explaining why it needed to come with. It took ten minutes of negotiation, but I got her backpack reduced by half the items then included her toy camera so she could "work" alongside me rather than chasing after Liam and demanding he pay attention to her, which I felt he would do.

My heart was in serious danger at the thought of him playing with our daughter. God, if he knew. *How would things change between us? Would he hate me? Or would he quit us cold, denying the chance at something more so he could be free to chase his dreams as a free agent, just as he'd made clear to me before?*

I shuddered at the terrifying thought. It didn't matter. Nothing would come of us spending time together, of him getting to know Lily more. He was too busy with football and school. The NFL Scouting Combine was on the not-too-distant horizon, and he needed to kill it in the competitions held over those four days.

I need to stop obsessing and worrying. Everything would be okay, despite how much my aunt had been hounding me to tell him ever since she'd met Liam the night he brought me home after finding Jackson dead in the fountain.

I bundled Lily up for the cold morning in the park then gathered her bag of supplies and my camera bag before getting us into the car and pointed in the direction of where we were meeting Liam.

It wasn't just about him or the team anymore. This campaign could be my ticket to a professional role if it worked. But every time he smiled at Lily or met my gaze with that intense focus, I wondered if I was getting in too deep.

It took five minutes to get to the park, just as fat snowflakes swirled lazily through the air, lightly dusting the bare tree branches and ground. Liam bounced on his toes not far from where I'd parked, his coat tossed on the hood of his truck, stretching his arms across his impressive chest. I tried to ignore how his dark-gray Under Armor shirt stretched across his broad shoulders and accented the rippling muscles of his arms and abdomen. He wore gray joggers that did nothing to hide his muscular thighs. I pushed out a breath, silently willing myself to get a grip as I climbed from the car and opened the back door to get Lily.

Liam was by my side before I noticed he'd moved. Lily squealed with delight when she saw him, making grabby hands that I ignored as I freed her from the car seat. She wiggled as I set her on her feet, then she launched herself at Liam's legs.

"Little butterfly!" Liam laughed as he caught her.

I watched as he lifted Lily effortlessly into the air, her laughter ringing out against the crisp winter air. The way they mirrored each other—her eyes, his dimpled grin—tightened something deep in my chest. It was only a matter of time before he put the pieces together. The thought terrified me.

"I was hoping you would come." He tickled her tummy after settling her on his hip with ease.

I secured Lily's stuff over my shoulder then went to lift my heavy camera bag, but Liam took it deftly from my hands and transferred it to his shoulder. I offered a shaky smile, telling myself not to get used to him helping or entertaining the fairy tale of him being a part of our lives. *It's only for a few more months.* I had to keep reminding myself of that, steadily ignoring the part of me that wanted to grow close to him.

I found a good spot, dropped Lily's bag, and motioned for Liam to hand me my camera equipment so I could set up. He set it beside me then put Lily down. She dragged her bag to him, chattering about everything in it as he nodded agreement. Once my camera was ready with the lens I wanted to use attached, I snagged Lily's toy camera and handed it to her. "Hey, baby girl, let's get to work, okay?"

"'Kay, Mama." Her expression turned serious as she mimicked my every move.

Liam chuckled. "God, she's so cute."

"Why don't you do some pull-ups then jog through that trail? Is there anything else you can think of that would be good for training?" I glanced at Lily. "Back up, Lils, so Liam can do his part."

Panic coursed through me, my heart hammering against my ribs, praying that he didn't put two and two together about how his name and Lily's both started with L. *What the hell was I thinking?* That I would never see him again. I'd been so naive. Lily did as I asked, her camera up and ready. I steadied her when she stumbled with her gaze focused on Liam and her camera.

Without being told twice, Liam went to the pull-up bars set at various heights on the workout portion of the structure set apart from the playground where Lily usually played. I was proud of myself for focusing on getting the shots I needed and ignoring the tension thrumming through me from how he interacted with our daughter.

I snapped pictures of Liam stretching, jogging, and doing various foot drills. He was so photogenic with his athleticism and gorgeous face. The scar along his cheek only enhanced that dangerous, intense edge, and I loved how focused he was in everything he did. Snow continued to swirl around us, peppering his dark-brown hair and only adding to the ambiance of the photo session. When I thought I'd gotten enough, I called him over, packing up my equipment. "I think I got all I need for now." Excitement buzzed through me as I visualized the article layout I could get started on, leaving sections blocked in for his volunteer work. During one of our library sessions, I'd also snapped a few candid shots.

My uncle's daunting D1 football schedule would be included. It was an insane regimen that all his athletes followed, beginning at five a.m. and ending at midnight. There was room for variation, but the most dedicated athletes were in the thick of it, following the timeline to a tee.

"Mama." Lily dropped her camera in my bag. "Swings?"

"Sure thing, Lily-bean." I adjusted her hat with the cute pink puffball on top. Her cheeks and nose were red, but she seemed warm enough. "Just let me put this stuff in the car."

Lily ignored me and raced toward the swings. I sighed then motioned to my headstrong daughter. "Can you?"

Liam laughed. "I got her." He took off after her, closing the distance in a few long strides, then swung her into his arms to her peals of laughter.

I stood frozen at the effortless affection that had developed almost instantly between the two. A shuddered breath left my lungs, and I shivered, reminding myself I'd done the right thing. *Right?* God, I couldn't go there. I pivoted on my heels and hurried to put everything in the car and lock it up before joining Liam and Lily. On a whim, I pulled my camera back out, leaned against the car, and snapped a few candid shots of Liam pushing Lily on the swing, both wearing carefree grins. I had to pause, hand to my chest, and blink past the mist in my eyes— they looked so alike. *How could he not see it?* I put my camera back in the bag then crossed the distance to them, leaning against the swing set pole.

Liam caught my gaze. "She's adorable. Is her dad in the picture?"

Fuck. "No, not really," I mumbled, busying myself with my phone and the text from my aunt. Grasping onto her message, I changed the subject so fast that he probably had whiplash. "Looks like we're having an impromptu barbecue with the football team tomorrow."

"Yep, Coach sent out an email mandating everyone to attend. We had an emotionally challenging meeting where everyone was informed about Jackson's death. They had counseling set up. It was tough. Now there's even more team building in the wake of finding out some disturbing information about Jackson's blood work."

"He told me." The easy levity present a few seconds ago dissolved at the thought of the strange substance found in Jackson's blood that might have caused his death.

I coaxed Lily from the swing, promising her she would see Liam tomorrow. He walked me to the car, helping to lock Lily safely into her car seat. When I closed the car door and turned, he hadn't moved and crowded me against the car. Snow kissed my face as I tilted it to meet his earnest gaze, my breath catching in my throat as he tucked a wayward strand of hair behind my ear. Then he bent and brushed his lips over mine in the lightest of touches that had me melting faster than the snowflakes on my suddenly heated skin.

The warmth of his lips lingered long after he pulled away, leaving me breathless and reeling. I wanted to believe it could mean something—this spark, this connection—but the reality of everything I hadn't told him loomed large between us.

He backed up, that mischievous, sexy-as-hell grin curving his lips, causing the dimple in his cheek to flash. "I'll see you tomorrow, gorgeous."

Words failed me, and I nodded, getting into my car as fast as possible. *I'm in so much trouble.*

As I drove home, Lily humming happily in the back seat, my chest tightened. Every moment Liam spent with her made it harder to hide the truth. *But what would it do to him if he found out now—so close to the combine, with his future on the line? What would it do to us?*

CHAPTER SIXTEEN

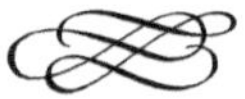

SKYE

The library was silent, save for the faint hum of the air vent and the scratch of Liam's pencil on paper. His brow furrowed as he worked through the equations I'd assigned, the flickering light overhead casting shadows across his face.

"You're close," I murmured, leaning to point at his mistake. My arm brushed his, and the brief contact sent a jolt through me that I tried to ignore.

Liam shifted, turning his head to look at me, his proximity making it impossible to breathe evenly. "Close isn't good enough," he said, his voice low, the usual humor replaced with something quieter, heavier. "I need to get this right."

The intensity in his gaze made my pulse stutter. "You will," I said softly. "You've been improving. You just need to—"

"To stop doubting myself?" he interrupted, a wry smile tugging at his lips.

I nodded, feeling my chest tighten. "Exactly."

The pencil fell from his hand, forgotten, as he leaned back in his chair and looked at me fully. "Do you doubt me too, Skye?"

The question caught me off guard, and for a moment, I didn't know how to answer. His eyes searched mine, not for validation about academics but for something deeper—something I wasn't sure I was ready to give.

"Liam…" I started, but the words stuck in my throat.

"You don't have to answer," he said, his voice softer now. "I just—I want to be someone you can trust."

The vulnerability in his tone cracked something inside me. "You've been showing me that," I whispered. "It counts for more than you think."

The air between us thickened, charged with words left unsaid. I tried to focus on the printout between us, but his hand brushed mine, deliberately that time. The warmth of his touch sent a ripple of electricity up my arm, and when I looked at him, the weight of his gaze made it impossible to look away.

"You drive me crazy, you know that?" he said, his voice low and rough.

"Liam—" I started again, but he moved.

Before I could stop myself—or him—his lips were on mine, soft but urgent. The kiss was a mix of pent-up frustration and something else, something I hadn't let myself feel in years. His hand cupped the back of my neck, and I melted, my resolve crumbling as I kissed him back.

The chair scraped loudly as he stood, pulling me with him, and suddenly, we were pressed against the edge of the table. My fingers curled into his shirt, and his other hand splayed against the small of my back, anchoring me in place.

When he pulled back, his breathing was ragged, and his forehead rested against mine. "I know this doesn't fix anything," he said, his voice unsteady. "But I can't—Skye, I can't pretend I don't feel this."

I swallowed hard, my chest heaving as I tried to find the words. "I don't know how to do this again," I admitted, the truth spilling out before I could stop it.

His hand tightened on my waist, grounding me. "We'll figure it out," he said simply. "If you let me."

The moment hung between us, fragile but electric. I nodded slowly, and though the future was still uncertain, for the first time in years, it felt like a step forward.

It was late, and the kitchen was quiet except for the soft clink of dishes and the occasional rustle of paper as Aunt Eileen sorted through a pile of mail on the counter. Uncle Tommy sat at the table, his head in his hands, the weight of the world etched into the lines of his face.

I rinsed the last of the plates and set them in the dishwasher, drying my hands on a towel before crossing the room. "You okay, Uncle Tommy?"

He didn't answer right away, and Aunt Eileen gave me a look that said, *Give him a minute.* But I wasn't sure we had that kind of time—not with everything hanging over him.

Finally, he let out a long sigh and straightened, rubbing his eyes. "I don't know anymore, Skye. Losing Jackson... I thought I'd seen the worst of it, but now it feels like the ground's shifting under me."

Aunt Eileen placed a cup of coffee in front of him and squeezed his shoulder before sitting down. "It's a terrible tragedy, losing someone so young. It's taken a toll on the team, on everyone. We'll get through this."

"It is. We've had several meetings and set up counseling for the players." Uncle Tommy shook his head. "This isn't something you just get through, Eileen. Jackson's death—it's changed everything. And now the questions... They won't go away anytime soon."

"What questions?" I slid into the chair across from him.

He looked up at me, his gaze heavy with exhaustion. "The police have questions, and now the university's digging into it more. I don't blame them, but it doesn't make it easier. They want to know what I'm doing to address the concerns about our leadership, and that spotlight, it's landing on the assistant coaches."

I leaned forward. "What do you mean?"

Aunt Eileen shot him a sharp look before speaking. "The assistant coaches have been under scrutiny since Jackson's collapse. With the way some players have been performing this season—huge gains in speed, strength, and endurance—people are starting to wonder if it's all as clean as it seems."

"They've explained it," Uncle Tommy interjected, though his voice lacked conviction. "I asked the coaches directly—point-blank—if anything illegal was going on. They swore there wasn't. They've had the athletes tested. No drugs, no enhancers. Just a new training program they've been implementing."

"And you believe them?" I asked carefully.

He rubbed his hands over his face, sighing. "I don't know. One or two of them seemed defensive, but that could just be because they feel like their methods are under attack. They claim the program is responsible for the players' performances. Better conditioning. Better drills."

Aunt Eileen made a sound in her throat, something between a scoff and a sigh. "It's hard to argue with the results. But it's also difficult to believe it's all as simple as they're making it sound. Especially given how quickly the improvements have happened."

My stomach twisted. "But Jackson..." I trailed off, unsure how to phrase my thoughts without accusing anyone outright.

"That's the thing," Uncle Tommy said, his voice low. "They swear Jackson was clean. He passed every drug test we gave him. I've even seen the tests. They keep pointing to preexisting conditions, overexertion—anything to explain it away. But none of it feels right."

I nodded slowly. "And the other players? Have they said anything?"

Uncle Tommy's jaw tightened. "Not a word. They're loyal to their coaches. They're defending them, saying it's all legit. But loyalty only goes so far. If something else is going on, someone will slip eventually."

"It's a tightrope," Aunt Eileen added, her gaze flicking between us. "If there's nothing to find, pushing too hard could fracture the team. But if there is something…" She trailed off, her lips pressing into a thin line.

Uncle Tommy leaned back in his chair, staring at his coffee. "I put some feelers out. Steve Mack, Jackson's position coach, was in talks with another college for a head coaching position. I just want to do right by these kids. But I don't even know where to start."

I placed a hand on his arm, squeezing gently. "I'll help you, Uncle Tommy. Whatever it takes, we'll figure this out."

His eyes softened, and he gave me a faint nod. "Just… be careful, Skye. If there's nothing to this, I don't want you stirring up trouble that could hurt the team. And if there is something…" His voice hardened. "The people involved won't take kindly to being exposed."

"I can handle it," I said.

Aunt Eileen's sharp look told me she wasn't convinced. "I know you think you can," she said, her voice firm. "But this isn't something we want you digging into because you took on an internship that involves the team."

"You might feel connected because you were the one who found Jackson, but this isn't something we want you looking into, Skye." Uncle Tommy leveled a stern gaze my way. "Leave it to the police to figure things out."

I hesitated before nodding. "I promise."

CHAPTER SEVENTEEN

LIAM

Kylian, Ares, and I got to Coach's house early to help with any needed prep for the mostly indoor gathering. It was an unseasonably warm day and most of us wouldn't mind being outside—which I was sure his wife would appreciate.

Since Kylian was the team captain, he'd planned to be there first thing anyway, and it just made sense for Ares and me to ride with him. Besides, I couldn't wait to see Skye and her adorable daughter again. Our kiss yesterday had played on repeat in my mind all night long. It was innocent, and I could've sworn it affected her the same way it had me.

I felt like I was walking a tightrope whenever I thought about it. The NFL was everything I'd worked for, but with Skye, it was like someone had tilted the balance, making me question what mattered most. I didn't have room for distractions, but maybe she wasn't one. Maybe she was the thing holding it all together.

During the car ride, Ares and Kylian grilled me about yesterday's photo shoot. I hadn't told them much, just that I'd learned Lily's dad wasn't in the picture—which left an opening for me to get closer to Skye. Her having a kid didn't scare me. I liked spending time with the little spitfire. If anything, Lily made me want it even more—to prove I could handle the responsibilities off the field as well as I did on it. But wanting and having were two different things, and I couldn't let my emotions screw up the biggest shot of my life. But I had thought it weird that Skye said the dad wasn't present, as I knew she and Mav were still close. *Could it be that he isn't the father after all?*

As Ares steered the conversation to the photo shoot, I tried not to let my face give anything away.

"Man, you're already halfway to playing house," Ares teased, leaning over the seat. "You and Skye tag-teaming bedtime stories yet?"

I rolled my eyes, but the thought hit harder than it should've. "She's got a kid," I said, lightening my tone. "Doesn't mean I'm stepping in."

Kylian chuckled, shaking his head. "Yeah, but you want to. You're not fooling anyone, Liam."

Maybe I wasn't.

It was the first gathering Coach Becket had held since he was hired my sophomore year. The team meant so much to me—everyone except Calvin, the second-string quarterback who was unfortunately present—and we'd all been there for each other through thick and thin. Aside from being with my sister, hanging out at Coach's house gave me the definition of family.

We helped Coach's wife set out the side dishes where we would be eating inside, and I chased Lily around the yard when she burst through the back door and made a beeline for me.

When I headed into the kitchen, Eileen handed me a stack of plates to carry to the tables inside, her gaze lingering on me longer than it should've. "You've got a way with kids, Liam. Natural, even." Her tone was light, but her eyes told another story—like she was piecing together a puzzle I didn't know I was part of.

"Kids are easy." I shrugged it off.

"Not always," she replied, her eyes flicking to Lily, who'd followed me in. "But you seem to have a knack for it."

Thirty minutes later, the rest of the team had mostly arrived, packing the yard with athletes. Skye found me and Lily just as Calvin strolled by, pausing with his signature asshole smirk as he checked her out.

"Hey, baby. When are you going to do a feature on me?"

I tensed, setting Lily down but keeping a grip on her hand so she wouldn't take off and get trampled by one of my teammates tossing a ball around. "Second string doesn't draw the crowd, Calvin."

His face turned beet red as he narrowed his eyes in anger then darted them to Lily for half a second. "Cute kid. Too bad my cousin Mav isn't here to play daddy to his daughter."

The smugness in his voice made my blood boil. Calvin wasn't just running his mouth—he was fishing for something. *Does he know Mav is the father? Or is he just poking at rumors?* Either way, the implication hit too close to home.

Skye whirled to face the asshole who would soon find my fist in his smug face. Her finger jabbed into his chest, and she bared her teeth at him. "You have no idea what you're talking about, so shut up and get out of my face." She bent, picked up Lily, and took off for the back door to the house.

That was my cue. I grabbed Calvin's jacket and hauled him close. Ares and Kylian converged from my peripheral vision. I didn't care, nothing would stop me from shutting the asshole up, but I wasn't stupid. There were too many witnesses, and our coach's presence stilled the violent reaction I wanted to unleash on him.

"Stay away from Skye and her daughter."

He smirked. "Funny how that bothered you so much. Bet she has a hard time looking at that ugly scar on your face. Probably why she dumped you in the first place."

"You're an idiot." The scar was nothing to me. I wasn't that insecure. "You talk to either of them again, and you'll regret it."

"You got nothing," Calvin taunted. "You're too much of a pussy to do anything to me with Coach so close by."

Kylian and Ares crowded us, giving me just enough coverage so no one would see what happened next. I buried my fist in his gut. Air rushed from Calvin's mouth as he bent over from the force of my punch. Ares wrapped his arm around Calvin, and I released his jacket as my friend led him to another section of the yard, saying that Coach would find out how Calvin had treated his niece and her daughter if he mentioned my hitting him. I didn't think the weasel would rat me out, but it was better with the threat in place.

As Calvin hobbled away, his words stuck in my head like a thorn. *"Too bad my cousin isn't here to play daddy." Skye had always been close to Mav, sure, but... could he be Lily's father?* She'd sounded like that wasn't the case when I asked about the father at the park. I clenched my fists, shoving down the thought. I didn't have time to chase shadows.

"What was that about?" Kylian asked.

I glanced at our QB1, then eyed the patio doors, fighting the urge to check on Skye and Lily. "Calvin was mouthing off. It was nothing. He was trying to hit on Skye and get a rise out of me." I laughed, the sound darker than I'd thought it would be. "He didn't expect Skye to hand him his ass, though. It was hot as hell."

After Calvin slunk off, the tension in my shoulders eased, but not entirely. Being part of the team wasn't just about stats or scouts—it was about showing up for the guys who relied on me, both on and off the field.

We put the incident behind us and mingled with our teammates—most of whom were outside at one of the tables—eating our body weight in food. Ares, Kylian, and I took turns at the grill, giving Coach a break. Even while grilling with Ares and

Kylian, I found my gaze drifting to Skye through the crowd. She laughed at something Eileen said, but the tension in her shoulders hadn't eased. Calvin's words lingered like a bad taste in my mouth.

After everyone had eaten, we had a short meeting about expectations. Coach's tone was heavier than usual, his words measured as he reminded us of the dangers of taking the easy road. His gaze locked onto each of us in turn. "Jackson's death wasn't just a tragedy—it was a wake-up call," Coach said, his voice steady but sharp. "You're under pressure. I get it. But cutting corners? Taking risks with your health to keep up? That's a fool's game. You've all got talent, but talent doesn't mean anything if you're not smart about using it."

The weight of his words hung over us like a cloud, and for the first time, I saw flickers of doubt on even Ares's and Kylian's faces.

The barbeque broke up, but Kylian, Ares, and I lingered to help clean up while the rest left. As I passed through the yard, my gaze caught Mav exiting the house next door and heading toward his car. *They're neighbors?* Calvin's smug words clawed at the back of my mind, each digging deeper. I quickened my pace, the fire in my chest demanding answers I couldn't ignore any longer.

I caught up to Mav just as he reached his car. My chest burned with jealous rage. "Hey!" I barked, my voice cutting through the relative stillness.

Maverick turned slowly, his expression wary but calm, like he'd been expecting me. "Cartwright." He leaned against his car. "What do you want?"

"What do I want?" My voice was as strained as the muscles in my back. The idea that he could be Lily's father made me want to lay into him, but I restrained myself. "Just had an interesting conversation with your cousin."

"Oh?" Mav's dark brows rose.

"Yeah, Calvin thought you should be next door playing daddy to your daughter."

Mav's lips twitched at the corners. "Okay and?" He scoffed. "I don't pay much attention to what Calvin says. He's an idiot."

"Tell me the truth. Are you Lily's father?"

Mav's eyes widened briefly before narrowing, his usual cocky smirk replaced by something colder. "You're seriously asking me that? Haven't we already had this conversation?"

"Answer the damn question." I stepped closer, my pulse hammering. His cousin was a mind fuck—the reason we were having the discussion again. I needed to hear the truth, needed to make sure before I let myself believe what was clawing its way into my chest.

Mav straightened, his arms crossing over his chest. "You're supposed to use your damn head, Cartwright. Skye is like a sister to me."

The weight of his words hit me hard. I wanted to call bullshit, to believe there was still some angle I hadn't seen, but there was no hesitation in his voice. No guilt. Just raw frustration.

Memories of every time I'd seen them together flashed through my mind, and I analyzed the interactions without the persistent red haze of jealousy I usually wore around them. I could see it for the first time—there never had been any romantic chemistry between them. *Protective?* Yes, absolutely. But that palpable chemistry that ignited whenever she and I were close was absent.

Anger laced my frustration and that goddamned panic of what-if because the timing was right. *So if it wasn't him... then that only leaves one answer.*

My stomach twisted. Lily wasn't just Skye's daughter—she was mine. I wasn't confused anymore, not about that. *But the reality of it? The weight of what it means?* That still hadn't settled. "You've been in her life this whole time. You had to know, right? Why the hell wouldn't you say something?"

Mav's gaze hardened, his voice dropping to a dangerous calm. "You think this is about me? This is about you not stepping up when it mattered. I've been there for Skye because she needed someone who wouldn't bail. Where were you, Liam?"

His words hit their mark, stoking the fire raging in my chest. I growled. "If you're not the father, then stop acting like her damn guardian."

Maverick took a deliberate step closer, his voice a low growl. "I'm not her guardian—I'm her friend. Someone who didn't bail when things got hard."

The accusation burned, but I couldn't let it go. The thought of what she'd done swung into another round of denial. "She would've told me if I was the father."

He stared at me for a long moment, the tension between us thick enough to cut. Then, with a slow shake, he said, "Ask her, Liam. If you want the truth, ask Skye. But if you're not ready to hear it, stop dragging me into your mess."

I swallowed hard, his words twisting like a knife. "You think I haven't tried? She won't give me a straight answer." *But did I actually ask her? Or did I ask a roundabout question about the father being in the picture?*

"That's on you to fix," he said, his tone softening slightly. "But don't come at me like I'm the enemy here. I've been there for her because she needed someone. And if you care about her —about Lily—you'll stop pointing fingers and figure out what the hell you want."

I stood frozen as he climbed into his car and started the engine. He wasn't my competition. He never had been. But if Mav wasn't the father, that only left one answer. *She'd known this entire time, and she never told me.* My stomach knotted, a slow, searing ache settling in my chest. *She chose to do this alone. She chose to keep me out of it.*

My hands fisted at my sides. The betrayal ran deeper than I expected, cutting through the anger and landing somewhere I wasn't ready to face. It wasn't just that Skye had kept her from me—it was that she never even gave me the chance to step up. The motor's hum faded into the background, his words echoing in my head as I made my way back to the barbeque.

Mav wasn't wrong. I had a lot to prove to Skye if I wanted her in my life—and I did. *And Lily?* I already cared about her like she was mine, and I wasn't about to walk away again. The anger and betrayal I felt wasn't as easy to let go of.

I shoved the difficult conversations to the recesses of my mind, not yet ready to have a confrontation with Skye. I needed time to process learning about who I was to Lily. In the meantime, I was determined to spend as much time with them as I could. I wanted Skye to see that I would be there for her and her daughter. I wasn't the same person as I was before.

Kylian and Ares sat at the kitchen table and chatted with Coach about scouts and prospects while I found Skye playing a board game with Lily and Coaches wife in the living room. Not ready to leave, I talked them into letting me join in and teamed up with Lily. One game turned into two before Lily's yawns came one after the other.

As Lily leaned against me, Skye's hands froze mid-motion, gripping the edge of the game board. Her lips twitched like she wanted to say something, but she packed up the pieces instead. The cautious way her eyes flicked between me and Lily made my chest tighten. She wasn't just protective—she was scared.

"You don't have to stick around," she said lightly, but something in her voice was cautious.

"I want to." I kept my tone easy.

Her shoulders stiffened like she was bracing for something I wasn't sure I could stop.

"Time for bed, Lils," Skye said, packing up the game. "If you go right up, I'll read you a story."

"No." Her arms crossed defiantly over her little body, and she flung herself against my side. "Want Liam."

Skye's lips pressed tightly together, and I laughed, lifting Lily to her feet. "Go get ready with your mom, and I'll come read you a story afterward."

The little negotiator grinned then raced up the stairs, Skye following with a perplexed expression as she glanced over her shoulder at me. That left me with her aunt, who stared intently at me again. Her look wasn't just surprised—it was conflicted. Like she wasn't sure whether to pull me closer or push me away. Lily's easy affection for me was adorable, but it felt like walking a minefield. *How long before Skye's walls come back up?*

I got to my feet and helped Eileen up, making a quick stop to tell Kylian and Ares I would be about fifteen minutes more.

The room felt different—charged with something unspoken. My pulse slowed, the tension thickening as my gaze flicked to the staircase where Lily had disappeared moments ago. She had grinned up at me, trusting and unguarded, and it hit differently now. The weight of it all settled, pressing in at the edges of my ribs.

Eileen's gaze lingered on me, unreadable—like she was waiting for me to say something, to realize something—before she quickly turned away.

But I already knew.

CHAPTER EIGHTEEN

SKYE

"Skye Finley." Aunt Eileen grabbed my arm and pulled me into her bedroom next to mine and Lily's. "That young man is amazing with Lily." My aunt crossed her arms over her chest and leveled me with the look that used to make me agree to anything she told me to do—but that was before I became a mom.

"Yeah, he is, but I bet that's because he doesn't have any of the responsibility weighing him down." I slapped my hand over my heart, frustration buzzing along my skin from the impossibility of our situation. "I know what his priorities are." Or I did, but trusting was difficult. "Just, don't push me on this. Please."

"He was young then, sweetheart." Aunt Eileen pulled me in for a hug, rocking slowly. "Everybody changes as they mature. It's not just about you, Skye. He has a right to know. Give him a chance. You and Lily are so special, and I know he sees it by the way he watches you when you're not looking."

A shudder racked my body, and I soaked up her support before pulling away. I had to make her understand why telling Liam was a terrible idea. "I can't put Lily through the heartache that's bound to follow telling Liam he's her dad. Can you imagine?" My voice rose, and I had to take several deep breaths to regain control. "He's on the verge of achieving everything he's ever wanted. A family isn't part of that plan, and I can't risk derailing his future—no matter how much I might want to. I can't do that to him, not when he specifically told me that was his end game and nothing, not even me, would distract him from reaching his goal."

"But—"

"No." I softened my voice. I didn't want to hurt her. I knew her ambush came from a place of love. "It can't just be about what I want. If I told Liam, he could lose everything important to him. Can you imagine Uncle Tommy finding out?" I whisper-shouted. "He would flip his shit if he learned one of his star players knocked me up. That could derail Liam's likelihood of interviews from scouts and field time."

"You really think your uncle would do that?"

I rolled my eyes. "Hell, yes."

Aunt Eileen paled, looking adequately chastised. "Well... okay. We'll keep this between us, at least until football ends." Fire returned to her soft brown eyes. "Then all bets are off because Liam should have things in order with an agent by then."

"No." I firmed my voice, willing her to see reason. "This needs to stay silent until after the draft."

Aunt Eileen shrugged, the corners of her mouth lifting with that mischievous expression that spelled trouble. I didn't like it.

She shook her head. "Sweetheart, people are going to notice. Lily's the spitting image of him—the eyes, the grin, everything."

"No one will notice. Lily isn't around the football players." I crossed my arms, mimicking her posture. We were at an impasse, but I would win.

"Except for today, especially when Liam was seen holding her around all of them."

"That's a low blow." I saw red. "Did you plan for this? Did

Uncle Tommy have all the ballers over for a team-building barbeque because you put the idea in his head?"

"Of course not. But even the most unobservant can see that Liam is so good with Lily. Maybe it's you who can't see that. All I'm trying to do is pull that rip cord." She rested her hand on my arm, probably in an attempt to get through the wall I'd erected. "Open your eyes and see what could be instead of worrying over heartache and loss."

My head jerked back as if she'd slapped me. "I know first-hand what loss feels like. Remember, I lost my parents. And when I found out I was pregnant, I knew the news wouldn't be welcome. The guy I was madly in love with didn't want a serious relationship with me. It was clear that a family would impede his professional trajectory."

The floor creaked faintly outside the door, and the hairs on the back of my neck prickled, but I was too focused on Eileen to care.

Frustration pinched Aunt Eileen's mouth, creating lines she hated along her upper lip. "But that's his daughter too. All I'm saying is Liam deserves to make the choice to be a father to his daughter. Tommy doesn't need to know until later if that's what's stopping you from telling him."

"So she is mine."

I spun to find Liam's tall, broad frame filling the door. His head was tilted back slightly, brows angled together, creating lines on his forehead. The scar on his cheek stood out, and a muscle jumped along his tense jawline.

Staggering back as if I'd been punched in the gut, I uncrossed my arms and held my shaking palms out against the anger and shock pouring off him. "Liam—"

"Lily's asleep." Guttural words shot through clenched teeth. "I was coming to say goodbye."

"Liam, I—"

"No." His response cracked like a whip as he retreated into

the hallway. "We're going to talk, Skye—about all of it. But not now. Right now, I can't even... How could you keep her from me?"

My breath caught, frozen in my chest. Liam's voice wasn't just angry—it was broken, raw, like every ounce of betrayal had poured out in those words. My hands trembled, the room spinning as if gravity had flipped. This couldn't be happening. He wasn't supposed to know—not yet, not like this. *Lily... Oh God, Lily.*

The air left my lungs, and I dropped to my knees as a full-blown panic attack hit me with the force of a tsunami. I couldn't even process how much he'd heard other than the part about Lily being his—I was well and truly fucked.

CHAPTER NINETEEN

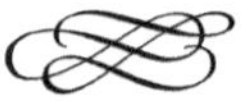

LIAM

Lily's my daughter. I'd asked Mav, and part of me had already known. But hearing it like that, hearing them confirm it—it still felt like a goddamn sledgehammer to the chest.

The truth wasn't unexpected—not really. That quiet, nagging thought had been buried in my subconscious from the second I saw her. The familiarity in her green eyes. The way Eileen had watched me, like she was waiting for me to see it, to put the pieces together. I had. I just hadn't wanted to believe it. Hadn't let myself. Because accepting it meant facing the reality that Skye had kept something that massive from me—had made the choice, alone, to raise our daughter without me.

My hands fisted at my sides, my breathing uneven. *She's mine. Lily is mine.* And I never had a fucking clue.

A crushing weight settled over me, pressing down on my chest like a full-body tackle I hadn't braced for. My legs moved before I'd even made the conscious decision. I rushed down the stairs and past the kitchen, where Kylian and Ares were still talking to Coach. One look, and they both straightened, quickly saying goodbye and hurrying after me.

Footsteps pounded behind me, and I quickened my pace, slipping through the front door and outside. The door never shut behind me—either it was Skye or the guys. I hoped it was the guys. With the way I felt, I was afraid I would say something to her that I couldn't take back.

A small hand locked onto my bicep and tugged. I fought the urge to yank my arm free and forced myself to turn and face Skye. Kylian and Ares stood on the front steps, the door closed behind them, wearing wary expressions as they gave us space.

Red rimmed Skye's eyes as she stood before me, her face unnaturally pale, and tears lined her cheeks. With no coat, she shivered from the cold December air, and I cursed, whipping off my letterman jacket and draping it over her.

"Don't even start." I crowded her, my fists clenching at my sides in pure frustration. "You knew all this time that Lily's my daughter, and you didn't tell me?"

Skye's trembling hand shot out as if to hold back the storm. It wasn't just that she'd kept Lily from me. It was what that meant—Skye didn't think I would step up. Maybe back then, she was right to worry, but not now. Not anymore. I just... I needed time to process.

I ignored the shocked "What the fuck?" that came from my friends and shook my head, taking a step back to stop her from getting closer. I clenched my jaw tight, my breath ragged as the weight of it all pressed down on me. *She knew. She fucking knew.* "You didn't just ghost me," I said, my voice rough. "You made a choice. You knew you were pregnant, and you decided to keep it from me. Two years, Skye. Two fucking years."

"It wasn't like that." Skye glanced behind her, pupils blown wide. "Liam, please. Keep your voice down. My uncle might hear you."

"I don't give a fuck." Two years of first steps, first words, first everything. I'd missed it all. Because of her. Because of me.

"Go inside, Skye," Kylian said. "You guys can talk somewhere else when Liam's had time to calm down."

"But…" Skye trembled, her gaze locked on me.

I averted my eyes. I couldn't even look at her right now. I had a daughter, and I'd missed two years of her life. *Just… fuck.* I ran my hands through my hair, gripping the strands tight. No—hurt barreled through me—I wouldn't let her get off that easy. I swung my gaze back to her, locking on like a heat-seeking missile. "How could you do that—not tell me? I've missed out on so much of her life—she doesn't even fucking know I'm her dad."

"I-I…" She faltered, her lips trembling before she squared her shoulders and lifted her chin. "You didn't want this, Liam. You made it clear that football came first. We weren't serious—your words. And I thought—I thought keeping you out of it was the best thing for Lily. For both of us."

"Bullshit." She knew better than that. "You're the one who ghosted me."

"Because you didn't want more!" Her voice rose with each word.

"Hey, guys." Kylian moved toward us, a glance behind him at the house. "This isn't the place or time for this discussion."

"Besides," Skye said as if Kylian never interrupted. "You're a shoo-in to be drafted to the NFL, and you *told* me nothing would get in the way of that—including a future with me."

"That's not what I meant. It didn't go down that way, and you know it." Anger rolled around in me at her snort. "You never told me, and I had a fucking right to know!"

Kylian and Ares moved fast then.

Ares clamped a hand on my arm, his grip firm but calm. "Not here, man. Take a breath."

Kylian shifted between me and Skye, his eyes sharp. "You won't fix this yelling on Coach's lawn. Let's go."

Each took one of my arms and pulled me back. Ares opened

the rear door to Kylian's SUV. It took both of them to shove me inside.

I wasn't having any of it, so I rolled down my window as soon as Kylian started the SUV. "How could you do this?"

"What would've happened if I hadn't, Liam? Football's always been your everything. You'd have seen us as a distraction. Lily and I—we weren't. I wasn't stupid. I heard Cassidy and Jennifer brag about you and warn me off too."

"No one has a right to speak for me. And who the fuck are they?"

"Your jersey-chasing posse."

Tears filled her eyes, but I felt nothing except anger for once.

"You would have left us."

"You don't know that," I growled. I wanted to be furious at her, to make her feel the weight of what she'd stolen from me. But some small, ugly part of me whispered that she wasn't entirely wrong. *Back then, would I have stepped up? Would I have chosen her and Lily over the dream I'd been chasing my whole life? Especially after that dressing down from our freshman-year coach?*

"It was easier this way. Besides, would you have wanted a family if you possibly had to forgo your dreams with football? I guarantee that your coach, and probably my uncle when he took over the position, would have lost their shit. You might not have gotten the opportunities you did if they'd known."

I hesitated. Not because I wanted to know or be a part of Lily's life any less, but because she wasn't wrong. I would have been riding the bench.

"I have my answer." She whirled around and ran into the house.

I had a sinking feeling about my intangible family's life.

"You need to breathe, man," Ares muttered as he got in the vehicle. "This isn't just about being pissed. It's about what you do next."

As Kylian's SUV pulled out of the driveway, I stared at the

house, its dark windows giving nothing away. A sliver of clarity returned. It wasn't over. She could run, but I wasn't letting her shut me out—not again. As we drove away, my thoughts wouldn't stop spinning. I'd missed all of Lily's beginnings. I couldn't change the past, but I sure as hell wouldn't miss any more.

The SUV ride was silent except for the hum of the tires on the pavement. My mind raced with everything I'd just heard. By the time we got back to the condo, my chest felt like it was ready to explode.

It was quiet when we walked in, the kind of stillness that didn't match the storm raging inside me. I paced like a caged animal.

"Liam, chill, man." Ares leaned against the kitchen counter. "You're not going to solve anything by wearing a hole in the floor."

Before I could snap back, Aurora and Brielle walked in, each carrying mugs of coffee.

Aurora handed one to Kylian before perching on the arm of the couch, her blue eyes zeroing in on me. "You look ready to explode," she said softly. "Want to talk about it?"

I scoffed, running a hand through my hair. "Talk? What's there to talk about? Skye lied to me. She kept my daughter from me for two years."

Aurora's mouth dropped open before she quickly closed it. "You're Lily's dad?"

Brielle raised an eyebrow. "And why do you think she did that?"

"Because she didn't think I'd step up." The bitterness in my voice surprising even me. "She thought I'd choose football over them."

Aurora tilted her head as she gnawed on her lower lip, worry darkening her eyes. "Would she have been wrong?"

Her words hit like a slap, and I stopped pacing. "What the hell is that supposed to mean?"

"She was nineteen, Liam," Ares said gently. "Nineteen, pregnant, and scared. From what we've heard about your disagreement freshman year, she had every reason to think you'd prioritize your career. And let's be honest—you probably would have."

I opened my mouth to argue but couldn't find the words. *Would I have stepped up back then?* The ugly truth was, I didn't know. Maybe Skye had been right to think I would see them as a distraction—just like my freshman coach, and my dad, would have said. But that wasn't who I was anymore, and I would prove it—to her, to Lily, and to myself.

"But that doesn't make what she did right," Aurora added, her voice firm. "You had a right to know. She should have trusted you with the truth."

Brielle nodded. "You have every right to be upset, but don't let that anger cloud what matters. Lily. She's what's important now."

Their words sank in, heavy but necessary. I dropped onto the couch, burying my head in my hands. "How do I make up for not being there?" Mav had been right. I'd bailed back then, but that didn't mean I had to keep running. I refused to let Skye shut me out.

Aurora leaned forward, her voice soft. "You start by showing Skye you're here to stay. She's scared, Liam. Scared of what you'll do, scared of what this means for your future. Prove her wrong."

Brielle smiled, her hand resting lightly on my shoulder. "And show Lily that her dad is someone she can count on, no matter what."

I nodded slowly, their words echoing in my head. They were right. It wasn't just about me and Skye anymore. It was about

Lily. I couldn't change the past, but I could damn well make sure she knew who I was moving forward.

148

CHAPTER TWENTY

SKYE

I ran inside, slamming the door behind me, shoulders tense as I prepared for a fight. My uncle must have heard my life imploding outside. But he wasn't standing there on the other side of the door, waiting to bust some heads—his football players', specifically. Instead, the TV blared with a movie, but no one was on the couch watching. Uncle Tommy's back was to me as he sat at the kitchen table across from my aunt, who briefly caught my eye and gave a barely noticeable shake of her head.

Tears ran like a river down my face, and I darted for the stairs before my uncle could see. *I'm failing everyone—Liam and Lily. And when my uncle finds out, him too. And my aunt?* She'd wanted me to tell Liam. They were all so disappointed in me, or would be. Liam was right—he deserved to know. Maybe things would have been different. *Or not.* I struggled to forget what he'd said to me when I'd known I was pregnant.

I flopped on my bed in the room I shared with Lily, too tired to even wash my face or change out of my jeans and long-sleeved shirt. I buried my face in the pillow, muffling a scream that clawed its way up my throat. The fabric soaked up my tears as I pressed deeper into the mattress, wishing I could disappear.

Liam's words echoed in my head, sharp and unforgiving, each cutting deeper than the last.

I shook from silent sobs, not wishing to wake my daughter. I had no idea how much time had passed before I fell into a fitful sleep, waking the next day like a truck had run over me during the night. Deep circles that no amount of concealer could completely conceal hung like moons under my eyes. It promised to be a hell of a Monday.

Lily was a bundle of energy, and Aunt Eileen had a doctor's appointment and left early, which meant I had to get my daughter to Little Sprouts Daycare before I went to school. I got her fed, dressed, and in the car in under an hour, which was a miracle. In the car, I caught sight of my reflection in the rearview mirror. The bags under my eyes were darker than I'd ever seen.

"Mama, when I see Liam?" Lily hugged two of the Disney princess dolls she'd taken a battle stance on bringing before getting into the car.

I didn't have the energy to fight her on the toys. Her big green eyes fixed on mine in the rearview mirror. I was so screwed. "I don't know, Lils. Probably in a couple of days, okay?" *Or never?* I had no idea what was going on in his head after yesterday.

I managed to drop Lily off at daycare without further incident and hightailed it to the class I was supposed to TA. I was thirty minutes late and beyond thankful Joe had answered my Hail Mary text for help. He'd covered for me, or at least was covering for me until I showed up. I didn't deserve such a good friend, and when I'd said as much, he'd replied that he had Megan thanks to my encouragement. We were all good.

By some miracle, I found a parking space in the student lot that wasn't too far from the science building, and I raced down the path to the door. I yanked it open and made a beeline for the stairs, only to skid to a halt when Professor White stood three feet from where I'd been heading. Bushy white eyebrows rose as he took in my disheveled appearance and frantic pace.

"Skye." He glanced at his watch. "Aren't you supposed to be TAing entry-level chemistry right now?"

"Yes. You're right. I'm so sorry, Professor White. I was running late, and Joe is covering for me until I could get there."

"The TA position holds a lot of weight, especially regarding financial compensation and connections that I assumed you planned to use for your future."

"I know." I'd dropped my chemistry major for marketing with a focus on sports and social media, though, so the TA position didn't hold the weight he was referencing. "It's a big deal, and I'm fortunate to work under you. I promise it won't happen again." Silence met my verbal barrage, and I couldn't stop myself from filling it. "You can count on me, Professor White. I will control everything—ah, my alarm clock—so I'm not late again."

He nodded, his lips curving slightly at the corners. "I know you will. Hurry along, then."

I mumbled something unintelligible and raced up the stairs to room 201, waving to Joe through the door's window. He said something to the class, gathered his bag, and met me in the hallway.

"Hey." I flashed a weak smile. "Thanks so much for covering for me."

"Yeah, no problem." His brows furrowed. "Are you okay? You look like hell. You got this?"

A chill crawled over my body to think about that night. "I'm good. Yeah. Again, thanks."

As I watched Joe walk away, determination mixed with my gratitude. I couldn't keep letting everyone else clean up my messes. Maybe I couldn't fix everything today, but I could start by showing up, even if it was thirty minutes late.

I hurried into the classroom, made my excuses, and went to work.

I finished that class and the next one scheduled immediately after. Both kicked my ass. I was dragging emotionally. Liam's expression—the hurt and shock followed swiftly by fury—destroyed me.

I stumbled down the steps and threw my weight against the doors closest to the parking lot. I was ready to fall face-first onto the couch while Lily watched cartoons. Rushing down the pathway, I lifted my too-heavy head and surveyed my surroundings, drawing up short at a familiar face.

Detective Cartwright blocked my path, a tight smile curving her face. Air whooshed from my lungs as I realized I couldn't escape last night—or what'd happened to Jackson.

"Hi, Detective. Were you looking for me or someone else?" *Please, please say someone else.*

"You're just the person I was looking for." She pulled a clear plastic evidence bag from her pocket. Inside was a laboratory sample bag with traces of powder.

My breath hitched.

"Do you recognize this?"

I moved closer, my heart pounding as I examined the bag. We often used the contaminant-free, wire-rimmed, ziplock-style bag in the science lab. It even had the university's abbreviated lettering on the right corner.

"I do. We use them in the chem lab," I said, my voice tight. My stomach dropped as I stared at the bag. *Is this another piece of the puzzle—or the start of a nightmare I can't escape? Professor White doesn't seem like someone who'd...* No. I couldn't let my mind go there. *But then again, how much did I know about anyone in the lab?* Megan's sharp comments about athletes flashed in my mind, and so did Joe's quiet intensity. Everyone had secrets, and Jackson's death felt like the key to them all.

She nodded. "It was found in Jackson's pocket. Can you tell me what Professor White is like?"

My throat went dry. "Professor White? He's—he's strict but

fair. I mean, he runs a tight ship, but he's not the kind of guy to… to…" My words faltered as the weight of her question settled in. *Was my professor involved in a student's death?* The idea of getting drawn deeper into the case sent a chill down my spine.

"I see." Her eyes narrowed as if gauging my reaction. "You're a TA for Professor White?"

"I am." *Is she pointing a finger at me? Why not?* Everybody else was. It had been the worst day, and I felt the start of a headache building.

"Who else has access to the lab?"

"Oh, there's me, of course, Joe Riken, and I guess Megan Elwood. We're the only assistants this semester. Nobody else should be there unaccompanied, but some grad students probably use the lab with permission."

She wrote down Joe's and Megan's names. "Can you think of any of them?"

"No, not really, I don't know of anybody who gets lab access. I just figure some might."

"I understand. If you think of anybody else who might have access to these, call me." She handed me her card before continuing toward the building, leaving me rooted to the spot.

I clutched the card, my mind racing. The lab. The powder. Jackson. And now Liam. Everything was unraveling faster than I could hold it together.

CHAPTER TWENTY-ONE

LIAM

"What are you going to do?" Aurora leaned into Kylian's side, where they sat together on the other couch.

I shrugged, still working to process what had happened yesterday. It was late, and we'd just finished a huge meal that Aurora had made. Kylian and Ares rallied around me, forcing me to return to our place after weightlifting rather than spending hours reviewing film like I'd planned. I knew our competition, as I'd poured over the footage for hours the past few days. They were right; I needed a break to think things through rather than avoid the issue.

"You like Lily, though," Ares said, pulling Brielle into his lap.

She looped her arm around his neck and leaned against him on the opposite end of the couch from where I sat.

"Don't you want to work things out with Skye?" he pressed. "Be a part of your daughter's life?"

"Yeah, of course I do." I scowled as a wave of possessiveness swept through me. "Knowing I'm Lily's dad changes things—it ties us together—and I would never abandon my kid."

"What about the NFL?" Brielle tucked a honey-blond strand behind her ear.

I raked my hand through my hair for the hundredth time. "I don't want to give it up, but maybe I can convince Skye to move to wherever I'm drafted so I can be a part of Lily's life—"

"And Skye's," Aurora interjected forcefully. "I know you're mad at her—and rightly so—but you're totally into her. There's no denying it." She rushed the words out when I opened my mouth to argue. "Can't you work past this?"

"I don't know." I forced a measured breath, working through things mentally before speaking. "I mean, yeah, I'm attracted to her, but I don't trust her. Not after she left me the way she did and withheld the news that I would be a father." I held up my hand when Brielle opened her mouth to counter. "I get it. I'm sure she was scared, but keep in mind, she had two-plus fucking years to come clean. I lost all that time with Lily."

"She shouldn't have kept this from you," Ares growled. "No matter what, remember we're on your side."

"We get that you're upset. Hell, I would be too," Kylian said. "But too much is at stake to let your feelings fester. Work things out with Skye."

"Every day you delay talking it out with her is another one you lose with Lily," Aurora chimed in. "We want the best for you, and I know you care about them."

I nodded. She was right. They all were, but I was just so damn mad at Skye. The worst of the shock had worn off, and I could think a little clearer. I could grudgingly understand why she hadn't told me. I was a dick about her wanting more of a commitment from me.

Honestly, even back then, I would have given it to her. Deep down, I knew she was the one for me, and it had scared the hell out of me, which was why I'd pushed her away. That was on me, and I would own that. She was right about Coach. Part of me still worried that when he found out, it would affect my future, but I had to risk it. I couldn't bear to lose Skye and Lily all over again.

Kylian was still talking, but I wasn't listening anymore. My thoughts were stuck on Skye—and Lily. I rubbed a hand over my face, trying to clear the memories clawing their way forward. It was no use.

Freshman year, the night we'd snuck onto the football field. Skye had been laughing, her head tipped back under the glow of the stadium lights. I'd been showing off, juggling the football like an idiot, and I remember how she'd stopped mid-laugh to look at me—really look at me.

"You know you're going to be unstoppable, right?" she'd said, her voice so certain it made my chest tighten.

I'd laughed it off, called her a dreamer, but the truth was, I'd needed to hear it. No one else had ever looked at me like that— like I could be more than just the next big NFL hopeful. Like I was already enough.

The memory hit harder now, knowing what I'd lost. She'd believed in me when I didn't believe in myself, and I'd thrown it all away.

Kylian's voice cut through my haze. "So, what are you going to do, man?"

I straightened, forcing myself back into the present. "I'm going to talk to her."

"We're here for you," Ares said.

"No matter what," Kylian reiterated as the girls got up and hugged me.

Goddamn, I loved them—they were my family. The three of us had already been through more than most would in a lifetime, and it'd bonded us. I was just so grateful for Ares and Kylian.

It was just past nine at night, but I couldn't wait any longer, now that I'd decided. I grabbed my phone from where I'd tossed it on the coffee table next to the game controllers and thumbed off a message asking if we could talk. A few minutes later, Skye texted that she was at my sister's and I could meet her there.

I didn't take long to get to Fiona's and let myself into her townhome. Dad was passed out in the recliner. Good. With my emotions all over the place, things would not go well if I had to deal with him.

I locked onto Skye as she sat across from Fio, hands wrapped around a coffee mug. I caught a little of their conversation before my impatience got the best of me, and I interrupted them. "Hey, sis. I need to talk to Skye for a minute."

"Ah, no." Fiona leveled me with her older sister's death stare. "Skye popped over to share info I need for the case. We'll be done in five." She waved me away. "Go. There's leftover lasagna in the fridge."

I hesitated, but my stomach won out. I loved Fio's lasagna. I forced myself to go into the kitchen and reheat food without stomping or slamming things—no need to wake Dad and have him be a part of, well, anything. When the microwave dinged, I took out the plate, leaned a hip against the counter, and dug in while eavesdropping on their discussion.

Professor White's name was mentioned, and my interest piqued. *They had a lead on Jackson's death?* Skye told Fio about his schedule, demeanor, and what she knew he was working on. They were wrapping up when I rinsed my plate and put it in the dishwasher. I wanted to ignore what I'd heard, but I couldn't. Besides, Skye wasn't getting out of talking to me.

"Why are you looking into the science department?" Broader questions rather than specific names could help me get an answer from Fio.

With a snap, Fiona shut her laptop and swiveled toward me from her spot at the table. "Just fleshing out the case. Jackson's blood work showed traces of something that didn't likely have anything to do with his heart condition."

"Unless he didn't know anything was wrong with his heart. Or did Coach say it was documented in the athletic portal?"

"It wasn't." Fio frowned. "It's possible he didn't want to share a condition that could limit his field time. Anyway"—shoving her chair back, she stood—"thanks for your help, Skye. If I need anything else, I'll be in touch."

Yeah, not so fast. I caught Skye's arm as she rounded the table to leave. "We need to talk first. I'm using your room, Fio." I didn't allow my sister to reply before dragging Skye through the family room and down the hallway to Fio's bedroom. With a firm click, I shut the door after we were inside.

I ignored the lavender bedspread haphazardly pulled up in Fio's attempt at making her bed or the pile of romance books on the nightstand that looked like they were about to topple over. It was so at odds with her hard-ass demeanor, but this was her inner sanctuary.

Back to the door, I crossed my arms over my chest, willing my voice to remain calm while Skye stared at me with wide, wary eyes.

"We can make it work." There, I got it out and didn't sound like I was about to tear her a new one.

"We can make what work?" Skye mimicked me by crossing her arms. "I've been doing fine with my aunt and uncle's help. Lily loves having them in her life. She has a stable and secure home. I don't want to rock the boat with you complicating things." She flung her hands out. "Then, when you get into the NFL, what then? You leave and never look back? I won't put my daughter through that kind of abandonment."

"*Our* daughter. And that's your MO, not mine."

She clamped her lips tight, her eyes briefly closing before she seemed to lose most of the fight. Her shoulders dropped about an inch before she nodded. "Yeah, okay. You're right. I didn't handle things well back then. You don't understand, Liam," she said, her voice breaking. "I've spent every day of the last two years wondering if I made the wrong decision. But I was alone, scared, and had to think about Lily first. I can't risk turning her world upside down now, not when she's happy and safe. Can you honestly say you would have welcomed the news that you were about to be a father when you only wanted to focus on your path to the NFL?"

"Yes!" I shouted then took a few seconds, willing my temper to calm the fuck down. "I would never have abandoned either of you had I known. I gave you a stupid fucking answer because I'd had a shitty meeting with my coach about being distracted and messing up, and I panicked. And look at what that cost me."

Skye shoved her hands through her long brown hair, pulling it away from her face. "We were both young, and I was so scared. I—I should have told you. I'm sorry." She whirled around and paced the small length of the room to the window and back to where I stood by the door.

"I want to spend time with Lily and get to know my daughter better."

"Of course. But—" She worried her full bottom lip with her teeth before releasing it. "I don't think we should tell her you're her dad yet. You need to get through the season and the combine. If my uncle—"

"I don't care about your uncle finding out."

Skye's humorless laugh filled the space between us. "You should. He's going to lose his mind when he finds out one of his star football players knocked me up and didn't stand by me."

"You didn't give me that choice. And I know my sister would want to be involved in Lily's life too." Fiona always had my back, even when Dad didn't. She would want to know Lily to make up for all the things Dad screwed up for us growing up. *But would Skye let her in?*

"And your dad?" Skye's brows rose. "I didn't meet him, but I saw him passed out on the chair when I came in."

"My dad is better left out of the picture."

Skye studied me a little too closely before nodding.

My blood pressure eased when I realized she let it go. "I want to tell Lily I'm her dad."

"Yes." She nodded slowly, drawing out the word. "But not yet. We'll spend time together with Lily, but I'm going to stay firm on not telling her until after the combine or when you know for sure you're getting picked up by a team."

"I don't c—"

"I *do* care," Skye snapped. "I won't block you from seeing Lily, but we will do this my way."

I clenched my fists, my body vibrating with frustration. *How could I agree to this? To wait when every instinct screamed that Lily deserves the truth?* But then I looked at Skye, the tension in her body, the fear she was trying so hard to mask. She wasn't just protecting herself—she was protecting Lily. And I couldn't be the one to rip that safety net away.

I recognized the stubborn set to her shoulders and the defiant chin tilt. I wouldn't risk pushing her. I didn't want her to disappear again. It was a fear I couldn't quite shake. I studied her, my anger fading into something else—something quieter, heavier. She was fighting for Lily the same way I wanted to. Maybe we weren't as different as I thought.

"Fine," I said, my voice low but firm. "We'll do things your way. But I'm not going anywhere, Skye. I'm here to stay."

Her shoulders eased just a little, and for the first time, I felt like maybe—just maybe—this wasn't completely broken.

CHAPTER TWENTY-TWO

SKYE

Lily's low whimper hurt my heart as I cuddled her in my arms. I rocked her slowly, waiting for the Tylenol to kick in and ease the pain. She'd had ear infections before, but never that bad. I glanced up when the door to my bedroom eased open, and Aunt Eileen peeked her head in.

"How's it going?" She kept her voice low so as not to disturb Lily, who needed to get some sleep. It was way past her bedtime.

"Could be better." I grimaced as Lily's sharp elbow jabbed me in the ribs.

That calculating gleam entered my aunt's eyes, and I shuddered.

"What?" I instantly regretted asking.

"You should call Liam."

"No." My reaction was immediate and defensive. I was her mom. I'd never needed his help before.

Aunt Eileen slipped inside and shut the door quietly behind her. "You told me you're trying to work things out, right?"

I reluctantly nodded, not liking where she was headed.

"He's upset about missing out on Lily's life. Well, this is a part of it. Let him share in her care."

I narrowed my eyes, not liking her thinking. "I know what you're doing."

A sly smile curved her lips. "Having a child isn't all roses, sweetheart. He needs to experience all of it, and what better way than to test out his long-term commitment?"

"Fine." She had me there. I'd confided in her more than once that I feared Liam would infiltrate our lives and leave us with broken hearts and a very confused little girl when he entered the NFL. I waved my aunt away and quickly texted Liam about Lily, asking him to come by.

"I'll keep Tommy busy when he gets home. I recorded the new episode for his favorite show. Plus, I made ribs."

"Devious."

He would be engrossed in the NFL sports documentaries my aunt was referencing. They were good. I'd binged *Receivers* as soon as it'd come out.

I regretted the text almost as soon as I sent it. I didn't need Liam's help, not really. But when Lily whimpered in her sleep, clutching me tighter, something inside me cracked. Maybe Aunt Eileen was right. If Liam was serious about being in Lily's life, he needed to see all of it—the sleepless nights, the worry, the love that consumed everything. I hated how much I wanted him to prove her right, how much I wanted to believe that he would stay.

When my phone chimed with Liam's response that he would be over in fifteen minutes, I relayed it to my aunt, whose grin stretched impossibly wide. I stuck my tongue out, but she missed that lovely expression, as she had already exited my room.

In slow, even movements, I rocked Lily from side to side in my arms while sitting cross-legged on the bed. Lily's breathing evened out as she fell into a light sleep. When my door opened, I didn't need to look at the time to know no more than fifteen minutes had passed. Liam quietly entered my and Lily's room.

Liam froze just inside the doorway, his eyes locking onto Lily curled against me. His shoulders, tense when he walked in, seemed to drop a little as he took her in. His concerned gaze crawled over Lily then me, and my cheeks heated in response. *Why did he have to be so intense?* My body should not react to him the way it did, especially after all our time apart after we broke up—if a two-month fling could even be considered a relationship.

I slowly exhaled and tried to control my pulse. That man took up way too much space in the room. "Hey."

He closed the distance between us, sitting beside me on the bed. "How's she doing?"

His voice was low and gravely, making my stomach clench. "The Tylenol kicked in, and she finally fell asleep. She'll probably wake in four hours in pain, though."

Lily's eyelids fluttered, and she let out a small, pitiful groan.

"Hey, kiddo," he said softly, crouching beside her. His voice was quiet, as though he was afraid to disturb her. "Not feeling too great, huh?"

"My ear hurts," she mumbled, barely lifting her head.

Something shifted in his expression—something I hadn't expected. It wasn't panic or discomfort. It was... focus.

He pressed a kiss to her forehead. "You're burning up," he said, his voice steady, but his eyes flicked to me, sharp with concern.

"She's been fighting it all day," I said, my tone clipped. I didn't mean to sound defensive, but the tension in my chest refused to loosen. "The Tylenol brought the fever down, though."

He didn't say anything, just grabbed the washcloth I'd left on the nightstand to dip it into the bowl of cool water. His movements were careful, precise as he wrung it out and folded it neatly before pressing it against Lily's forehead. "There you go,

Lil," he murmured, his voice softer than I'd ever heard it. "This'll help."

I stayed rooted in place. Lily didn't flinch, didn't twist away like she usually did when someone who wasn't me tried to help. Instead, she sighed, her tiny body relaxing slightly under his touch. It shouldn't have surprised me, but it did.

He stayed like that for a few minutes until Lily's breathing evened out. I untangled my legs and stood with Lily in my arms. Liam beat me to her bed and moved the covers out of the way so I could lay her down. He covered her when I carefully extracted my arms. We both waited a few tense seconds before returning to my bed.

The room had no space for any other seating, not with both our beds, the dollhouse in the corner, or her overabundance of toys spilling out of the pink-and-purple chest. I scooted back to lean against the headboard, and Liam did the same. Our shoulders pressed together, and it took everything in me not to move away. It didn't mean anything—he was only there for Lily, not me.

"I know you're busy. I shouldn't have asked you to come," I said, though part of me was glad he had. Lily's soft breathing filled the quiet, but the tension between us buzzed louder than any words. I threaded my fingers together on my lap to keep from fidgeting.

"I just want to be here with you both." His deep voice rumbled.

I glanced at him out of the corner of my eye, his profile caught in the soft glow of the bedside lamp. His jaw was tight, a muscle ticking there like he was holding something back. But his eyes—dark and full of unspoken emotions—drew me in despite myself.

"I don't want you to feel obligated, Liam," I said quietly, though the words wavered, betraying me.

His head turned, his gaze locking on mine with an almost physical heat. "I don't feel obligated, Skye. I *want* to be here. For her, yeah, but also for you."

My chest tightened, my gaze dropping to my hands knotted in my lap. "Why? We've been fine. I've been fine." Even as the words left my mouth, I wasn't sure I believed them.

He shifted beside me, and I felt the weight of his movements before I saw them, the mattress dipping as his knee brushed against mine. He didn't pull away or apologize, and the contact sent a ripple of awareness up my spine.

"I know you have. You're stronger than I'll ever be," he said, his voice low and rough. "But just because you *can* do this alone doesn't mean you should have to."

The words hit harder than I wanted to admit, and my throat tightened. "It's not like I had a choice."

The bitterness in my voice came unbidden, sharp, and raw, but Liam didn't flinch. Instead, he leaned closer, his arm brushing mine. The warmth of his skin seeped through my thin sweatshirt, and suddenly, it felt like there wasn't enough air in the room.

"I know I screwed up," he said softly, each word deliberate and weighted. "I should have been there from the start. If I'd known—"

"You didn't know because I didn't tell you," I interrupted, my voice trembling. "And I had my reasons, okay? It wasn't just about protecting her. It was about protecting me too."

The silence between us crackled with tension, and I could feel his eyes on me, searching. I didn't pull away when he reached for my hand, though I told myself I should. His fingers slid over mine, warm and calloused, and I hated how much I liked the weight of his hand. Letting him in meant risking everything. But as his thumb brushed over my knuckles, I felt the tiniest flicker of hope. It scared me more than anything.

"I get that," he said. "I don't blame you for doing what you thought was best. But I'm here now, Skye. And I'm not going anywhere—even if you try to push me away."

My pulse pounded in my ears, and I stared at our hands, the simple contact unraveling something inside me. "It's not that easy," I whispered, but I could hear the hesitation in my voice.

"Maybe not," he admitted, his tone gentle. "But we can figure it out. Together. You don't have to trust me all at once. Just let me prove it to you. For Lily. For you."

His words tugged at a part of me I'd buried long ago, a part that still ached when I looked at him too long. Slowly, I turned to meet his gaze again. His face was so close, his expression open and unguarded.

"I don't know if I can," I admitted, my voice barely audible.

"You don't have to know right now." Liam's free hand came up, brushing a loose strand of hair from my face. His fingertips skimmed my temple, lingering just long enough to make my breath hitch. "But let me try."

The room felt impossibly small, the tension between us sharp and electric. My eyes searched his for something I wasn't sure I could name. And there, in the silence, I found sincerity, hope, and maybe even the man I'd once thought he could be.

His shoulder pressed into mine, solid and warm, and I hated how much I noticed it. I wanted to lean into him, even as my mind screamed to keep my distance. But the quiet conviction in his voice chipped away at my defenses.

"Okay," I murmured, the word escaping before I could second-guess it.

His lips curved into a slow, cautious smile, and his thumb brushed over my knuckles again, a silent promise in the touch. "Okay," he echoed.

I wanted to believe him, to trust that he would stay, but the fear was still there, curling tight in my chest. Even as his hand lingered over mine, warm and steady, the knot in my stomach didn't loosen. I wanted to believe him, to trust that he would stay. Yet the memories of his absence and my loneliness whispered their warnings. Still, as I glanced at him, his expression open and unguarded, something inside me softened. Liam's smile did something to my chest I didn't want to name. Maybe, just maybe, we could figure this out. Together.

CHAPTER TWENTY-THREE

LIAM

I watched Skye for a moment, trying to find the right words. The weight of everything said and unsaid hung between us, thick and oppressive. Finally, I cleared my throat. "Do you have… pictures?"

She looked up, startled. "Pictures?"

"Of Lily," I said, my voice softer. "From when she was a baby."

Her brows knit together, and for a second, I thought she would say no. But then she nodded and pulled her phone from her pocket. "Yeah. Give me a second."

I stayed still as she scrolled through her photos. She hesitated before pausing on a picture, her movements careful, like she was bracing for impact. Wordlessly, she handed me the phone, already queued to what she wanted me to see.

My breath caught at the first picture. Lily, tiny and swaddled in a pale-pink blanket, her little mouth open in a yawn. My chest tightened as I flipped to the next image. Each photo was a snapshot of a moment I hadn't been part of—her first gummy smile, her tiny fingers clutching Skye's hand, her wobbly first steps.

"She's perfect," I said, my voice thick.

Skye's lips curved into a faint smile, but it didn't reach her eyes. "She is."

I scrolled back farther and froze. The image wasn't of Lily. It was of Skye—her stomach rounded, her hand resting protectively on the swell. She was laughing at something off camera, her hair falling in loose waves around her face.

"You're beautiful," I murmured, barely aware I'd spoken aloud.

Her head snapped toward me, her eyes wide as she shifted closer, her body pressed against my side to see what I was looking at. "That's… I mean, that's Lily."

But it wasn't. Not entirely. I wasn't just looking at Lily in that moment. I was looking at her. At Skye, carrying Lily, glowing with something I couldn't put into words.

Another picture stopped me cold. Skye in a hospital bed, holding a tiny, wrinkled Lily against her chest. Her hair was damp, her face pale and tired, but her expression was fierce, almost defiant, as she stared into the camera.

"I wish I could've been there for you." The words slipped out before I could stop them.

Her breath hitched, and she looked away, her fingers brushing the edge of the phone. "It wasn't easy. But we managed."

"I should have been there." My voice was low, rough.

Her head tilted slightly, like she couldn't decide if she wanted to believe me. "Maybe," she said quietly. "But back then…" Her voice trailed off, and she shook her head. "I didn't give you the chance to be there for me."

"I'm here now," I said firmly. "I can't change the past, but I'm here now. For you. For Lily."

She didn't respond immediately. Her gaze lingered on the photo, and I thought I saw something crack in the walls she'd built around herself.

"I want that." She nodded, her voice barely above a whisper.

———

Sliding into the booth across from Fiona, I barely had time to pick up the menu before she leaned forward, eyes sharp and locked on me like a hawk zoning in on its prey.

"What's going on, Liam?" she demanded, skipping past any semblance of small talk.

"Good to see you too, Fio," I muttered, flipping the menu open to avoid her gaze. The scent of coffee and fried bacon filled the small diner, mingling with the low hum of conversation around us.

Fiona tapped her nails on the cracked vinyl of the booth seat, her sharp gaze never leaving mine. "Don't deflect. You're acting weird." She tilted her head, her ponytail swinging, and she pinned me with the look that had intimidated me since I was twelve. "Does this have anything to do with Skye?"

My fingers curled into the edge of the menu, my stomach tightening at the inevitable conversation I'd been avoiding. I wasn't sure I was ready for this—admitting it out loud made it all the more real.

I exhaled slowly, setting the menu down. "Yeah... it does."

Fiona tilted her head, curiosity flickering across her face. "Okay... and?"

I hesitated, rubbing the back of my neck before forcing myself to meet her gaze. "She has a daughter, Fio."

Her lips parted slightly in surprise, but she didn't jump to conclusions. Instead, she waited, giving me space to continue.

"A little girl." The words felt heavy as I said them out loud. "She's... she's about two, maybe three."

"Oh my God. Holy shit," she whispered, leaning back in her seat like the realization had knocked her over. Her expression softened, the initial shock giving way to something else—understanding, maybe even something protective. "Liam…"

I swallowed hard. "She's mine. She didn't tell me. I had no fucking idea." My hands fisted on the table as the memory of Lily's bright green eyes hit me again. "Fio… she looks just like me."

Silence stretched between us, the weight of my confession settling like a stone. Fiona reached across the table, squeezing my wrist. She didn't let go, her grip grounding me in a way I desperately needed. "Jesus, Liam. That's a lot."

I let out a shaky breath, nodding. "Yeah. It is."

I let my head fall back against the booth, staring at the ceiling like it had the answers I couldn't seem to find. My hand tightened around the menu. *How many times had I played this scenario out in my head?* Telling my sister, explaining it, owning it. But now that it was real, its weight settled on my chest like lead. There was no point in lying, not when Fiona's bullshit detector was as finely tuned as a scout's stopwatch.

"When did you find out?"

"Not until a couple of days ago." I pushed a hand through my hair, frustration bubbling up again. "Skye didn't tell me when she found out she was pregnant. She had her reasons, and honestly, I get it. But it's not any easier to swallow."

"Okay, I'll trust you on that one. Just for the record—I'm not happy you didn't know." Fiona's expression softened, her shoulders relaxing slightly. "And now? What's going on with you two?"

I laughed, short and humorless, slouching back in the booth. "I'm trying to figure it out. I want to be there for Lily, for both of them, but it's complicated. Skye doesn't fully trust me—neither of us trusts the other, actually. But I don't blame her. Back then, I wasn't exactly someone you could count on."

I couldn't stop thinking about Dad. About the way he used to sit in that recliner, the TV blaring, a beer clutched in his hand like it was the only thing tethering him to reality. I didn't want that for Lily. I wanted to be the dad who showed up, who stayed. But wanting wasn't the same as knowing how.

She gave me a long, hard look before reaching for her water and taking a slow sip. "So, what are you doing about it?"

"I'm trying," I said, my voice quiet, deep-seated fear rearing its deranged head despite the decision, the determination to be there for them. If I could confide in anyone about my worries, it would be my sister. She had the same emotional scars. "But, Fiona… I don't know if I can pull this off. Considering where we came from—how Dad was, how Mom bailed—I don't have a great blueprint for being a parent."

Fiona winced, her fingers tightening around her glass. "Yeah, we didn't hit the jackpot with role models, did we? Mom left us like we were trash, and Dad…" She trailed off, shaking her head. "He hasn't been Dad for years. Just a bottle with legs."

A bitter laugh escaped me. "Exactly. So, what makes me think I can do this? That I can be enough for Lily? For Skye?"

She leaned forward, her voice soft but firm. "Because you're not Dad, Liam. You're not Mom either. You care. You're trying. You're someone your friends have been able to count on in any situation. That's already a hell of a lot more than they ever did for us."

Her words hit me square in the chest, and I stared at the table. "It doesn't feel like enough."

Fiona's hand covered mine, grounding me. "It's enough. And even if you're not sure, I am. You're brave for even taking this leap. I'm not sure I could do it. But you? You're already halfway there."

I shook my head, but her grip tightened. "That's a lie. You could do it. You've been there for me."

"That's easy. I'll always be there for you. But relationships?" A humorless laugh spilled from her lips. "But I'm not the one we need to focus on. It's you—and, Liam, I mean it. You've got me in your corner, okay? Whatever you need, whatever *they* need—I'll be there. You're not alone."

I swallowed hard, her words breaking through some of the doubt wrapping around me like chains. "Thanks, Fio. That means more than you know."

"And Skye?" Fiona asked, her gaze piercing. "What's your plan there? I've gotta tell you, I'm not thrilled she kept her pregnancy—*Lily*—from you. With that said, let's move forward. Do you want to be with her? Because if you do, you've got to show her—and not just with Lily. She needs to know you're all in."

Her words acted like a visceral map I didn't know I needed. "You're right. I need to show Skye I want her and that I'll be there for her too.

She smiled and leaned back. "Good. Now, let's order before I start gnawing on this table."

I picked up my menu only to lower it when she spoke.

"But seriously—don't think I'm letting you off the hook. I want updates—regular ones. And I want to spend time with my niece. That's nonnegotiable."

A grin tugged at my lips despite everything. "Deal."

As the waitress came by to take our orders, I felt a small flicker of hope. Fiona's belief in me didn't erase all the doubts, but she was right. I wasn't alone. I wasn't my dad. I could be more for Lily and Skye. It wouldn't be easy, but if I'd learned one thing from football, it was that the hard-won victories were the ones that mattered most.

CHAPTER TWENTY-FOUR

SKYE

I stretched my arms above my head, feeling the tension in my shoulders pull tight before finally releasing. The last stack of graded finals sat neatly on Professor White's desk, a triumphant finish to a grueling evening of red ink and second-hand stress over the periodic table.

I glanced at the clock—almost five. I had a night game to cover soon. After putting everything away, I bundled up to leave the building. I shoved my hands into my jacket pockets as I stepped into the hallway, the cool air of the building brushing against my skin. The campus was eerily quiet, the kind of silence that made every sound echo just a little too loudly.

Guilt ate at me as my sneakers squeaked against the linoleum. Fiona's questions about Professor White lingered in the back of my mind, and I couldn't shake the heavy weight of my answers. I hadn't said anything damning—just observations, facts—but even those felt like betrayals when stacked against the backdrop of a student found dead. The thought sent a shiver down my spine.

I was just past the dimly lit rows of lockers near the lab

rooms when I heard voices—familiar voices. I slowed my steps, my heart skipping a beat. Around the corner, just at the edge of the hallway leading to the lecture halls, Joe stood with one of the football players who was also in my entry-level science TA session. My brows furrowed. Joe was usually the epitome of easygoing—sarcastic and teasing in that big-brother way—but his posture was stiff, his body angled slightly away like he was trying to hide whatever was happening.

I shifted to the side, staying hidden in the corridor's shadows.

Joe's hand dipped into his sweatshirt pocket, emerging with a small baggie. My stomach dropped as he passed it to the football player, who accepted it with a glance over his shoulder before shoving it into his pocket.

It wasn't vitamins or supplements—it was drugs. It had to be. And Joe wasn't just involved, he was the one supplying them. A cold certainty settled in my chest. Joe was the dealer. The signs had been there all along, but now, there was no mistaking it. The question wasn't whether he was guilty—it was how far this went. *Who else is involved? Megan? The research group? The entire department?*

I covered my mouth with my hand, willing myself to stay silent. This couldn't be happening. The athlete—*what's his name? Tyler? No, Marc*—his effort in class had always been mediocre at best, but recently, something about him had shifted. His performance on the field had caught the coaches' attention, drawing praise that seemed too sudden to be entirely earned.

I didn't want to believe it, not about Joe. But he was standing there, casually handing off something to a student athlete like it was nothing.

A sick sort of dread curled in my stomach. Joe's words from a few weeks ago echoed in my head, his tone sharp with concern as he warned me about getting too involved with Liam.

"Guys like that will ruin you, Skye. They take what they want and leave the rest in pieces." How hypocritical could he be?

I stepped back, the motion too quick and clumsy, and my sneaker squeaked against the floor. Both of their heads whipped in my direction.

Panic surged through me as I spun on my heel, forcing myself to walk—no, run—down the hallway. My pulse thundered in my ears as I reached the building's exit, shoving the heavy glass door open and practically bursting into the cool night air.

The dark campus stretched before me, the faint hum of a streetlamp overhead doing little to calm my nerves. I didn't stop moving until I reached the parking lot, ducking behind my car to catch my breath.

What the hell did I just see?

I leaned against the cold metal, my hands trembling as I pressed them to my temples. Joe wasn't just my friend—he was one of my *safe places*. The one person I trusted to have my back in this hectic world of school, TA-ing, and balancing mother-hood. *And now...*

My stomach churned. I couldn't go back inside. Not tonight.

Sliding into my car, I locked the doors. My forehead rested against the steering wheel as I tried to steady the wild thrum of my heart. I whipped out my phone and called Fiona, quickly relaying everything to her about what I'd seen, and what it could've been about. *Maybe. Maybe I was mistaken and it was an innocent mistake?* God, I hoped so, but it was unlikely.

After she thanked me for the information, she told me under no circumstances to go near the suspects.

I needed to figure out how deep this went and who else was involved—from a distance. But I couldn't shake the feeling that I was teetering on the edge of something far more dangerous than I'd ever anticipated.

The stadium buzzed with energy that seemed to pulse in time with the music blasting through the speakers. Fans waved banners and screamed themselves hoarse as the game unfolded under the stadium lights.

My camera was a comforting weight around my neck as I moved along the sidelines, snapping shots of the action.

I let the excitement fill me, chasing away some of the worry. This was my element—the organized chaos of the game, the tension hanging in the air like static electricity. It was exhilarating, the perfect distraction from the tangled mess of emotions I carried like an overstuffed suitcase.

But no matter how hard I tried, my gaze returned to Liam. His sharp focus on the field mirrored the stability he'd started bringing to my life—a stability I desperately needed with everything else spiraling out of control.

Through my lens, I captured him in motion—cutting through the defense with a sharp precision that made my breath catch. His attention was razor-sharp, his body coiled with strength and determination. It struck me then how Liam's unwavering commitment wasn't just about the game but about who he was. And despite all the doubts swirling in my head, I found myself trusting him in a way I couldn't with anyone else. I'd seen him play before, but this was different. Or maybe I was different.

I shook my head and aimed my camera elsewhere. My job was to cover the team, not obsess over Liam. But when his eyes briefly met mine after a perfectly executed play, my pulse skipped. It was a fleeting moment, but it steadied something inside me, like an anchor in a storm.

As the game progressed, I shifted the camera angle, aiming at the jubilant faces of the crowd, but I kept drifting back to Liam.

I caught him mid-play and realized how much I'd started leaning on him lately. It wasn't just Lily—it was me too. He wasn't perfect, but he was honest, and that mattered more than anything.

I lost myself in the excitement swirling around me, snapping pictures like crazy, itching to edit and post them as soon as possible. During halftime, I uploaded a few stellar ones with catchy phrases to encourage engagement. The second half flew by, but I found myself zeroing in on a couple of players.

Marc, the second-string tight end, juked past a defender, his movements too precise, too powerful for someone who'd struggled to keep up just weeks ago. My stomach twisted. The improvement wasn't just surprising—it was uncanny. And as much as I wanted to dismiss it as hard work, I couldn't unsee the connections forming from spotting him in the science building.

The game ended in a roar of victory, the team rushing the field. As the players celebrated, my eyes found Liam again. He was in the center of it all, grounded and unshakable. I let the mayhem fade for a moment, anchoring myself in the one thing that felt solid—him.

My camera hung loosely around my neck as I scanned the players, the coaches, and the euphoric fans. My mind raced, recalling Megan's offhand comment about muscle recovery and stamina. *Is that what I'm seeing here?* The science nerd in me wanted to chalk it up to rigorous training, but the unease in my gut said otherwise.

She and Joe had been working on research about performance enhancement in athletes. Megan had mentioned it casually in passing. At the time, I'd been too busy to consider it. But now, with what I'd witnessed, the idea clung to me like a burr.

I didn't want to know. Not really. But ignoring it wouldn't make it go away—and if there was one thing being Lily's mom had taught me, it was how to face what scared me most. Whatever was happening, I couldn't look the other way.

Something was off—Joe's exchange in the hallway, the sudden improvement of certain players, Megan's comments about performance enhancement. It all felt too connected to ignore. If I wanted answers, I would have to dig for them myself.

Joe wasn't just my friend—he was a peer I'd trusted in this whirlwind of school and motherhood. And now, that trust felt like it was crumbling to dust, leaving a hollow ache in its wake. *Was this the same guy who covered for me in class when I was late? The one who teased me endlessly but never let me down? How could he be hiding something like this? Or is Megan the culprit—is she using him? Could it be that he isn't aware of her real agenda?*

Something was gnawing at me, and I couldn't shake it.

I needed to know if there was even a chance that he was involved in something bigger—something that could explain the sudden changes I saw on the field. And Megan's research might be the key to finding them.

My gut screamed at me to stay away, to keep myself as far from this as possible. *But I can't. If there's a chance I could clear Joe's name, I had to take it.* Aside from that, someone else might get hurt—or worse.

Without really thinking, I pulled out my phone and texted Megan.

Me: *Where are you? I need to talk.*

Her response came quickly. *In the science building. What's going on?*

I didn't bother replying. I was already weaving through the crowd, my feet carrying me away from the stadium and toward campus.

Megan was waiting for me outside the lab, her arms crossed against the cold. Her red scarf stood out against her dark coat, and she gave me a curious smile as I approached.

"Hey, what's up?" she asked.

"I want in on your research group," I said, the words tumbling out without preamble.

Megan blinked, startled by my sudden urgency, but I couldn't slow down. If there was a way to figure out what was happening—who was involved and why—this was it. It was risky, but doing nothing wasn't an option. Not when athletes were dying, and the research could be tied to it. It might be dangerous, but I would never know the truth unless I got close. I would have to be careful—stay on the edges, ask the right questions. I couldn't let them suspect I knew anything.

Megan's eyebrows shot up, and for a moment, her expression faltered. "You want to join?" she asked, her tone caught between curiosity and something else—wariness maybe.

Something in her voice was off, like she was testing me. I nodded quickly, keeping my expression neutral. "I've been curious about your work for a while. I think it could be important."

Megan studied me for a beat longer then smiled—less enthusiastic, more controlled. "All right. I'll talk to Joe."

The thought of facing Joe again made my stomach twist. I didn't know if I could look him in the eye, not after what I'd seen. But I had to find out what they were hiding—and I had to play it smart, so to hide my anxiety, I quickly added, "It's research, and I'm invested." *Invested in nothing happening to Liam.*

"Okay. That makes sense. I suppose we could use your insights from the social media angle to track trends and patterns in player activity. Are you sure, though? I know you've got a lot going on."

"Yeah, I'm sure," I said quickly. "I just… I think this could be important."

She studied me for a moment then nodded. "Okay. Let's get you looped in."

We walked into the building together, the fluorescent lights buzzing faintly overhead. My thoughts raced as Megan started explaining some of their findings, mentioning Joe's contributions and the different angles they were exploring. I hoped the research would help me understand what I'd seen. But as I listened, the knot in my stomach tightened. Part of me wasn't sure I wanted to know the answers.

CHAPTER TWENTY-FIVE

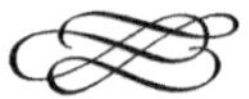

SKYE

The scent of garlic bread and simmering marinara greeted me as I stepped into Fiona's townhouse, Lily balanced on my hip. Her tiny hands clutched her favorite stuffed bunny, the one she refused to go anywhere without. Liam was right behind us, the booster seat we'd brought dangling from one hand. His other grazed my lower back in a way that sent a mix of comfort and nerves through me.

"It smells amazing," I said, my voice overly bright as Fiona appeared in the kitchen doorway.

She grinned, wiping her hands on a dish towel. "Thanks. Spaghetti is kind of my go-to, but I promise it's edible."

Lily squirmed in my arms, and Fiona's gaze softened as she crouched slightly to Lily's level. "Hey, sweetheart. You like spaghetti?"

Lily nodded shyly, her face half buried in Bunny's worn ears.

"She's a picky eater," I said apologetically. "But she usually goes for pasta."

"Well, good thing I made enough to feed an army." Fiona's voice dropped, her grin becoming conspiratorial. "There's also dessert, but that's top secret until we've all earned it."

Lily's eyes widened slightly at the mention of dessert, and I couldn't help but smile.

Fiona straightened, her gaze flicking between Liam and me. "I know Dad wasn't supposed to be here—I'm sorry." She winced, glancing at Lily too. "He's at the table, and he's... well, you'll see."

"It's fine." I tried to smooth things over, settling my hand on Liam's arm in reassurance.

He studied me for a moment, no doubt judging my sincerity before he muttered something under his breath that sounded suspiciously like a curse before brushing past me. "Let's just get this over with."

I followed him into the cozy dining room, my nerves buzzing like a live wire. The table was already set, the centerpiece a simple vase of wildflowers that looked like they'd been hastily thrown together. It was charming in a way that fit Fiona perfectly. Liam's dad sat at the head of the table, a drink in his hand and a critical eye on us as we entered. His presence was heavy and oppressive.

"Didn't think you'd actually show," he said to Liam, his tone dripping with something I couldn't quite place—*disappointment? Contempt?*

"Good to see you too, Dad." Liam's voice was tight. He pulled out a chair and placed the booster seat for Lily without even looking at his father, the gesture seeming instinctive.

I eased Lily into the booster seat and took the chair next to her that Liam pulled out for me. Her little legs swung as she clutched Bunny tighter.

Fiona appeared with a serving bowl heaped with spaghetti, her cheery energy doing its best to offset the tension. "Let's eat before it gets cold." Her smile appeared forced as she set the bowl down with a clatter.

The meal started quietly, the clinking of forks and occasional compliments for Fiona the only sounds. I tried to focus on Lily, cutting her spaghetti into manageable bites and encouraging her to eat.

"Cute kid," Liam's dad said suddenly, his gaze sharp as it landed on Lily then Liam. "You said she's yours, right?"

"Enough, Dad." Liam's stony gaze locked on his dad in challenge. "You're being rude."

The question wasn't directed at me, but we still hadn't told Lily that Liam was her father. I forced down the panic and plastered on a smile I didn't feel, determined to take point. I kept my voice even. "She's my daughter."

As Liam's hand brushed mine under the table, a warmth spread through me, unexpected but welcome. I found myself wanting to rely on him. Especially seeing how he handled his father, the way he stayed calm even when it was clear he wanted to explode—it made me feel as if he really could be the kind of person Lily and I needed.

His father grunted, taking another swig of his drink, the ice clinking loudly in the glass. "Doesn't look much like you."

Before I could respond, Fiona jumped in, her tone breezy but with an edge that left no room for argument. "That's because Lily's adorable. Clearly got all her good looks from her mom."

Liam snorted, and I shot Fiona a grateful glance.

"You must be quite the multitasker, huh?" Liam's dad mused, a hard look in his eye.

"Enough." Liam snapped, low and controlled, his gaze locked on his dad until the uncomfortable weight of silence hung over the table.

The conversation shifted after that, with Fiona doing her best to steer it toward neutral topics. I could feel Liam's tension radiating off him, his posture stiff and his jaw tight as he engaged only when absolutely necessary.

Liam's father leaned back in his chair, his sharp eyes fixed on me like he was assessing a weak opponent. "So, Skye," he said, the words laced with condescension, "what exactly is it you do?"

I stiffened, my grip tightening around my fork. "I go to Fall Lake University, and I'm the social media manager for the football team." I worked hard to keep my voice steady.

"Social media, huh?" His tone made it sound like I'd said I sold knockoff watches on a street corner.

Liam's jaw ticked, his gaze darting between me and his father. Under the table, I felt the warm brush of his hand against mine. Before I could react, his fingers closed over mine in a firm squeeze—not too much, just enough to say, *I've got you.*

My shoulders relaxed slightly, and I glanced at him. His expression didn't waver, but the corner of his mouth twitched, just enough to let me know he wasn't about to let his father's attitude go unchecked.

"Social media is a huge part of modern sports," Liam said evenly, his voice carrying just enough edge. "It keeps fans connected, grows the brand. It's one of the reasons our team gets so much national attention. You'd know that if you kept up with anything at all."

His father's nostrils flared, but before he could respond, Fiona jumped in with a story about Liam's childhood antics, deftly steering the conversation in another direction.

Liam's hand slipped away, but the warmth lingered. It wasn't much, but it was enough.

"Skye," Fiona said after a while, her voice cutting through the lingering unease. "You're doing an amazing job with Lily. I don't know how you manage classes and everything else."

I blinked, caught off guard by the genuine warmth in her tone. "I have help," I admitted, glancing at Liam. "More now than I used to."

Liam's lips quirked into a small smile, and Fiona nodded approvingly.

"Well, if you ever need more help, you let me know." She grinned. "I mean it. You've got enough on your plate."

Her words shouldn't have made my throat tighten, but they did. I managed a quiet "Thank you," my fingers tightening around my fork.

By the time dessert—homemade brownies—was served, Lily was yawning, her head resting against my arm. I excused myself to get her settled on the couch in the living room with a movie, thanks to Fiona. When I returned, Liam was alone in the kitchen, rinsing plates while Fiona kept Lily entertained. Their dad sat at the table as he nursed what I suspected was another mixed drink.

"You okay?" Liam asked, his voice low as he stepped closer. His concern was genuine, and for a moment, I saw the Liam I'd fallen for back in freshman year—not the football star or the man still figuring himself out, but someone who cared deeply.

I nodded, though the knot in my stomach hadn't entirely loosened. The glimpse at his family life—thanks to his dad's demeanor—told me more than I thought I would learn just from sharing a meal with them. I caught a flicker of something in Liam's eyes—determination, maybe, or regret. It was hard to tell. "Yeah. Just tired."

Even with the uncomfortableness of his dad's presence, the weight of Liam's and Fiona's support throughout dinner settled over me, something I could get used to.

<hr>

Liam

As I stood in the kitchen, stacking plates with Skye, I could hear Fiona in the living room, her animated voice likely coaxing Lily into coloring or playing with one of the toys we'd brought over as the movie played in the background. I couldn't help but smile at the sound of Lily's soft giggles. At least someone was enjoying themselves. Skye excused herself to check on Lily, and I took the opportunity to speak to the problem in the room—or my life, really.

Still at the dining table, Dad slouched in his chair. As I approached, I caught the faintest whiff of Jack Daniels.

"Will there ever be a time you don't drink?" I accused.

He smirked, swirling the liquid in his glass like he was proud of it. "What do you care? Not like I'm driving anywhere."

I bit back the urge to snap at him. It wasn't the time. Skye had already been on edge all night, and I wasn't about to make things worse with a shouting match.

Speaking of Skye, she appeared in the doorway just then, holding Lily's bunny in one hand. "I think we're going to head out," she said, her voice tight.

"You don't have to leave yet." I took a step toward her. "Fiona's with Lily—"

"No, it's okay," she interrupted, offering a strained smile. "She's getting sleepy anyway. Thanks for dinner."

I wanted to argue, to tell her to stay, but the look in her eyes stopped me. She was done for the night, and I couldn't blame her. Being around my father was a mistake, I should never have agreed when Fiona put on the pressure about dinner. We should have done something elsewhere, without Dad.

"I'll walk you out." I grabbed her coat from the back of a chair.

We didn't say much as I helped her get Lily bundled up, the quiet between us heavy with unspoken tension. Once they were in the car and pulling away, I headed back inside, my jaw tight as I closed the door behind me.

Dad was still at the table, his glass now empty but his smirk firmly in place. "Looks like you've got your hands full"—his voice dripped with mockery—"playing house with a kid that isn't even yours. That's bold, Liam. Real bold."

"Watch it," I warned, my voice low.

"What?" He leaned back in his chair with that same smug look he always had when trying to provoke me. "I'm just saying it like it is. You can play house all you want, but it won't last. Love never does. You of all people should know that by now."

I felt like I'd been sucker punched. "What's that supposed to mean?"

He shrugged, reaching for the bottle of Jack Daniels I hadn't noticed sitting on the buffet along the wall, behind a vase, and near his chair. "Look at your mother. Things were great between us until you and Fiona came along. Then it all went to hell. Kids complicate things, Liam. They ruin everything."

I stared at him, my hands clenched into fists at my sides. I should've been angry—furious—but instead, all I felt was a deep, aching sadness.

"That's not what's gonna happen to me." Despite my best efforts to steady it, my voice trembled.

He barked a bitter laugh. "Oh, isn't it? You're a damned fool if you think otherwise. And you're a bigger fool for thinking you can do any better."

For a long moment, I didn't say anything. I just stood there, staring at the man who had spent years making sure I knew how little he believed in me in everything except maybe football —and for that I suspected it was only because he saw me as a meal ticket.

As Dad spewed his usual bitterness, I felt the familiar sting of his words, the doubt he'd planted in me years ago. It was possible I wasn't cut out for this—being a father, building a family. But then I thought of Lily, her tiny hand clutching her bunny, and Skye, standing tall even when she was clearly over-whelmed. They deserved better. I could be the one to give it to them.

The memory of Fiona's voice floating in from the living room, soft and gentle as she talked to Lily, sifted through my mind. I thought of Skye, her hands trembling as she tucked Bunny into Lily's bag. And Lily herself, looking up at me with those big, trusting eyes.

"You're wrong." I squared my shoulders, my voice firm. "Love isn't the problem. You were." I turned and walked away before he could respond, heading to the living room where Fiona sat on the couch.

Fiona looked up at me, her brow furrowing. "You okay?"

"Yeah," I lied, sitting down beside her. "I'm fine."

"You're nothing like him, you know," Fiona murmured, her hand resting on my arm. "You've already proved that."

Her words settled something deep inside me, the knot of tension loosening just a little. "Thanks, Fio," I said, my voice rough. "I just hope I don't screw this up."

I didn't just want to prove my father wrong—I needed to.

CHAPTER TWENTY-SIX

SKYE

The tension in my chest didn't ease, even as I drove farther from Fiona's house. My fingers gripped the steering wheel, my knuckles white as I glanced in the rearview mirror. Lily sat quietly in her car seat, clutching Bunny like it was her lifeline. At least she wasn't about to lose it—unlike me.

Liam's father's words replayed in my mind on an endless loop, sharp and cutting. I couldn't shake how his smirk lingered, or the way his gaze seemed to peel away every layer of my composure as he remarked on Liam's involvement with Lily. *"Doesn't look much like you."* And if that wasn't hurtful enough, I got the distinct impression that he thought I viewed Liam as a meal ticket by his veiled comments.

As I turned onto a quieter road, my thoughts were interrupted by the steady glow of headlights in the rearview mirror. Hot tears pricked at the corners of my eyes, my nerves stretched to the breaking point after meeting Liam's dad. I blinked them back, focusing on the road. The last thing I wanted was to cry in front of Lily. Not when I'd embarrassed myself enough by letting that man get to me.

The streetlights grew fewer as I turned onto my usual route

home from school, hoping the drive would help clear my head. But the ache in my chest only deepened. Liam had defended me. That much was clear. He'd been firm, protective even. But the fact that his father thought so little of me—or maybe so little of Liam—hurt more than I wanted to admit.

As I replayed the evening in my mind, the constant glare of headlights behind me began to tug at my attention. At first, I dismissed it as paranoia—just another car on the road. But as the miles passed, unease crept in.

I glanced in the rearview mirror again, checking on Lily. The bright headlights hurting my eyes. *How long has that car been following me? Since I left Fiona's house?*

Something about the way the car hung back, just far enough to stay in view but not close enough to feel intentional, sent a chill crawling up my spine.

I inhaled deeply realizing how much darker it was with the trees looming overhead, their branches cutting shadows across the road. My heart skipped a beat. *Plenty of people take this road— but where are they tonight?*

I took a sharp left onto a narrower road, sure I would shake my shadow with this move. The dark trees pressed in from both sides. My pulse quickened as the headlights stayed behind me, unwavering. When I slowed, they slowed. When I sped up, they surged forward.

My grip on the wheel tightened. *It's just a coincidence.* But deep down, I knew better. My breath hitched as I sped up more, despite the road's winding curves. The car followed without hesitation.

"Okay," I whispered, glancing at Lily in the mirror.

Her little head rested against her car seat, unaware of the danger. That steadied me. I couldn't panic—not with her in the car.

The other vehicle surged forward, cutting around me with a roar of its engine then swerved sharply in front. I slammed on the brakes, the tires skidding on roadside gravel. Our car jerked sideways, the world tilting as we careened into the ditch. The airbag deployed, slamming into me before it deflated. The metallic tang of blood filled my mouth. The world tilted, and for a moment, everything was silent—until Lily's scream pierced the haze.

I blinked hard, trying to focus. The car was tilted awkwardly. I twisted to the side, my gaze frantically searching out Lily, but she was safe in her car seat, her bunny now on the floor.

"Lily," I croaked, my voice trembling with my frantic need to get my daughter out of the car.

She cried, her tiny hands gripping her car seat straps, but she was safe. Fear fueled me as I unbuckled my seat belt.

Before I could reach for her, I heard it—the crunch of boots on gravel. Every instinct screamed at me to get my daughter out, to run. My door was yanked open. A sweet-smelling cloth covered my mouth. I struggled, holding my breath for as long as possible after that first inhale, but it was no use. My eyes fluttered closed, and the world went black.

CHAPTER TWENTY-SEVEN

LIAM

The only sound in the garage was the rhythmic thudding of my fists against the worn leather punching bag. Each strike was a futile attempt to shake off the weight pressing on my chest. I didn't hold back—strikes landed with a ferocity that sent the bag swinging, the chain above it groaning in protest.

My knuckles stung where the tape had shifted, but I didn't care. Pain was easier to deal with than the simmering rage I felt toward my father. He would never change. No matter how much time passed, he would always have that way of cutting me down and making me doubt everything I thought I knew about myself.

The door to the garage creaked open, and I knew it was Fiona before she said anything. She could always find me when I was like this.

"You're going to break your hand," she said, her voice cutting through the sound of my fists colliding with the bag. "Don't risk that. Not with football."

"I'll live," I muttered, hitting the bag again.

She didn't respond immediately, but I could feel her

watching me. Finally, she stepped closer, crossing her arms as she leaned against the wall.

"Liam, you have to stop letting him get to you."

I froze, my fist poised midair before I let it drop to my side. My breathing was heavy, and sweat trickled down the back of my neck. "I'm not letting him get to me," I denied.

Fiona raised an eyebrow. "Really? Because from where I stand, it looks like you're imagining his face on that punching bag."

She wasn't wrong.

I sighed and grabbed a towel off the nearby workbench, wiping my face. "He just… he knows exactly how to push every damn button. It's like he enjoys it."

"Of course he does." Fiona's tone softened as she moved to sit on the bench near me. "That's who he's always been. But, Liam, you don't have to let him define you."

I sat next to her, the towel draped over my shoulders.

"Sometimes, I feel like, no matter what I do, I'm going to turn into him," I admitted.

Fiona's eyes widened slightly, then she shook her head. "You're not him. I've told you that many times before—you've got to believe it. You never were. Liam, I know our parents messed us up—Mom leaving, Dad drinking himself into oblivion, the insults—but that's not you. Look at how you are with Lily."

I glanced at her, surprised.

"She adores you," Fiona continued. "And you don't even realize how much you've stepped up. Seeing you with her gives me hope that we can both break the cycle. Their curse doesn't have to be ours. We are not them. Look at us. We've already become better people than they ever were. Seeing you with Lily makes me believe in us and that maybe someday I'll be able to find what you have for myself."

Her words hit me hard, the knot in my chest loosening just a little.

"Thanks."

One word—but she acknowledged the depth behind it with a small smile. "Don't thank me. Just believe it." Fiona squeezed my shoulder before standing.

The garage fell quiet as I wiped my face, the rhythmic squeak of the still-swaying punching bag chain fading into silence. My phone buzzed on the workbench, breaking the silence like a warning.

"Hello?" I answered.

"Liam," Eileen's voice was quiet. "Is Skye there? She texted she was on her way home over an hour ago, but she's still not home. I've been trying to reach her, but her phone must be dead."

"No, she left almost two hours ago now."

"Are you sure?"

"Yeah, she left right after dinner. Maybe she went to the lab? No, she wouldn't take Lily."

"Her phone's going straight to voicemail. Where could she be?" Eileen's voice stretched with fear and worry. "I can't reach Tommy. He's stuck in a meeting, and my car is in the shop."

"Wait, you're saying she didn't make it home at all?"

"No, she didn't. Let me check my app, see if I can find where she is." She paused to work with her phone. When she spoke again, I could tell I was on speaker. "She's on Elm Street, that's a back road. Why would she have taken that?"

My gut twisted. That road was secluded—too secluded. "Can you send me her location? I'll find them." My heart pounded. "I promise, Eileen. I'll find them both."

I hung up and turned to Fiona, who was watching me, her expression mirroring my dread.

"What's going on?" she asked.

"Skye and Lily never made it home." I grabbed my keys off the counter, phone in hand.

Fiona's face paled, but she didn't hesitate. "I'm coming with you."

She grabbed her coat as I relayed what little information I had.

"Liam," Fiona said as she buckled into my truck, her mind clearly racing. "Skye's been digging into the investigation. What if someone noticed? Maybe something she photographed..." She trailed off, frowning. "Do you know where she'd go if she were in trouble?"

The thought made my blood run cold. "I don't know," I admitted, closing my door. "If this is about the investigation and someone took her, they don't know what they've started." My grip on the wheel tightened, my knuckles white. "Whoever's responsible will regret ever putting them in danger." I would stop at nothing to bring Skye and Lily home safely. I finally had them in my life, and I would not lose them again.

CHAPTER TWENTY-EIGHT

SKYE

The world swam as I pried open my heavy eyelids, a dull pain radiating through my skull. The last thing I remembered was driving home from Liam's. It was dark. There were headlights… It took a moment for the cloudiness to clear, and when it did, panic slammed into me like a freight train. My arms were pulled behind me, wrists bound painfully tight. A glance down revealed ropes cutting into my legs, holding me to a hard metal chair.

"Lily!" I rasped, my throat dry.

Her cries were high-pitched, desperate. I turned my head, my heart sinking. She was still strapped into her car seat, deposited a few feet away. Her little body trembled with sobs as she clutched her bunny tightly. Her red cheeks glistened with tears as she looked at me with wide, terrified eyes.

"It's okay, baby," I said, my voice hoarse. "Mommy's here."

"Well, isn't that sweet?"

The voice sent a cold wave of dread down my spine. I twisted as much as I could, and there he was—Joe, pacing in the room like a caged animal. We were in the chemistry lab. I recognized the industrial counters, the shelves lined with neatly labeled chemicals. It was late, and no one else was around, or they would've heard Lily's cries. That combined with the probability that he'd parked directly behind the building to enter near the lab killed any hope that someone would've seen him with a crying child and an unconscious woman.

"You just couldn't leave it alone, could you, Skye?" Joe snapped, running his hands through his messy hair.

"Joe…" My voice wavered, but I forced myself to sound calm. "What are you doing? Why—why would you drive us off the road?"

"You." He jabbed a finger in my direction. "You couldn't just stick to your little TA duties and keep your nose out of things. No, you had to poke around. Asking questions. Taking pictures. God, you're so predictable."

"I don't know what you're talking about."

"Oh, don't play dumb." He grabbed a crowbar off the counter, gesturing wildly with it. "You think I don't know about the research? About how you were sniffing around Megan's project? How long until you connected the dots and figured out what I've been doing?"

"What have you been doing?" I asked, stalling for time. My mind raced as I glanced at Lily, praying for a way out.

Joe scoffed. "Untraceable performance-enhancement drugs. You know, the drug that's making all those benchwarmers look like superstars? That's me, Skye. My formula. And you were this close to blowing it all up. But that's only part of it. I had plans. So many. Foxglove—my research."

"But the performance-enhancing research was Megan's." I needed more information and time.

"Part of it was. While Megan researched the negative side effects of performance enhancers, I used her research to hone an undetectable formula for college athletes. But foxglove was my true claim to fame. The performance-enhancement stuff was just a side hustle."

My mind spun as I worked to make the connection. The sudden improvements on the field, Jackson's death. It all clicked together in a sickening puzzle. But I had no time to dwell. My eyes darted to Lily, her trembling hands clutching Bunny, and a fierce resolve took hold. I had to get her out of here—no matter what. "The football player who died—"

"That wasn't supposed to happen!" Joe shouted, his voice cracking. "I didn't know he had any of the performance-enhancement stuff left. When I found out he had a heart condition, I switched out the product. The idiot took too much. He must have used both the performance enhancer and my foxglove treatment at once. If he'd only taken the new sample I'd given him, he would've been fine, possibly even healed. I didn't mean for it to happen. But I won't let you ruin me over it."

I stared at him, horrified. *Human trials.* The unethical reality of what Joe had done slammed into me like a punch. "So, what's the plan, Joe? You think you can just… what? Get away with this? With taking me and my daughter hostage?"

His eyes darted to the gallon of acid on the counter, and I swallowed hard.

"You don't get it, do you?" Joe's voice hitched, and for a moment, he looked less like the man with a crowbar and more like the friend I thought I knew. "This is my chance. My one shot to matter, to be someone. To change medical history with my formula containing digoxin extracted from foxglove. It would cure atrial fibrillation, something Jackson had. And you —you just had to ruin it by getting involved and telling the police."

"Joe, listen to me. Lily's a little girl. Let her go. She doesn't have anything to do with this."

Joe hesitated, his grip tightening on the crowbar. His eyes flickered with something—*guilt?*—but it vanished as quickly as it appeared.

He shook his head. "Too late for that."

CHAPTER TWENTY-NINE

LIAM

The soft glow of the streetlight cut through the darkness on the sideroad, illuminating the outline of a car that looked like Skye's in the ditch. My heart beat against my ribs as I pulled onto the side of the road. Gravel crunched under my tires as I stopped the truck abruptly, my chest tightening at the sight of Skye's car.

The front end was crumpled. From what I could see, the car was empty. No Skye. No Lily.

"Damn it," I cursed, throwing my truck into park. Before I could move, Fiona's hand shot out, her voice sharp.

"Wait." Her gaze locked on mine. "Stay calm. Don't touch anything. If they're not here, this is bigger than a crash."

I hesitated, my hand gripping the door handle. "Fiona, Lily could be in danger. We don't have time for—"

"We make time," she interrupted, her tone firm but steady. "If this is connected to what Skye told me earlier, then we need to handle this carefully. Let me assess the scene first."

She got out, her movements precise as she pulled on gloves from her coat pocket. I followed, my chest burning with barely restrained panic.

Fiona crouched near the car, her flashlight cutting through the shadows. Her trained eyes scanned the area while I fought the urge to run straight into the woods lining the side of the road and shout their names. She pulled out her phone, called the station, and reported the accident.

A familiar Jeep pulled up behind my truck, and Maverick jumped out, his expression as grim as I felt. "Where is she?"

Eileen must've called him. It made sense that he would show up. "Not here."

Maverick's jaw clenched as he surveyed the wreckage. "Where's the ambulance? If they were injured—"

"There wasn't one," Fiona interjected, rising to her feet. "The scene is off. The driver's door is open, the car seat missing, and in addition to the damage on the front of the vehicle, there are tire marks on the road. Whoever was here likely caused the accident and left on their own. The girls might have been taken."

My stomach churned at her words, and I glanced toward the car.

"Damn it," I muttered, running a hand through my hair.

Fiona straightened, her voice sharp as she stepped toward us. "Skye called me before your last game and told me she saw Joe handing a football player something suspicious—a plastic bag—at the science building. She said it didn't look right. Do either of you know anything about that?"

I shook my head. "She didn't tell me anything about Joe after the game."

"Me either." Mav frowned.

Fiona's lips pressed into a thin line. "I haven't managed to take Joe in for questioning. He was due to come to the station tomorrow. His involvement changes things, and the scheduled interview would have added another level of panic. If Skye saw him hand off drugs or something illegal, she might have become a liability to him."

"And if she called him out on it…" Maverick trailed off, his face darkening.

"That gives him motive," Fiona finished. She pulled out her phone and started dialing.

"I reported Skye and Lily missing from the scene, but I need to flag Joe as a person of interest." Fiona moved a few steps away as she placed the call.

Mav turned toward me, his mouth compressed into a harsh line. "We need to find that fucker."

We were in agreement. "I don't know him well. Do you? We need to figure out where he would've taken them."

Maverick crossed his arms, his gaze narrowing. "Skye mentioned once how territorial he was about his lab. If he wanted control, that's probably where he'd go."

Fiona returned and caught the tail end of our brief conversation, her fingers flying over her phone as she relayed the situation to dispatch. "That makes sense."

My fists clenched at the thought of Skye and Lily trapped with someone who wanted to do them harm. "Then we're wasting time. Let's go."

Fiona's hand shot up, stopping me in my tracks. "No. You're not charging in blind. If Joe's there and he's unstable, you'll only escalate the situation."

"What are you saying?" I demanded.

"I'm saying we do this right," she said firmly. "I'll contact backup. You and Maverick stay close, but let me lead. If Joe sees you and feels cornered, it could make things worse for Skye and Lily."

Maverick put a hand on my shoulder, his grip steady. "She's right, Cartwright. We go in hot, we risk blowing it. Let her handle it."

Every instinct screamed at me to act, but Fiona's unwavering calm and Maverick's steady logic held me in place. I nodded reluctantly. "Fine. But we're not waiting for backup. Let's move."

Fiona hesitated but didn't argue. She gestured toward my truck. "We'll take one vehicle. Stay quiet, and do as I say."

As we climbed in, I clenched my fists, my jaw tight. Skye and Lily needed me. And I wouldn't let them down.

The drive to the university was a blur of tension and silence. Fiona sat in the passenger seat, her phone pressed to her ear as she coordinated with dispatch, her tone clipped and professional. "We're en route to the science building. Suspect is possibly holding two hostages. Name: Joe Riken. Male, mid-twenties. Potentially armed and dangerous. Standby for confirmation on-site."

Maverick leaned forward from the back seat, his hands gripping the headrest. "How sure are we about this?"

"It fits," Fiona replied, her voice steady. "If he's trying to control the situation, he'd pick somewhere familiar, somewhere he can manipulate."

"And the lab is isolated," Maverick added grimly. "No one would stumble in on him by accident."

My knuckles turned white against the steering wheel as I pushed the truck faster. My thoughts kept flashing to the scene of their damaged and abandoned car.

Fiona's voice broke through my thoughts as I whipped into the nearly deserted parking lot behind the science building. "Liam, slow down. We can't afford to draw attention."

I forced my foot off the gas, though my chest burned with the need to get there faster. Every second felt like an eternity. When I threw the vehicle into park, Fiona was out of the truck before I could cut the engine. She gestured sharply for us to follow, her movements precise and purposeful with her Glock at the ready but pointed down and at her side.

"Stay behind me," she ordered, her voice low but firm.

The three of us moved quickly but quietly through the back entrance, Fiona leading the way with her flashlight cutting through the dim hallways. The air was heavy, the silence broken only by the faint hum of the building's fluorescent lights.

My pulse thundered in my ears as we approached a closed door near the end of the hall. That was when I heard it—Joe's muffled voice, sharp and frantic.

"Do you think I wanted this?" A loud crash like something metal hitting the floor.

Then Lily's cries pierced through the door, high and trembling with fear. "Mommy!"

Every muscle in my body coiled, ready to break down the door, but Fiona's hand shot out, pressing against my chest.

"Wait," she hissed. "We need to know what we're dealing with on the other side."

"I don't care," I growled, my vision narrowing. "Lily's crying—"

"Think, Liam," Maverick cut in, his voice low but firm. "If we go in without a plan, we risk making it worse."

Another loud crash sounded from inside, and Fiona's jaw tightened. "I'll open the door. You two follow my lead. We need to keep him distracted long enough to secure Skye and Lily."

I nodded sharply, every nerve screaming for action as Fiona reached for the door handle.

The second I saw Skye tied to that chair, my vision went red. Even from the sideview I had, I could tell she was pale, her wrists raw from the ropes biting into her skin. Lily's cries tore through the room, her little voice shaking with fear. *And Joe?* That bastard stood there with a crowbar like he was ready to use it.

I didn't think. I just moved.

"Get away from them!" I roared, sprinting toward Joe.

He swung the crowbar, the sharp whistle of metal slicing through the air. I ducked low, the motion throwing me off balance but not enough to stop me. The counter edge jabbed my hip as I lunged forward, my shoulder slamming into his chest.

The impact took him to the floor with enough power to make the crowbar clatter out of his hand. Joe let out a guttural shout, struggling beneath me, his movements sluggish from the force of my tackle.

Unable to stop myself, I slammed my fist into his face. "You're done," I growled, my voice shaking with rage.

Behind me, Fiona moved in swiftly, her gun trained on Joe as I pushed off him.

"Stay down," she barked, but he wasn't going anywhere. I'd leveled him.

Mav moved around them as Fiona snapped the cuffs onto his wrists. Lily whimpered, and he dropped to his knees before her, cooing softly that she was okay as he deftly unhooked the straps that held her in her car seat.

I didn't wait to watch Fiona drag Joe up. My focus was on Skye. "Skye!" I hurried to her side. Her eyes brimmed with tears as I worked to untie her, my hands clumsy with urgency.

"Liam," she choked out, her voice breaking.

"You're okay." I released the last knot and pulled her into my arms the second she was free.

Her eyes frantically tracked her daughter. "Lily!" she cried out, dropping to her knees before Lily and pulling her into her arms as soon as Mav had her free.

Mav shifted back, and I knelt beside Skye, pulling her and Lily into my arms, needing to feel them both whole and safe. Lily fisted my shirt with one hand, her other arm wrapping around Skye's neck, her sobs muffled against her mom.

"I've got you," I murmured, holding them close. "I've got both of you."

Skye practically collapsed into me, her body trembling against mine. I pulled her closer into my chest, holding on tighter than I probably should've, but I couldn't let go. Not yet.

"Are you okay?" I asked, my voice rough, the words catching in my throat.

She nodded, but her grip on my shirt said otherwise. "Joe?"

My hand slid up to cradle the back of her head. "Fiona has him. You're safe. Everything will be okay."

Skye let out a shaky breath, her forehead dropping against my chest, Lily tucked between us. Relief flooded through me, but it didn't erase the image burned into my brain: Skye tied to that chair, her face pale, her eyes wide with fear.

"I thought I'd lost you," I whispered, the words slipping out before I could stop them. "Both of you."

Her head lifted, her red-rimmed eyes locking onto mine. She looked as wrecked as I felt, her tear-streaked face lit only by the dim light filtering through the lab. "You didn't."

"I can't lose you, Skye." A tremor shook my body. "Either of you. I don't know what I'd do if—"

"Liam..." Her voice wavered, and I saw the tears welling in her eyes again.

"I mean it." I held her gaze. "You're everything. You and Lily —you're my everything."

Her breath hitched, and for a moment, neither of us moved. The world around us—the sirens, the voices—faded into nothing. There was only the three of us, my lifeline that I vowed never to let go.

CHAPTER THIRTY

LIAM

The lights buzzed overhead, harsh and cold against the sterile walls of the hospital. We'd arrived in an ambulance because I was taking no chances with Skye or Lily's well-being. The exam went well with very little wait. After having seen the doctor, we were left in the ER until the nurse came with discharge papers.

It was eerily quiet, the earlier nightmare replaced by an uneasy calm. Skye sat on the exam bed, Lily curled in her lap, her tiny fingers tangled in her mom's hair. Lips pressed softly to Lily's temple, Skye whispered soothing words I couldn't quite make out.

Fiona had just stepped out after checking on us to head to the precinct, leaving me hovering near Skye and Lily, wanting to slam my fist into Joe's face all over again for putting them in such a fragile state. I shoved my hands into my pockets, knuckles still raw from the earlier scuffle.

"Mr. Cartwright?" A nurse called from the door, her tone clipped but polite as she entered, handing me the discharge papers. "They're cleared to leave. No serious injuries."

Relief washed over me like a wave, but it didn't chase away the lingering anger—or the guilt. We listened to her brief instructions about rest, echoing everything the doctor had already told us. I nodded my thanks, swallowing the lump in my throat, and walked toward them.

Skye met my gaze as I approached, exhaustion etched into every line of her face. Her eyes, though rimmed with redness, softened. Lily stirred in her lap, lifting her head to look at me, thumb still tucked into her mouth and her bunny clutched tightly to her chest.

"Hey, Lilybug," I said softly, crouching to her level. "You ready to go?"

She nodded, her little voice a whisper. "I wanna go with Mommy."

"You will," I promised, glancing at Skye.

Skye's hand trembled slightly as she pushed a stray hair out of Lily's face. "Thank you," she murmured. Her voice was barely audible, but I caught it. "For coming. For not giving up."

I swallowed hard. "I'll never give up on you. On either of you." I would raze the world to keep them safe.

The drive to the police station was a blur. Skye sat in the back seat with Lily, holding her close. Her aunt and Coach had blown up my phone, only calming after they heard Skye and Lily were given a clean bill of health and that we would meet them at the police station.

Fiona had arranged for us to give statements, and despite the tension still thick in the air, Skye insisted on going. "I need to see this through," she'd said, her tone resolute.

The station was a stark contrast to the hospital—a cacophony of ringing phones, shuffling papers, and low conversation. As soon as we walked through the doors, a voice cut through the noise, trembling and thick with emotion.

"Skye!"

Eileen Becket—Skye's aunt—hurried across the room, her hands clasped to her mouth, tears streaming down her face. She was a blur of movement as she rushed to her niece and scooped both Skye and Lily into her arms.

"Oh, thank God." She sobbed, pulling them close. "I was so scared. When you didn't come home after letting me know you were on your way… I didn't know what to think."

Skye clung to her aunt, her own tears spilling over as Lily burrowed into her shoulder.

"We're okay," Skye whispered, her voice soft but steady.

Eileen pulled back just enough to cup Skye's face, her tear-filled eyes scanning every inch of her niece like she needed to see for herself that she was truly there. "You're sure? Are you hurt? What about Lily?"

Skye shook her head, brushing her fingers through Lily's dark curls. "We're fine. Just… shaken up."

Eileen's gaze flicked to me, her expression softening despite the worry still etched into her features. "Liam." Her voice broke, and she reached out to squeeze my arm. "Thank you. For bringing them back."

I nodded, words sticking in my throat. "I'd do it a thousand times over."

Fiona stepped forward then, gently placing a hand on Eileen's shoulder. "Let's give them a moment to catch their breath before we take statements. There's a quieter room in the back."

Eileen nodded, her arm still wrapped protectively around Skye and Lily as she guided them toward the room Fiona mentioned. I stayed rooted in place, watching until they disappeared down the hall.

"Cartwright. Son."

The deep, familiar voice cut through my thoughts, and I turned to see Coach standing near the front desk, arms crossed, his expression unreadable.

"Coach," I greeted him, my voice low as I approached.

His sharp gaze studied me, and for a moment, I felt like I was back on the field after a bad play.

"Before you follow your wife," I started, "I need to tell you something."

"Let's talk." He gestured toward a side office.

I followed him in silence, my chest tight with the weight of what I was about to say.

Once the door closed behind us, he leaned against the desk, arms still crossed. "What's on your mind?"

I hesitated, my throat dry as I stood before my head coach, the man who had become a pillar of strength and reason over the past three years he'd been in my life. "It's about Lily."

His brows furrowed, thick, bushy mustache pulling down with the corners of his mouth, and for a moment, I thought he was going to cut me off. But he stayed silent, waiting.

"She's mine," I said, the words tumbling out in a rush. "I didn't know until recently, but she's my daughter. I swear, if I'd known—"

"I know, Liam," he interrupted, his voice calm but firm.

The words hit me like a freight train. "You... knew?"

He sighed, running a hand over his weary, stress-lined face. "Not at first. But over time... Lily's grin, her dimples, and the color of her eyes... Then the way you looked at her, at Skye over these past weeks—it wasn't hard to piece together."

"Why didn't you say anything?" Shock held me suspended.

"Because it wasn't my place," he said simply. "I knew Skye had her reasons for keeping it from you. And I knew you'd figure it out when the time was right."

I shook my head, my hands splaying wide at my sides. "I wish you would've told me."

He stepped closer, his tone softening. "You think I didn't want to? That it didn't kill me to see you trying to navigate life without knowing the truth? That my niece held the information close to her heart, choosing to navigate motherhood on her own? I had to trust that she had her reasons. And, Liam, you needed to come into this on your own. You needed to be ready."

His words sank in slowly, the initial hurt of another person keeping the truth from me bleeding into something else, something I couldn't quite name.

"That's why you've been so hard on me," I realized. "On Ares and Kylian too. You've been pushing us all this time."

He nodded. "Why do you think I called you three leaders? Why do you think I demanded more from you than anyone else? It wasn't just about football, Liam. It's about the kind of men you need to be. On the field. Off it. In life."

I blinked, the weight of his words settling over me. All the times he'd called me "son," all the extra drills, the lectures in his office about life and how we needed to step up and do the right thing, the tough love—it all made sense. It hit me in that moment. He'd done more for me than just be a coach. I finally understood why I never wanted to let him down, why I listened closely when he spoke.

"You're more of a father to me than my own ever was," I admitted, my voice breaking.

Coach's expression softened, and his eyes held a warmth I hadn't seen before. "Why do you think I've always called you son? I've seen the man you're capable of being. And standing here now, seeing the way you've fought for Skye and Lily—I couldn't be prouder. You've earned my respect, Liam, and the family you have now reflects the kind of man you are. Remember that."

The door opened behind us, breaking the moment. Fiona stood there, her expression a mix of relief and urgency. "I need a quick statement from you, Liam. And Skye and Lily are ready to go."

I nodded, glancing back at Coach. "Thank you," I said quietly.

"For what?"

"For believing in me. For being there, even when I didn't realize it."

He clapped a hand on my shoulder, his grip firm. "Go take care of your girls, son."

That was all I wanted.

CHAPTER THIRTY-ONE

SKYE

The house was silent, the kind of silence that only came after an epic storm. The soft hum of the heater kicking on and the faint creak of floorboards under Liam's steps felt magnified in the stillness. Outside, the wind rattled the windowpane, a sound so sharp it made me cringe before I could stop myself.

I couldn't shake the weight of the night. Filing statements at the police station with Fiona's help had been surreal, every detail dragging us deeper into the reality of what Joe had done. The scandal was already unraveling—players, coaches, even administrative ties—and my uncle was buried in the fallout. My aunt had stayed behind at the office with him, working late after getting assurance that Liam would keep watch over us.

But knowing we were safe didn't quiet the anxiety twisting in my chest. My hands trembled as I double-checked the locks on the front door for the third time then moved to the windows to check each latch. Every shadow felt like a threat. When I drew the curtains tightly closed, it felt less like shutting out the world and more like bracing against it.

Lily was curled on the couch, her tiny hands gripping her

bunny like a lifeline. Liam sat beside her, his large frame fitting awkwardly but protectively in the corner of the cushions. His arm stretched along the backrest, a silent barrier between her and the world.

"Skye." His voice was soft, a nudge to bring me back to the room.

"I just need to check—"

"You've checked everything twice," he said gently but firmly. "Come here. Sit with us."

I hesitated, glancing toward the kitchen window as though it might suddenly fly open. But the warmth in his voice and the steadiness in his gaze pulled me back. I crossed the room and sank into the space he'd saved for me, tucking my legs beneath me.

Liam shifted slightly to make room, his shoulder brushing against mine. "It's okay," he murmured. "We're safe."

Lily leaned against me, her soft sniffles fading as exhaustion took over. "Mama," she mumbled, barely audible.

"I'm here, baby," I whispered, kissing her temple.

Liam reached across, his fingers brushing against mine in a silent offer. I took his hand, his callouses rough but grounding, and let out a breath I hadn't realized I was holding.

Lily's breathing steadied, her little fingers loosening their grip on her bunny. Liam glanced at me, a silent question in his eyes. I nodded, and he stood, lifting her with a gentleness that caught me off guard. He carried her toward my bedroom, his movements careful, as though she might shatter if he wasn't steady enough. I followed, the heaviness of the night pressing on me. She still clutched her bunny in her tiny hands as he carried her. Liam cradled her with a tenderness that made me ache.

Once she was tucked into the middle of my bed, she reached out instinctively, grabbing for both of us. I slid in on one side, and Liam hesitated momentarily before settling on the other.

"I can sleep on the couch," he said quietly, his voice laced with reticence.

"Stay," I replied, surprising even myself. The word came without thought, only instinct. "She needs us both tonight."

Something about him was so steady, so solid, that it made me feel a little lighter.

We lay in silence for a while, the kind that wasn't uncomfortable but carried more than words ever could. My head spun, my thoughts chasing themselves in circles, but when Liam shifted closer, the turmoil in my mind stilled for a moment.

He reached out slowly, hesitating for just a second before his hand brushed mine. My breath caught, but I didn't pull away. His fingers slid over mine, warm and firm, and when I glanced at him, his gaze was even.

Lily's little hand found my shirt, clutching tightly, while her other reached for Liam. He let go of me and took it without hesitation, his larger fingers curling protectively around hers.

For a long time, we lay in silence. The streetlight outside cast faint stripes across the ceiling, and the rhythmic sound of Lily's breathing became the room's anchor.

"She's stronger than I thought," Liam whispered after a while, his voice barely more than a breath.

"She is," I agreed, my gaze fixed on her peaceful face. "But tonight… tonight was too much."

He didn't respond immediately, and when I turned my head, I found him watching me. His expression was a mix of exhaustion, guilt, and something softer—something that made my chest ache.

"Skye, I'm sorry," he said finally.

I frowned. "For what? You saved us."

"For not being there sooner. For not being there at all before now. If I'd known…" He trailed off, his jaw tightening.

I reached out, my hand resting lightly on his arm. "You're here now. That's what matters."

His eyes searched mine, and I felt seen—not as the woman who had to have all the answers or the mom who had to hold it together but as just me.

"Thank you," he said, his voice thick. "For trusting me. For letting me be here."

I didn't have words, so I squeezed his arm gently before pulling my hand back. I did trust him. *How could I not?* He'd constantly proven how he'd changed, and I believed him—he was there for us, no matter what.

Lily shifted between us, her little hand tightening on Liam's. The sight made something inside me twist. I wasn't used to sharing this space—this role—with anyone else. But seeing him with her, how he instinctively protected and comforted her, I realized how much I wanted it for her—for us.

His hand curled protectively around Lily's. It was such a simple gesture, but it spoke volumes. He wasn't just saying he would be there—he was proving it.

"I'm not the guy I was back then," Liam said quietly, possibly reading something from my expression. "I know I have a lot to prove, but I'm willing to do whatever it takes. You don't have to trust me all at once. Just… give me a chance."

His words were simple, but they hit something deep inside me. The walls I'd spent years building felt less like a fortress and more like glass—fragile and already laced with cracks.

"I trust you, but I'm scared," I admitted, the words trembling as they left my lips. There would be so many changes, and the NFL would come knocking soon.

"So am I." He released Lily's grip, laying her palm on his chest before taking mine in his again. His thumb brushed over the back of my hand. "But we don't have to figure it all out tonight. Right now, we're here. That's enough."

I turned to look at him, his profile faintly illuminated by the light filtering through the curtains. He looked exhausted but resolute, his hand never letting go of mine.

"All right," I whispered.

His lips curved into a faint smile that felt like a promise. "Good."

I let my eyes drift shut as Lily's breathing steadied, her small body curled against mine. The cracks in my world, once jagged and threatening to swallow me whole, didn't feel like a weakness anymore. They felt like openings—places where the light of Liam's love and unwavering commitment could seep through, warming the parts of me I thought would stay frozen forever. And I let myself believe in something more than survival. I believed in us.

CHAPTER THIRTY-TWO

LIAM

The energy in the stadium was electric, the crowd's roar vibrating through my chest as I stood on the sideline, helmet in hand. Fall Lake University had come alive for this playoff game, the stands packed with screaming fans waving banners and wearing every shade of our school colors. We had a real shot at the championship—it didn't get bigger than that.

Coach clapped me on the shoulder, his grin wide but determined. "Focus, son. One play at a time."

I nodded, adrenaline already thrumming through my veins. This game wasn't just about getting into the championship. It was about proving that I was more than my mistakes, more than my father's doubts, that I was good enough to go into the professional league. It was about Skye, Lily, and the life I was determined to build for us.

I took in my teammates, the ones who had cleared the grueling interviews to determine who was involved and who wasn't after Coach Becket learned of the scandal. Coach Mack and Coach Ramirez were absent. The story hadn't broken yet, thanks to Fiona. She'd done what she could to keep things under wraps, at least until after today's playoff game. It was my chance, as well as my teammates', to prove ourselves on the field while scouts watched.

The coin toss resulted in our offense taking the field. The game was a grind from the first snap. Michigan's defense was relentless, but we were sharper. I could feel the rhythm of the team clicking into place. Kylian's passes were lasers, precise and impossible to miss. On a third and long in the second quarter, he launched a deep spiral downfield, and I pushed every muscle in my body to get under it. The ball hit my hands like it belonged there, and I bolted toward the end zone, leaving defenders in my wake.

The crowd erupted as I crossed the line. My teammates mobbed me, their voices blending into the deafening roar of the fans. It wasn't time to celebrate. We were there to win and immediately got back to work.

"Hell of a play!" Kylian shouted, slapping my helmet as we jogged to the sideline.

Our defense held the opposing team and in no time at all, we were back on the field. The roar of the crowd faded into the background as I stood on the line of scrimmage, my eyes locked on the defense. This was it—third and long, our playoff hopes hanging by a thread.

I braced at the scrimmage line, my knuckles whitening, but my mind wasn't on the play. It was on them. Skye. Lily. I could see Lily's face, scrunched up in concentration as she colored at the kitchen table, the way she'd looked at me last night when I tucked her in, her small arms wrapping tightly around my neck like she didn't want me to leave. And Skye. Her voice soft and loving when she whispered good night. I wasn't just playing for me anymore. I was playing for them.

The ball snapped, and I surged forward, adrenaline pounding in my veins. I couldn't let them down. Not now. Not ever again.

We kept the pressure on, and by the time the clock hit zero, the scoreboard flashed our victory in bold numbers: 38–24. The Falcons were headed to the championship.

The field was chaos, teammates celebrating, the band blasting the fight song, and fans screaming from the stands. Kylian was being interviewed by a reporter, but I noticed a scout for Tampa Bay and Buffalo hovering nearby. I'd barely made it off the field when a man in a sharp suit appeared at the sidelines, clipboard tucked under his arm.

"Liam Cartwright?" he asked, extending a hand.

"Yes, sir." My heart pounded.

"Jimmy Garrett, scout for the Baltimore Ravens." His handshake was firm, his tone businesslike but laced with enthusiasm. "We've been watching you all season, and I have to say, today sealed it. We're very interested. We'll be in touch soon to talk details."

The words landed like a bolt of lightning. It was the shot I'd been chasing since I was a kid. "Thank you, sir," I said, my voice steady despite the storm inside me.

As Garrett walked away, my thoughts reeled. The Ravens—an actual NFL team—wanted me. I barely had time to process the moment when Mark Thompson with the Kansas City Chiefs approached, cutting through the crowd with purposeful strides.

"Cartwright," he called, his voice carrying over the noise of the sidelines.

"Yes, sir." I turned, meeting his sharp gaze.

He extended a hand. "Today confirmed what I already suspected—you're the kind of player we're looking for."

I blinked, my brain scrambling to keep up. "Thank you, sir," I managed, shaking his hand.

"Not just your athleticism, though that's impressive," he continued, his voice steady and confident. "Your ability to read the field, adjust under pressure, and connect with your team—

that's what separates the good from the great. And you, Cartwright, have greatness written all over you."

A grin broke across my face, wide and uncontainable. "I appreciate that, sir. It means a lot."

"Don't let it go to your head," he said with a wink, his tone warm. "We're putting together a plan to meet soon. Keep your phone on, and we'll reach out."

"Yes, sir. I will," I promised, my voice still shaking with disbelief as he gave me a nod and disappeared into the crowd.

Two scouts. Two teams. Two opportunities I'd only dared to dream about. I couldn't wait to tell Skye. The buzz of the moment hadn't faded when I felt a familiar gaze on me. My eyes found Skye near the social media tent, her camera slung around her neck, a knowing smile tugging at her lips. She was watching, waiting, and somehow, she already knew what had happened.

I crossed the field in a few long strides, skirting around Ares as he chatted with San Francisco's scout, my grin breaking free. A wide smile tugged at Skye's lips as I reached her.

"Not bad, Cartwright," she teased, her voice warm.

"Not bad?" I repeated, stepping closer. "That was a playoff win. I think I deserve a little more credit than that."

She rolled her eyes, but her smile widened. "Fine. You were great."

After a beat of silence, she stepped closer, her hand brushing mine.

"You really were great," Skye said quietly.

"I couldn't have done it without you." My voice was just as low. "You and Lily. You're why I'm here, Skye. My motivation and why I'm doing all of this."

Her breath hitched, and for a moment, I thought she might pull away. But then she surprised me, her fingers brushing against mine before curling around them.

"You were incredible," she said softly, and for the first time, I believed every word.

I wanted to share everything with her, no more secrets, not more walls. Never again. "You're not gonna believe the conversations I had with some scouts," I said, breathless.

"Try me," she teased, tilting her head.

I told her about the Baltimore and Kansas City scouts and the chance to make it to the NFL. Her reaction was immediate—her arms around my neck, pulling me into a tight hug.

"That's amazing, Liam," she said, her voice muffled against my shoulder. "I'm so proud of you."

"We're doing this together, Skye." My voice held conviction. "The decision, the move, us being a family with Lily. I'm not going without you both by my side every step of the way."

When she pulled back, her eyes shone, and the stadium's noise faded for a moment. "I love you. And I want that too."

Her words hit me deeper than I let on. I wasn't just playing for me anymore. This win, this opportunity—it was for all of us. "I love you, Skye. I think I have from the moment we met all those years ago. I was just too stupid to realize it."

Later that night, after the stadium lights dimmed and the crowd dispersed, ESPN broke the news. The TV in the locker room glowed as anchors detailed the fallout from Joe's arrest:

"Two assistant coaches at Fall Lake University—Steve Mack and Mike Ramirez—are under investigation for their involvement in distributing an undetectable performance-enhancing drug developed by graduate student Joe Riken. The scandal has rocked the football program but left Head Coach Thomas Becket untouched, with sources confirming he was unaware of the scheme and is aiding the police and university during the investigation. The university has fully cooperated with authorities, distancing itself from the accused and ensuring the team remains eligible for postseason play."

The locker room went silent as players absorbed the report. Coach Becket had kept us shielded, working relentlessly to separate the guilty from the innocent. Despite the scandal, he'd made sure we could play clean—and win.

When the segment shifted to the victim—Kyle Jackson, the wide receiver whose death had sparked the investigation—a somber mood settled over the room. The scandal wasn't just a betrayal of the team; it had cost someone their life.

My gut churned as the segment played. Coach Mack and Coach Ramirez had betrayed everything the team stood for. But Coach Becket had worked tirelessly to protect us, to make sure we could step onto that field with our heads held high—that was what saved him from the university benching him for the remainder of our season. It helped that the guilty parties were discovered—and Professor White and Megan Elwood had been cleared of any involvement. I glanced around the room, seeing the same anger and relief on my teammates' faces. We'd earned this win, clean and fair, and no one could take that from us.

"Listen up." Coach stepped into the center of the room. "What happened off the field doesn't define this team. We play clean. We play fair. And we win because we've earned it." His voice was firm, unshakable. "Now, go enjoy the win tonight. You've earned that too."

CHAPTER THIRTY-THREE

LIAM

The crowd's roar still rang in my ears as I stepped into the quiet corridor outside the locker room. My heart raced—not just from the game but from the scouts, the victory, and the weight of what it all meant.

Skye was waiting for me near the exit, her camera slung over her shoulder. She wasn't smiling, but her eyes were soft, warm in a way that made the stadium noise fade into the background.

"Hey," I said, my voice hoarse from shouting plays.

"Hey yourself," she replied, her lips twitching into a small smile. "Congratulations, again. You were… incredible out there."

The pride in her voice hit me harder than any tackle. "Thanks." I took a step closer. "I couldn't have done it without you. Without Lily."

She opened her mouth to respond, but I couldn't stop myself. "Come here," I murmured, pulling her into a hug.

She melted against me, her arms circling my waist, and I couldn't hold back anymore. "Skye, I know I said it before, but I'm not going anywhere. Not without you and Lily. Nothing else matters." I cupped her face, tilting her chin so she would look at me. "Not with how I feel about you. About us."

She didn't respond with words, but the way her hands gripped my shirt told me enough. I leaned down, brushing my lips against hers, softly at first. The kiss deepened, her fingers tangling in my hair as I pressed her against the wall, the world narrowing to just her. My hands slid down to her waist, pulling her closer, and when she whispered my name, it was my undoing. We broke apart only when we were breathless, and I rested my forehead against hers.

"Okay, no more doubts. I'm fully in this with you." Her smile was blinding as she rested her hand over my heart.

"I promise I'll be here for you, Skye." I meant every word. I knew how lucky I was to have a second chance with her. A chance with Lily. "Every step of the way."

Her gaze flicked toward the hallway, a mischievous glint lighting her eyes. "You know," she began softly, her lips curving into a sly smile, "Aunt Eileen has Lily. We have some time."

It took me a second to catch her meaning, but when I did, heat flared low in my chest. "Yeah?" I murmured, my hand sliding to her hip. "Where exactly were you thinking we should go?"

She nodded toward the training room. "It's empty."

I didn't need to be told twice. Taking her hand, I led her down the quiet corridor, slipping into the dimly lit room, shutting and locking the door behind us. The faint scent of antiseptic lingered in the air, but I couldn't care less. All I could see, all I could feel, was her.

Skye leaned back against the counter, her hands pulling me closer, her gaze steady and unguarded. "You really meant what you said?" she asked, her voice soft but filled with certainty. "That nothing else matters?"

I stepped closer, framing her face with my hands, my thumbs brushing gently over her cheeks. "Nothing, Skye. Not the NFL, not football, not anything. You and Lily—you're it for me. My life starts and ends with you two."

Her lips parted slightly, her eyes searching mine, and I couldn't hold back. The words that had been burning in my chest for weeks slipped out before I could second-guess myself.

"I love you, Skye. I've loved you for as long as I can remember, and I can't imagine a single day without you and Lily in it. I don't want to. We've talked about you both coming with me wherever I'm drafted, but that's not enough. I want to give you everything—because you and Lily are my everything."

Her breath hitched as I reached for her hand, clasping it tightly between mine. "I planned to do this better, to have a ring and make it perfect, but I can't wait another second to ask you. Marry me, Skye. Be my family. Let me be yours."

Her eyes shimmered with tears, a soft, radiant smile breaking across her face as she nodded. "Yes. I'll marry you, Liam."

Relief and joy crashed over me, leaving me breathless as she tugged me down to her, her lips pressing against mine in a kiss that held nothing but love. I wrapped my arms around her, pulling her flush against me, my heart hammering as the moment sank in. She was mine. She had always been mine.

When we broke apart, her fingers traced along my jaw, her voice steady and full of emotion. "I've never been surer of anything in my life, Liam. You and Lily—you're everything I could ever want."

I smiled, brushing my thumb along her cheek. "And you're everything to me."

She leaned up, capturing my lips in another kiss, and this time, it was full of promise. A future. A family. Us. Together. Forever.

Skye

Liam's mouth moved possessively over mine, and I moaned into the kiss, molding myself to his body. He wound an arm around my waist, holding me against him as my knees buckled, the heat from his hands stirring a need I couldn't resist. With him, it was easy to forget my surroundings. And watching him play today, there was something electric, promising. It had affected me so much that I couldn't wait to be in his arms.

I buried my fingers in his hair, tilting my head for a better angle to deepen the kiss.

I needed more from him, more than words, more than promises. My hands slid from his hair, down the solid line of his shoulders, and I leaned back in his arms, searching his eyes. Every unspoken feeling between us burned there, and the weight of it left no room for doubt. When his lips brushed mine, soft at first, tentative, I was undone. I melted into him, my heart pounding in sync with his. Falling for him was inevitable, like gravity pulling me closer, holding me captive in the only place I ever wanted to be.

Heat sparked where his fingers trailed along my skin, spreading like wildfire through my body. He angled my head to deepen the kiss, his touch igniting every nerve ending with a breathless intensity. A soft gasp escaped me as I clung to his shirt, my fingers curling into the fabric like it was the only thing tethering me to reality. Letting him go wasn't an option—maybe it never had been.

Without breaking the kiss, he scooped me into his arms, the motion fluid and effortless. My legs instinctively wrapped around his waist, and I buried my face in his neck, the faint scent of him overwhelming my senses. He carried me across the room to one of the massage tables, lowering me gently onto the edge. The moment he pulled back, a soft whimper escaped my lips, the absence of his kiss a sharp ache I didn't know how to endure.

He reached up, tucking a loose strand of hair behind my ear.

His fingers lingered as they traced the curve of my cheek. His thumb brushed over the pulse fluttering at the base of my throat, and I couldn't look away from him. His touch, his gaze—it all felt inevitable, like it had been written in the stars long before either of us knew what we meant to each other.

"Skye," he murmured, his voice low and rough, sending a shiver down my spine.

His thumb trailed over my bottom lip, and I exhaled shakily, nerve endings sparking to life under his touch. Time seemed to stand still. In his eyes, I saw everything—love, desire, certainty, all my emotions mirrored back at me. I didn't just want him in the moment. I wanted every moment, every day, every lifetime with him.

We moved at the same time, our lips colliding in a kiss that was anything but tentative. It was fierce, all-consuming, a declaration of everything we'd been holding back. His hands cradled my face, angling me to deepen the kiss, and I let myself fall completely. My fingers fumbled with his shirt, tugging at the fabric until my hands found warm skin, his muscles taut under my touch.

The sharp intake of his breath against my mouth sent a thrill through me, and when his fingers found the hem of my shirt, my breath caught. We peeled away layers with reverence and urgency, each piece of clothing discarded as if shedding the barriers between us. When he pulled me back into his arms, skin to skin, it was like the world outside this room ceased to exist.

His touch wasn't just heat—it was comfort, connection, everything I never realized I was searching for. As his lips trailed along my jaw, down the curve of my neck, I knew the feeling wasn't fleeting. It wasn't just desire—it was love, raw and unfiltered, a love that promised more than that moment.

Sensual promise flickered in his eyes, dark and unyielding. The heat rolling off him was almost tangible as he crowded closer, and I instinctively hooked my leg around his waist, drawing him in. His hand moved up the curve of my thigh with agonizing patience, his touch igniting every nerve it grazed.

The flex of his broad shoulders sent a shiver down my spine as he guided my hand above my head, pinning it there. My fingers twitched in his grip, desperate to roam over the sculpted lines I couldn't stop devouring with my eyes.

I trembled, desire coiling tight within me as his mouth left mine to press hot, lingering kisses down my neck. When his teeth scraped the sensitive spot where my neck met my shoulder, I gasped, a dizzying rush overtaking me. My hand found his shoulders, greedily tracing the ridges of muscle that shifted and tensed under my touch.

He released his hold on me and cupped the back of my neck, angling my head, his lips brushing mine in maddening strokes, teasing and unrelenting. I writhed against him, the subtle friction of his kiss sparking jolts of electricity that shot straight through me. Every caress sent waves of fire skittering across my skin, leaving me a trembling mess. Leashed power thrummed beneath my fingertips, his strength barely contained, and I moaned as he deepened the kiss, his tongue coaxing, commanding.

My body was alive—hypersensitive, pulsing with a rhythm only he could set. I was unraveling, every touch, every kiss, pulling me further under his spell. Need tore through me, and I arched as his length pressed against my hot core, slicking the way for his entry. Nails digging into his trim waist, I urged him to hurry.

When his fingers traced my seam, I cried out, arching higher to meet him. Feverish nerve pulses shot through me when his thick length plunged inside, stretching me, and I exploded around him in quivering convulsions.

I clung to him while my head swam as sensation after sensation crested in waves, following each powerful thrust. His corded muscles flexed and bulged beneath my fingertips. When he slid a hand between our bodies to dip between my folds, teasing the sensitive bundle of nerves there, I cried out, throbbing around him.

He trailed heated kisses along my neck, whispering my name. Then his moan vibrated against my skin, and he chased my climax with his own, heightening my aftershocks.

Cradled in the strength of his embrace, I slowly regulated my breathing, neither of us willing to move. When he finally pulled out, I whimpered, wanting him all over again, despite knowing we only had moments before we needed to get dressed and leave for obligations that couldn't wait, but right then, none of that mattered. The world outside could keep spinning, but in here, time slowed down, allowing us to savor the stolen seconds.

With every shared glance, every whispered word, and every lingering touch, we etched the moment into our memories, a secret oasis we could revisit when the weight of reality pressed down on us again.

I clung to him, my heart pounding, and in his arms, I didn't just feel safe—I felt whole. Together, we were everything I'd ever dreamed of and more, a world waiting to be discovered, one breathtaking moment at a time.

EPILOGUE

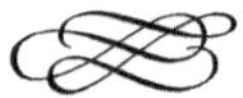

SKYE

One year later...

The late-summer sun painted the house in a golden glow as I stepped onto the back porch, my phone in hand. Not long after Liam joined the Kansas City Chiefs, I'd applied for a PR position, and based on my success with the Fall Lake University Falcon's social media, I'd been hired as an assistant. I loved my job, and working at the same facility where Liam was made it even better.

The Chiefs' Instagram needed fresh content, and I'd quickly learned that nothing fired up fans like action shots and behind-the-scenes glimpses. I snapped a quick photo of Liam's cleats and helmet resting on the back porch steps, covered with grass stains from practice. It was the kind of detail that told its own story—a grind-it-out day that fans loved. I added it to my drafts, brainstorming a caption to get the comments rolling.

My gaze drifted to the backyard, where Lily twirled in the grass, her laughter carrying on the warm breeze. Her "Big

Sister" T-shirt stood out like a beacon, the pink letters bold against the white fabric. I couldn't stop staring at it.

"Lily," I called, my voice soft but steady, "it's almost time to meet Daddy for dinner."

She skipped over, her little hand slipping into mine, warm and familiar. I glanced down at the sparkling diamond on my finger, the sunlight making it dance. That ring wasn't just a symbol—it was a promise that Liam and I had fought so hard to keep.

Inside, the sound of the game replay filled the house. Liam's name rang out, the announcer's voice full of excitement. "Let's talk about Liam Cartwright," the commentator's voice boomed. "He's been nothing short of spectacular this season. Another stellar performance on Sunday—two hundred fifty yards, two touchdowns, and a clutch scramble to seal the win. The Chief's starter is proving he's the real deal, and the league is noticing."

I couldn't help but smile, pride blooming in my chest. Witnessing Liam step into his own on the field was everything I'd known he was capable of—and more. He'd earned every bit of that praise.

"And it's not just Cartwright making waves," the second commentator added. "It's worth noting that he's part of a rare trio of standouts from the same college team. Kylian Wilder, now Miami's starting quarterback, has been electrifying the league with his precision passes and clutch plays. Meanwhile, Ares Bellingham has become a household name as San Francisco's star tight end, dominating the red zone with a physicality that's almost impossible to defend against."

"Three NFL stars from one university," the first commentator chimed in. "It's a testament to the kind of talent Fall Lake University can produce. They didn't just play together—they thrived together. You don't see that kind of chemistry and competitive fire come out of one program very often."

My heart swelled at the mention of Liam's closest friends. It wasn't just his journey that had come full circle—it was all of theirs. From their college years at Fall Lake to making their mark in the pros, they'd fought side by side for everything they had. Knowing they were still part of each other's lives, even as they carved out their individual legacies, made their success more meaningful.

I grabbed my bag and ushered Lily out the door, driving the short distance to the Italian restaurant we'd made our go-to since moving to Kansas. As we walked in, I spotted Liam instantly. His shirt clung to him, his hair damp and messy, and his signature grin lit up the room when he saw us.

"Hey, there's my girls." He scooped Lily into his arms.

"Daddy!" she squealed, wrapping her arms around his neck.

He kissed her cheek then leaned over to kiss me. "You two are my favorite part of the day."

"Guess what, Liam?" I tried to keep my voice casual, though my heart practically pounded out of my chest.

"What's up?" He looked between me and Lily, his brow furrowing.

Lily grinned, pointing at her shirt. "I'm gonna be the best big sister ever!"

For a split second, he froze, his eyes locked on the words. Then, his head snapped up, his gaze finding mine. "Are you serious?"

"Yep." I nodded, tears blurring my vision as I smiled. "We're doing it all together this time."

He set Lily down carefully, his hands shaking as he reached for me. The look in his eyes—pure joy, disbelief, love—was everything. He pulled me into his embrace, his voice a whisper against my ear. "I can't wait, Skye. For all of it. With you."

I wrapped my arms around his neck, breathing him in, feeling the steady rhythm of his heart against mine. This was it. This was everything. "Good thing we're getting married in two weeks, or my dress would need to be altered."

"If you'd given in to me, we would already be married," he teased.

I shivered, remembering all the ways he'd tried to persuade me to move up the wedding, claiming he wanted the world to know I was his forever. These had been the best hours—months—of my life, and they'd resulted in the gift we would be welcoming in about seven months. My hand smoothed over my still-flat abdomen as happiness bloomed inside all over again.

Lily tugged on Liam's hand, breaking the moment. "You happy, Daddy?"

He crouched down, scooping her up again. "Happy doesn't even come close, butterfly."

And as we stood there, the three of us—and the promise of one more on the way—I couldn't help but think how right it all felt. We were building something unshakable together—a life and family, one step at a time.

Thanks so much for reading my work. I hope you enjoyed it! As you know, an author's career is built on reviews. If you have a few moments, please consider leaving a review or rating for
RED ZONE.
amymckinleyauthor.com/pages/reading-order

Looking for your next book to read? Check out more books by
Amy McKinley/Isla Vaughn at amymckinley.com

ALSO BY ISLA VAUGHN

Sports romance books by Isla Vaughn

Hidden Valley Elite Series

Savage Start

Savage Lies

Savage Truth

Brutal Days

Brutal Nights

Cruel Start

Cruel Hate

Cruel Love

Wicked Games

Wicked Ends

Fall Lake Ballers

Quarterback Keeper

Pump Fake

Red Zone

Standalone Titles

Shattered Ice (coming soon)

Isla Vaughn also publishes under *USA Today* bestselling author Amy McKinley.

Mafia Elite

No Way Out

Blood Oath

Born in Darkness

Savage Secrets

Ruthless Heir

Collateral Damage

Rivals

Gray Ghost Novels (Former Navy SEALs)

Moments That Define Us

Broken Circle

Eye of the Storm

Beneath the Surface

Vantage Point

Covert Threat

Marked for Death

Deadly Isles Special Ops (Navy SEALs)

Twisted Secrets

Bound by Secrets

Forged by Secrets

Standalone Titles

Shattered Melody

Siren's Call: Cursed Seas

Fake Fiancé (A Second Chance Office Romance)

Moonlit Destination Series

Moonlit Whisper

Moonlit Kiss

Moonlit Mirage

Five Fates Series

Hidden

Taken

ACKNOWLEDGMENTS

To my family—thank you for your love, encouragement, and patience through every deadline and writing session. Your support means everything.

I'm beyond lucky to be surrounded by such brilliant critique partners who challenge, encourage, and help shape these stories into something better than I could've done alone.

Candace Irvin—your unwavering support and thoughtful feedback have been an anchor throughout this process. I honestly don't know what I'd do without your keen insight and incredible friendship.

Huge thanks to Emily Albright, Kristin Kisska, and Jessica Riley Miller—you've all jumped into the chaos with me and offered your time, creativity, countless read-throughs, and encouragement. I couldn't ask for a better crew to brainstorm with and lean on.

To Colleen Noyes and the amazing team at Itsy Bitsy Book Bits—thank you for your hard work, passion, and dedication that helps each release reach the readers who'll love it most. I'm so grateful to have you in my corner.

The ever-talented TE Black Designs continues to bring my vision to life with gorgeous covers, and Red Adept Editing makes the final polish process smooth, professional, and collaborative. I feel fortunate to work with such a stellar team.

To all the phenomenal readers and bloggers—thank you for riding along with me on this journey. Your support, reviews, and messages mean more than I can ever say. If you haven't already, join my newsletter so you don't miss out on upcoming releases and behind-the-scenes updates.

With all my heart—thank you.

ABOUT THE AUTHOR

Isla Vaughn is the author of the Hidden Valley Elite and Fall Lake Ballers series. Her romance books are full of complex characters, strong alpha males, and the fierce women who bring them to their knees. When not writing, she can be found daydreaming about owning a beach house, reading, or drinking too much coffee.

facebook.com/author.IslaVaughn
instagram.com/islavaughnauthor
tiktok.com/@islavaughnauthor
goodreads.com/islavaughn_author
bookbub.com/profile/isla-vaughn

9 781951 919719